BECAUSE OF ELLISON

By M.S. Willis

This is a work of fiction and any resemblance to any person, living or dead, any place, events or occurrences, is purely coincidental. The characters and story lines are created from the author's imagination or are used fictitiously.

Because of Ellison: Copyright © 2014 by M.S. Willis

ISBN: 978-0-9915666-3-1

mswillis@mswillisbooks.com

http://www.facebook.com/mswillisbooks

OTHER BOOKS BY M.S. WILLIS

Control Series

Book One – Control

Book Two – Conflict

Book Three – Conquer

Novella - David

Estate Series

Prequel – Joseph Fallen

Book One – Madeleine Abducted

Coming in 2014

This book is dedicated to all those who will fight, who are fighting, or who have fought. This is dedicated also to those who battle beside the ones they love.

Table of Contents

Prologue

- 2064 -

The light clinking of wine glasses and hushed coughs and murmurs filled the room as Hunter McCormick stoically walked a path to the front podium. Every step that he took resonated through his old bones while the droop to his shoulders reminded him of how exhausted he'd become over the many years of his life.

Reaching the steps leading up to the stage, Hunter mentally prepared to give his speech as he lifted one foot in front of the other and ascended the stairs to give his speech. It was here that he was determined to reveal the inspiration behind his accomplishments. He intended to lie to his audience, to feed them useless medical information, and a grand vision for his achievement because he knew that no person in the room would believe that a simple girl from an impoverished town had unknowingly brought about the greatest medical achievement of the century.

Memories of sundrenched days spent hiking and fishing rebounded in his thoughts and battered at his wearied soul as he gradually scaled the stairs. A smile so bright it could illuminate the darkest of nights was seared into his memory and he smiled back. His old lips cracked at the motion, but there was no way to prevent smiling in return when it came to her.

Reaching the podium, Hunter placed the tattered pages of his speech on the smooth wooden surface. The audience became motionless and silent, almost impassive in their tension as they waited to hear what he had to say. Scanning the typewritten letters, words and sentences of standard and acceptable medical dribble, he shook his head quickly before crumpling the pages and tossing them over his shoulder. Focusing once again on the audience, Hunter cleared his throat and remained quiet while he readied himself to tell the entire room about the person who'd inspired everything that he'd done.

"I had a prepared speech." His voice fractured; age taking its toll on his once sturdy vocal chords. "In that speech were the ramblings of a physician who'd found a cure for one of the cruelest diseases known to man. They were carefully arranged words about science, about the pursuit for the cure, about the ravages of an illness and how it affects the vitality, well-being and life of a patient and that patient's family." Pausing, Hunter gathered his strength, steeled himself to keep from breaking down when discussing her. "But ... those words weren't what mattered. None of those things were the reason I labored and fought as hard as I did all these years."

The audience sat in reticence as Hunter laughed to himself, remembering back to a blonde haired girl who glowered at something he had to say; one who always watched him with blue eyes as boundless as the sky. Turning his attention back to the audience, he commenced his speech.

"Her name was Ellison James ... and she was the biggest bitch I'd ever met in my life." He paused, waited for the collective gasps to quiet throughout the room before continuing.

Waving their reaction away with his hand, he said, "Don't be shocked by my candor, if El was standing in this room with us right now, she would agree." He

2

laughed again, not able to keep a straight face while thinking of the woman he'd loved. "She had an answer for everything, and most of the time, I didn't like it. But she was an unbelievable person. She cared about humanity, she was dedicated to nature, and she believed strongly that people should use their talents to not only benefit themselves, but to benefit others around them."

His face straightened, his brows furrowed, but he was determined to tell the story. His voice cracked again as he confessed, "If you want to know the reason why millions of people will now be saved, I'll be honest with you and I'll tell you that there is only one simple answer ... "

"It was because of Ellison."

Chapter One

Fifty Years Earlier

My eyes peeled open to discover horrendous tentacles of sunlight somehow intruding around the edges of the blackout curtains in my bedroom. A headache pounded at the back of my skull and I questioned whether someone had hit me with a baseball bat when I'd been too fucked up to notice. The slumbering body of my girlfriend, Tiffany, weighted down my right arm and her body heat was causing the skin between us to become sticky with sweat. Looking away from the obtrusive light, my eyes located the slowly spinning blades of the ceiling fan with clumps of dust clinging to the blades as they spun. The room was stifling and my mouth was hot and arid as a desert. Sitting up, I pulled my arm out from under Tiffany, callously dumping her to the floor.

"What the fuck, Hunter?!" With her piercing, high-pitched voice screeching in outrage, she pushed herself up into an unsteady standing position, rubbing at her elbow to lessen the sting from its impact with the ground.

Cautiously, I turned my head to look at her, in no way attempting to hide my disgust with the irritating sound of her grating voice. The scowl on her normally perfect face deepened at my obvious contempt. Her mahogany brown hair was matted from sleep and the makeup she still had on from the night before was smeared across her features. When I failed to respond, she turned towards the bathroom, giving me the finger before entering the room and slamming the door closed behind her.

It was the summer after I graduated high school and I lived in a guesthouse on my parents' sizeable estate. I had a fast, ridiculously expensive car, a hot girlfriend, and a full-ride scholarship to an elite college that I had absolutely no interest in attending.

And to be straightforward with you, I couldn't have cared less about any of it.

Ennui with life had instilled itself in me by the time I was 13 years old. School was too simple because I was a genius. When the school decided to test my IQ at the ripe old age of 10, the administrators and teachers danced themselves around in confidence that I would be a testament to their ability to … well … administer and teach. But it wasn't their accomplishment; it was simply nature. I'd always been superior in my intelligence; most of the time it served as a detriment to my wellbeing. It's what led me to the lifestyle choices I made as I grew older. Those choices started with alcohol. By the age of 14, I'd found a comfortable numbness inside the blanket with a twelve-pack or bottle, but, eventually, I grew bored with that as well. By the time I was 16, I'd progressed to drugs and girls in a quest to test the boundaries of a mundane existence.

For the majority of my life, I had absolute freedom. Except for the once a month lecture on responsibility I'd been forced to endure, my parents were typically too busy to pay attention to what I was doing with my time. They looked to my grades as an indication of my progress and a scale upon which to base their success in parenting. When I'd finally figured out their non-attention, I was delighted to find that as long as I aced my classes and endured the lectures that accompanied my major screw ups, I could get away with just about anything else. Technically, I moved out of my parents' house and into their guesthouse by the time I was 15; they didn't notice until two years later.

Forcing myself out of bed, I snatched my jeans from the floor, pulling them on my body one uncoordinated leg at a time. My balance was off and it took several attempts to perform a function as simple as dressing. The room would spin every so often and the pounding headache that was pulsing in my head only grew more intense as blood coursed its path through my body. After finally donning my pants, I had to immediately sit down again.

Grasping my head in my hands, I attempted to control the headache that ceaselessly battered at my skull. The only noise in the room was the light whistle of wind from the revolving blades of the fan and the clattering of objects from Tiffany blowing off steam in the other room. My phone chirped while I waited patiently for her to emerge from the room so I could ask her to leave. Was I an asshole for kicking her out immediately? Yes. But I couldn't help that the sound of her voice was like torture when I was hungover. Refusing to open my eyes, I reached to the side table and my hand fumbled over several objects before finally finding the phone. Still cradling my head in one hand, I brought the phone down and flicked the side button to reveal a text from my mother.

"Get your ass over here this instant, Hunter!"

"Fuck." A single syllable utterance, and my water starved throat screamed with burning pain. Forcing myself from the bed once more, I staggered to the bathroom door and leaned on it heavily while banging my hand against the white painted wood. Tiffany opened the door so quickly I almost fell into her from the loss of balance. She stared up at me with brown eyes filled with disdain, her tanned arms crossing themselves over her fake breasts and she bent one leg forward, waiting for what I had to say.

"You need to go, my mom wants to see me." Although, I was annoyed at having to cross the grounds of the property in vivid sunlight to answer my mother's call, I was pleased to have an excuse to get rid of my girlfriend.

"Whatever, asshole. I know you wanted me out anyway." Straightening her spine, Tiffany pushed past me, knocking me back into the frame of the door. I ignored her. Rolling my eyes, I stumbled towards the sink, flicked on the water and stuck my head under the faucet. I felt all ate up — like something had scratched away at my insides all-night long — reduced to a thirsty dog. I managed to turn on the faucet. My tongue lapped at the water hungrily, desperate to reintroduce moisture into my dehydrated body. After taking my fill, I turned off the water and looked up into the mirror above the sink. My normally clear blue eyes appeared hazy and my light brown hair was sticking up in a typically messy style. While perusing my haggard state, I realized that my bladder was demanding relief. I must have pissed for 15 minutes before finally shaking myself dry and meandering back into my bedroom.

A weak smile pulled at the corners of my mouth when I discovered that Tiffany had left. I knew I would hear from her within the hour and that she would lay into me as only she knew how, but I couldn't help but feel gratified by the momentary break. I didn't love her - didn't even know what love was - but I played a part in the relationship anyway for the easy ride and status of dating the hottest girl in school. She was your typical popular girl. Her beauty was a thing to be admired, but her intelligence was laughable and being around her was only beneficial when I was too fucked up to notice. I tried talking to her once about this fleeting idea I had that there was more to life; this feeling I had that something was lacking, that we, as a society, were missing out on something much bigger than us. She laughed in response, flicked her hair back and told me to get over it before reminding me that we were wealthy and had it all. I never tried talking to her about much else after that.

Shaking myself of sluggishness, I quickly pulled on a wrinkled t-shirt and a pair of sunglasses before exiting my dimly lit house out into the garish light of day. Crossing the property swiftly, I noticed an unusual detail out of the corner of my eye, but brushed it off without considering it further. The guesthouse stood atop a hill behind my parents' house and I was thankful for the downward slope that made the dreaded journey much easier to manage. The steep incline would be a bitch to climb on my return trip, but I put that thought out of my mind when I finally reached the main house. Moving through the back yard, I located my mother staring into the pool. Her hands were on her hips and the grimace on her face was a warning that something was amiss. Slowly, I made my way over, noting how the bushes that lined the pool had been knocked down and long trails of leaves and dirt were strewn out from the shrubs in the direction of the water. My mother's head turned towards me before I reached the pool deck and her hand instantly pointed down.

"Care to explain, Hunter?"

Looking towards the water, I noticed the leaves that were floating along the reflective surface; swirls of dirt wound their way through as the jets circulated the water. Shrugging my shoulders, I looked up at my mom. "Explain what? I didn't knock the fucking bushes over."

Her face contorted into an agonized frown and her hands came up to pinch at her temples as she responded. "Look IN the water."

Taking a few more hesitant steps, I glanced down into the deep end of the pool. My eyes bugged out and my body lurched in reaction to what I saw.

"Fuck."

One would have overlooked it if he or she had simply passed by without taking a look into the depths of the water. The black paint of my BMW blended perfectly with the lagoon-colored stone surface of the pool and bits of chrome shimmered as sunlight reached through the water, barely brushing against the silvery accents.

My heart leapt into my throat and I swallowed hard to keep it down with my stomach.

"As I was saying: Do you mind telling me why your CAR is at the bottom of our POOL, Hunter?!"

My mouth fell open so that I could respond, but no sound came out and my jaw was left dangling open in utter and humiliating shock. Spinning on my heel, I peered up the hill towards the guesthouse and determined what oddity had caught my attention just moments before. My car was not where I normally left it. Tire tracks shredded the grass where they had voyaged down the steep incline, apparently gaining enough speed to power the vehicle through the shrubs until finally landing at the bottom of the pool. My eyes blinked ... once ... twice ... before I turned back to the intimidating glare of my mother.

I spun my cognitive wheels as quickly as I could and spit out a load of bullshit, hoping it would appease the quivering beast of a woman that stood in front of me. "Well, holy shit! I can't believe the engineers and architects that designed this place didn't consider the placement of the pool. *Clearly*, designing a driveway to sit at the top of a slope that leads down towards a pool was poor site planning. You should call them immediately and demand compensation."

We both crossed our arms over our chests — me in indignation and my mother in absolute and unadulterated fury. "Don't give me that shit, Hunter! How did this happen? Cars don't just roll forward by themselves. Did you even bother placing the car in Park when you came home last night?"

I didn't know. My memory of the night before was foggy at best. I'd taken Tiffany to Ethan's house for a party. There were red solo cups and party favors consisting of any drug a person could want. I had a blast — I thought. But in reality, I wasn't even quite sure how I'd gotten home. Had Tiffany driven? Or was it me? It must have been Tiffany. I would have never done anything this moronic.

"Tiffany drove us home last night, she must have parked the car too close to the ridge. Again, better site planning would have prevented this event. I mean, what type of professional would place a ... "

"That's it!!" Throwing her hands up, my mother growled before turning and stormed towards the French doors at the back of the house. Motioning towards me, she indicated that I was to follow her inside. Kicking at some loose dirt with my foot, I shoved my hands in my pockets and paced behind my mother before being led into the living room. My father was on the phone glancing over some paperwork that was scattered haphazardly across the cherry wood sofa table. His eyes shot up as my mother and I entered the room and he excused himself curtly before throwing the phone to his side and standing up.

"Hunter, this is the last fucking straw, son. When your mother and I discovered that *car* in our *pool* this morning, I almost marched up to your house to beat your ass for such an irresponsible fucking stunt! Do you have any idea how much this is going to cost me? That car was brand new, not to mention what damage it did to the surface of our pool! What the hell is your problem?!"

Straightening my shoulders, I backed away from my father to place distance between his wrath and my body. I stared at his face, which had turned a light shade of purple, and noticed that his hair appeared to be standing on end.

"It was an accident ... "

"You know what, Hunter? We're done with your *accidents*, which is really just your excuse for your total lack of responsibility. You need to grow the hell up, son. You are 19 years old, *could* have graduated at 17, but instead, you didn't want to put in the extra work to build up your credits faster. You have a full ride to Harvard and you cannot expect to pass as easily through that school with the same habits you had in high school. You need to start taking your life seriously. Your mother and I have supported you thus far, but that support will end if you don't get your shit straight. On top of that, your lifestyle is seriously in question. We both suspect that you are not only drinking, but doing drugs as well. In fact, why are you swaying back and forth now? Take off those fucking sunglasses so that we can see your eyes. Are you drunk at this very moment or what?"

My entire body tensed as I attempted to continue standing in an upright position. I hadn't noticed that I'd been swaying, but given how hung over I was, it was highly possible. I wanted to sit down, but knew that doing so would only prove his point. Reaching up, I removed my sunglasses, only to be met with the knowing stares of my parents and I instantly regretted not using eye drops before coming to the main house.

My father crossed his arms over his chest and one eyebrow arched on his face. "Just as I thought, your eyes are bloodshot as hell." Stepping closer, he sniffed at the air around me. "You smell like alcohol and cigarette smoke."

I had nothing to say. Although my brain on normal days performed like a well-oiled machine, the alcohol and drugs I'd likely ingested the night before acted like a gunk that was gluing up the gears. I couldn't come up with one intelligible sentence that would have any effect on reducing my father's anger. Thus, I did what any normal, 19-year-old would do: I stared at him dumbfounded and kept my trap shut. I might have been thinking slowly at that moment, but I was still rational enough to realize that sometimes it's better to remain quiet and take the heat than to open your mouth and stir the pot.

"Sit down, Hunter, before you fall over." My father's voice had taken on a defeated tone suddenly. But was my father defeated — or was I?

Sitting on the couch, I leaned back into the overstuffed cushions and stretched my long legs out in front of me and crossed one ankle over the other. If I was being made to sit, I knew a lecture was coming — and if I had to endure the lecture, I was going to make damn sure I was comfortable while doing so.

My parents took a seat next to each other on the couch facing me. Their mouths were moving and I knew they were talking, but all I could hear was discordant sounds and disembodied voices as my conscious thought floated off into thoughts not yet explored.

Bored with the repetitive pep talk that I'd heard my entire life, I allowed my mind to wander aimlessly. I remembered there was another party I was looking forward to attending that evening until I realized that getting there would be complicated given the fact that my car was at the bottom of the swimming pool. Nodding my head at my parents and putting on my 'serious' face, I was inwardly plotting how I would convince them to loan me another car out of my father's impressive collection — at least until they bought me a replacement.

My parents' mouths continued to move and I continued nodding at what I knew were the important parts:

"We won't be here forever ... "

"Learn responsibility so you can support yourself in the future ... "

"Life is not about having fun only ... "

"Your future depends on the decisions you make now ... "

As long as I pretended to be paying attention, my parents would be satisfied. In all honesty, I could have typed out a script of this lecture, had them sign it and then promised to read it once every few months so as to avoid any unnecessary lectures in the future. By the time my mind had moved along to trying to remember what happened the night before, I heard the strangest thing.

" ... Living with your uncle in Florida for the summer ... "

What the hell?! Those words were NOT part of the script.

Straightening in my seat, I held my hands up to silence my father's tirade. "Whoa, what?! Run that Florida part past me again, please."

"Well, it's about time you pay attention to something I'm saying." My father's voice dripped with condescension. "Your mother and I have decided that you've had it too easy in life and as a result, you need to straighten out your priorities. We are sending you to live with your Uncle Bill for the summer. He'll put you to work around the house and you'll find out what it is like to live in poverty rather than having everything handed to you. It'll be good for you. I came from nothing, son, and I worked my ass off to get where I am today. There is no way in hell that I'm going to allow you to continue behaving like a delinquent teen. You are going to grow up, or you are going to be on your own. Do you understand me?"

My eyes shifted between my mother and father. They both had their arms crossed over their chests and their faces indicated they meant business. I had to get out of this. Taking away my last summer before college would completely ruin my life. Okay — not my 'life', but still; it would ruin my summer before college.

Clearing my throat, I threw on my but-I'm-you're-little-boy type pouty face in an appeal to break down the weakest link — mom. If I could get my mother to waiver in her decision, my father might crack as well.

"Listen, I'm sorry about the car and I'm sorry about your pool. I'll make sure it never happens again, but you two can't be serious about sending me to Florida. I haven't seen Uncle Bill since I was five. And doesn't he live out in the middle of nowhere? How will hanging out in a swamp teach me anything? If you two have to punish me, don't you think it would be better to have me here where you can keep an eye on what I'm doing?"

The looks on their faces told me that I was getting nowhere with my argument — fast. My head was still pounding, and I continued to grapple with the glue gunking up my grinding gears, so it became impossible to argue. Reality suddenly became sadly apparent:

I had nothing.

And I was going to Florida.

Chapter Two

The unfortunate thing about being a child in an overly wealthy family is that parents could afford annoying conveniences such as private planes. Rather than getting a few days ... or hell ... a few hours to think of a way out of exile, I was rushed like a captive to the guesthouse, forced to grab clothes and was abruptly packed onto my father's jet faster than I could process what was going on. By the time I hit 40,000 feet above ground, my fate was sealed.

My parents made sure to strip me of everything: my phone, my iPod, my laptop, my iPad — everything. If it could be plugged in, it was taken away. I didn't even have a chance to type up a quick plea on my social networking sites for one of my friends to swoop in and rescue me; and if my car hadn't been taking a cool dip, I might have considered making a break for it. My credit cards were the next to go. I never realized my dependence on plastic until I watched in dismay as my mother ripped the rectangular lifelines out of my wallet before brusquely handing the emptied leather shell back to me. The only thing left in it was my ID and the fake one hidden behind it.

I took the opportunity of the flight to catch up on some sleep. About two hours into my snooze, the pilot's announcement that we'd reached Florida woke me up. Looking out the window, I groaned to discover that the miniature cities that I'd watched passing by on my way out of New York had turned into a bunch of — well — green, as far as the eye could see. Every once in a while I would spot a spattering of gray, which I assumed could have been what Florida considered a *city*. I struggled to determine if I would survive the infinite amount of wilderness that apparently ran amuck in this godforsaken state. I was a city boy through and through. Nature and I had never really shaken hands except for the manicured lawns of my friends' parents' estates and the occasional family vacation I'd taken when I was a child. Not to mention the bean sprout I grew in Kindergarten. I'd named him Earl and we were pretty tight until I forgot to water him for a month and he bailed on me. The experience proved a person couldn't trust nature. If you didn't give nature what it wanted, it wanted nothing to do with you. I haven't trusted it since.

For the next hour or so, I looked around the cabin of the plane while idly tapping my fingers on my legs. The lack of technology was getting to me and I was like an addict missing his next fix. I tried to formulate ways to get a message to my friends back home that I was in need of liberation. I considered smoke signals, carrier pigeons and even Morse code. Unfortunately, modern convenience had all but extinguished the need for archaic modes of communication and my friends would be none the wiser as to what I needed even if I was able to get the message out. I was screwed and I knew it. And I was extremely unhappy about my parents' decision to force me into exile. What was I going to do in the middle of nowhere for three long months? This wasn't punishment; this was torture. There were parties I was missing and alcohol that would fall down the throats of some other lucky bastard while I was holed up in the middle of the woods fixing shit. I didn't deserve this.

The plane finally landed in the middle of nowhere and the pilot emerged from the cockpit a few minutes later with a large smile plastered across his genial face. "We've arrived, Mr. McCormick. A business associate of your father's is waiting on the runway to escort you to your next destination."

I looked up into the brown eyes of the pilot. His tanned face bore the fine lines of an aged man, yet the silvered hair at his temples gave him a distinguished look. Standing up on cramped legs, I reached into the stowaway compartments to extract my bags. I fished out my sunglasses and threw them on my face before stepping out the door and descending the stairs. I found the pilot shaking hands with another man I didn't recognize who was dressed much like my father in a top of the line pinstriped suit. The man turned to smile at me before waving me over to where they stood.

"Hunter!" The unidentified man strode purposefully towards me holding his hand out in greeting. Grasping my hand firmly, the man introduced himself. "My name is Robert Klimpt. I'm a business associate of your father's. He called and asked me to authorize clearance for his plane to land on our private runway. I'll be escorting you to the front of the neighborhood to where your uncle is waiting. It's good to meet you. You look very much like your father."

Pulling my hand back to my body, I nodded my head, mumbled an unintelligible response and soon, we were making our way to the golf cart waiting nearby. Another 10 minutes passed as Mr. Klimpt babbled on about his business dealings with my father. We reached a large iron gate at the front of the community and between the thick iron bars, I could see a red truck that looked like it hadn't been washed since it was built, which would have been roughly 1972. The red paint had faded and was broken up from rust spots, dents and dings that littered the metal surface. Beside the truck, stood a man who I assumed was my Uncle Bill together with a petite blonde girl. Both were dressed in plain white shirts and cutoff jean shorts and, whereas Uncle

Bill was wearing flip-flops, the girl next to him wore no shoes at all. Her hair was styled into a short bob and it bounced around above her shoulders as she animatedly spoke. The man smiled down at her every so often between taking puffs on the cigarette he was smoking, but his eyes locked on me as soon as I approached the gate.

"Well, damn, Hunter! Look at you! I've seen the pictures your mom has sent me, but I didn't think you were as big as you are! How tall are ya? Six foot five?" My uncle's voice was rough from years of smoking and his skin resembled a worn and wrinkled shirt. He was about as wide as I was tall and a veritable wall of muscle. After letting out a howling cackle that could wake the dead, he motioned to the little blonde beside him. "You remember your cousin, Lily, right? We're both really excited to have you stayin' with us this summer."

I slowly stepped out of the golf cart after the gates slid open and grabbed my bags before heading over to where they were standing. Once I'd exited the cart, Mr. Klimpt promptly said goodbye and hightailed it as fast in the opposite direction as the battery-powered engine of that cart could go. Turning back to my Uncle, I huffed out in resignation and threw my bags over my shoulder with one hand while reaching out to shake my uncle's hand with the other.

"Uh, yeah, I remember Lily. Hey." I waved down at the small girl and her smile beamed up at me, bright as sunshine.

"Hunter!" She bounced in my direction and took me into the biggest hug she could manage. "I really am glad to see ya. I told my best friend all about ya and she's excited as all hell to meet ya."

Damn, that girl talked fast ...

"Watch the language, baby girl." Bill looked down in Lily's direction with a fake glare that was quickly replaced with a smile.

Lily shrugged her shoulders. "Let's get a move on. I'm losing precious time in the sunlight standing around here." She turned suddenly and bounced her way over to the truck. Bill chuckled and clapped me on the shoulder as he said, "We'd better get going, son. You keep those girls out of the sun for too long and their heads start turning in circles on their shoulders. It's scary shit."

I nodded silently and followed behind him. It was going to be one hell of a summer, but there was nothing I could do but suck it up and get through it.

~   ~   ~

The trip to my Uncle's place was cramped as we tried to fit ourselves into the cab of the truck. Lily babbled on about all the things they did in Florida, while I smiled and did my best not to look at the never-ending sea of green that passed the windows as we drove. Most of the activities mentioned by Lily included a lot of being out during the day and sleeping at night. I cringed at the thought, concerned that the circadian rhythm I'd worked hard to establish over the past few years of my life might get thrown off. As it was now, it was 3:00 in the afternoon and I should have still been sleeping in my bed with another two hours to spare.

Pulling up to the house, my eyes once again bugged out from my head as Bill parked the truck in a wooded lot. The property was somewhat hidden from the road by the tree line and there was only one other house to the left of Bill's. I looked over the metal roofs of both houses and then focused my attention on the aluminum siding on the shack, er, house I would be occupying. The little remnants of paint that remained on the siding looked awkward against the gray aluminum that was mostly exposed. The house was raised up from the ground and wooden lattice lined the bottom. A questionable staircase led up to the front door, and by the time the truck was in park, Lily had jumped out and was bounding her way up those stairs, quickly disappearing into the interior of the building.

I climbed out of the truck and my shoe landed firmly in a mud puddle. "Shit!" While I pulled my sodden shoe out of the brownish liquid, my uncle chuckled.

"Yeah, you got to watch out for those. It rains every day in Florida, son, and the lack of concrete makes walking around the property a bitch at times. You'll get used to it though." Chuckling again, he clapped me on the shoulder as he led me towards the house. "I know the place don't look like much. That's why I was real pleased to hear that you'd be coming down this summer to help me fix it up. In fact, I got the materials ready that you'll need to scrape and prep the siding before we paint it. I figure, if you get started now, you should have a lot of it done by suppertime at seven."

We were making our way up the rickety staircase just as Lily came bounding through the door, nearly taking me out in her path. "I'm off, Daddy! El and I will be in our normal spot if ya need me."

Lily disappeared in the direction of the other house as I was led inside. I wasn't impressed with the mismatched furniture and the scraped up wooden floors of the place. Bill made a point to quickly show me the bathroom and my room, giving me just enough time to set my stuff down before whisking me back in the direction of the living room. Leading me out a back door, Bill stepped out onto an open porch that was littered with machine parts and a deadly mix of different chemicals, separated out in bottles. If this place ever caught on fire, we were screwed.

Bill started pulling out different scrub brushes and spray bottles of clear liquid and handed them to me. "Sorry for the mess, son, but I don't have time to deal with this shit and keep my auto shop going. I'd have Lily do it, but while the girl is good at reading and looking pretty, she doesn't have a clue when it comes to tools of manual labor. Having you come down really is a blessing in disguise. It'll be good to have some more testosterone around the place. Now, I gotta go back to work, but all you'll need to do is spray that paint thinner on the paint that's left and give it a minute before scraping it off. Should have no problem with it considering how old it is. After you're done with that ... " Bill reached over and picked up a one-gallon paint canister and a paintbrush. " ... You're going to be applying a layer of primer. You're a smart boy, you should have no problem figuring it out."

I took the canister and brush from Bill's hands and Bill turned to immediately exit the porch. Making my way back through the house, I decided to tackle the front elevation first. Stepping out onto the rickety staircase, I heard a loud slap of metal against metal and jumped back thinking the whole damn house was about to come down. Turning my head, I looked to the house on the right and saw Lily and another girl in their bathing suits as they were propping a ladder up against the side of the roof. Lily giggled at something her friend had to say and then turned to look at me in a failed attempt to be discreet. I noticed anyway.

Shaking it off, I jumped down the stairs and went to work scraping paint. The creak of the ladder caught my attention again and I watched as both girls climbed up onto the roof, stepping around carefully in their flip flops while retrieving padded mats that were secured to the roof by rope. Laying their towels down on the mats, they eventually plopped themselves down to soak up the sun. I took a second admiring the body of Lily's friend, but they were at such a distance, I couldn't really make out much more than the fact that she was thin, had some nice curves, and wore a small yellow bikini.

Over two hours into my chore, I had the last specks of paint stripped from the siding and was beginning the task of slapping on primer; a task that would be carried out with a delicate hand and attention to detail because I was a perfectionist. It's important to know this fact in order to understand what was about to happen. At times, my love of perfection could be a good thing. I aced tests and excelled at any video game I played; but on the flip side, and where my perfectionism was a bad thing; I could get crotchety when I was focused on my task and something came along to fuck it up.

After applying a coat of primer to the first quarter of the front wall, I sat admiring the fact that the paint job was flawless. Brush strokes were minimal and the application of the paint had been even over the entire surface of the siding. No drips had occurred and I was preparing to move on to the second quarter.

Yes. It's primer. But like anything of value, a solid and well executed foundation is essential to the overall quality of the job — much like what I keep hearing about love — if you don't have something of quality to base a relationship upon, eventually it will crumble down. It's a weak analogy, but one that might help the romantic understand how I view things.

Just as I was standing up to move my tools to an area to start 'Primer — Phase Two,' a truck pulled up in the dirt lot in front of the neighbor's house. The engine was loud, the tires were huge and I briefly wondered if a stepladder was required to step down from the beast of a truck that may or may not have been street legal. Turning my attention back to the primer, I noticed out of the corner of my eye as two large men climbed out and made their way to the front door of the house. Dressed in head to toe camouflage, both men looked as if they'd just come off a hunting trip. Opening the front door, one man disappeared into the interior just before a litany of curse words sounded from the house.

Two dogs, one that was black and looked to be a mix between a greyhound and a terrier, and a white one that was smaller than the first, came bounding out of the house.

"Sasha! Bear! You get your flea-ridden asses back here!" The man who hadn't yet stepped into the house yelled after the mutts and I turned my full attention to find that those 'flea-ridden' creatures were making their way towards me at top speed.

By the time they reached me, they were covered in mud from running through the multitude of puddles that were speckled across the dirt lots. My hands were filled with brushes and scrapers and I stepped back in a failed attempt to dodge the airborne furballs as they lunged in my direction. When their muddy bodies struck mine I was forced backwards into the wall of primer perfection I'd just accomplished. My anger was immediate and those dogs were going down.

Dropping a brush from my hand, I picked up the heavy canister of primer, and with a feral scream I swung out at the dogs and stepped forward in an attempt to force them away from the house.

The dogs were able to dodge the swinging paint can, opting at that time to run in circles around me, happily barking as if we were playing their favorite game. Using the momentum of the can, I swung around in circles with them, noticing how they continued to kick up mud, dirt and leaves onto the wall of the house. The entire section I'd just completed was destroyed and it would take another day just to scrape the siding clean again. By that point, I was no longer speaking a recognizable language. My anger at the dogs had reduced me to a basic and primal form of communication consisting of random grunts, growls and the occasional snort. My adrenaline was on overdrive as I rotated with the rabid beasts and while I was swinging around for the second time, I saw a streak of yellow just before I was tackled to the ground.

We landed in a puddle, the mud from which splashed up into my eyes, momentarily blinding me. It gave my attacker an advantage, one that she immediately exploited. Straddling my midsection, she pushed herself up, holding my shoulders down with her hands.

"What the fuck do you think you're doing, asshole?! Leave my dogs alone before I have to break both your fucking legs and shove my foot so far up your ass you'll be able to taste my nail polish."

My hands quickly traveled to my eyes, wiping away as much of the mud that I could. Blinking two or three times, I was finally able to squint up at the mud-covered and snarling blonde.

"What the fuck do you have to say for yourself? They're *small* dogs that were just trying to play with you. That paint-can could have hurt them, you piece of shit!" Slamming her hands down onto my chest, the girl pushed herself off of me and walked over to check out her dogs.

I sat up, attempting to wipe more mud from my face, and stared out at an angry, trembling, and beautiful girl, covered head to toe in mud — and not much else.

25

Rage swirled in her eyes as she glared over at me while she consoled the frightened dogs. "Well? Are you going to say anything or are you just going to sit there staring at me with your mouth wide open? I don't understand how everyone is calling you a genius considering you're acting like a damn fool at the moment."

My eyes glanced at the ruined wall, instantly stripping me of my shock and replacing it with vehemence so intense, I saw red.

Standing up, I asked, "Did you see what your *mutts* did to the wall I just painted?!" I took a step forward with my finger pointed directly in her face.

Lily ran over to where her friend and I stood, immediately moving between us and placing her hands out to ensure we remained separated. "Guys! Stop it! Calm the fuck down."

I didn't look down at Lily because my stare down with her friend had not yet finished. Her blue eyes shone out at me, a scowl peeking out from the mud splashed and smeared over her face.

"Hunter McCormick, you better look at me right this second!" Lily's voice took me by surprise; the use of my full name snapped me into a Pavlovian response instilled by my mother's classical conditioning as a child. My eyes shot down to Lily to find that she was smiling back up at me in apology.

"Hunter, I'd like to introduce you to Ellison James."

Chapter Three

Ellison

He was an asshole. An angry, dog beating, asshole who was creepy as all hell because of the way he kept staring at me. It was a good thing Lily had gotten between us because one more word out of his mouth and it would have met with the back of my hand.

While we continued to stare each other down, my brother, Jake, and my ex-boyfriend, Finn, wandered over to see what all the screaming was about.

Jake opened his big mouth first, amused at the situation, to say the least. "What the hell is going on over here?" His words were barely discernible due to his laughter. Finn didn't seem as amused by the muddy debacle.

Lily and Hunter turned to look in Jake's direction and I noticed how Hunter took a step back after seeing Jake up close. At six foot four, and three feet wide, Jake was definitely not someone with whom you would want to get on their bad side. Add to that, his shaved head and long beard and you had an intimidating looking man that most people would try to avoid. Although Hunter had a good inch of height on Jake, he was nowhere near as thick and, thankfully, realized that fact and backed down as soon as he set eyes on my brother.

Finn just stood there eyeing me with obvious disapproval as if I'd intended to roll around in the mud with a complete stranger in nothing but a small yellow bikini.

After eyeing Hunter for a few seconds longer, I gave my final warning. "I'm mean it. Stay away from my dogs. They weren't trying to hurt you."

Hunter seemed to calm down and stepped towards me causing Jake and Finn to step forward as well. Seeing that he was outnumbered, he stopped short, but reached his hand out to shake mine. "I apologize. I wasn't trying to hurt them. I normally love dogs. I just lost it when they messed up the paint job. My name is Hunter, by the way, it's *nice* to meet you."

I continued eyeing him, not in a forgiving kind of mood and definitely not interested in accepting his hand. "Whatever, Hunter. Just keep your distance and control your temper. They're defenseless animals."

A sigh escaped his lips while his eyes traveled between Lily, Jake, Finn and me. "Listen, I'll say it again: I wasn't attempting to hurt the dogs. But, I think I deserve an apology for the dogs ruining the wall."

I looked him over, but my anger wouldn't allow me to feel sorry for the destruction of the wall and therefore, I couldn't apologize. Reaching for Sasha and Bear, I grabbed their collars and limped them towards the house. My ankle was killing me and I just wanted to get away from the situation. When I first spotted him swinging that paint can out at the dogs, I jumped from the rooftop, injuring my ankle from the impact with the ground. It didn't stop me, though. I was on a rescue mission and I didn't allow the pain to get in the way of my objective.

After this experience I wanted nothing to do with Lily's cousin, despite Lily's assurances that he would be a great person to have around for the summer. She'd talked him up like he was a superhero, constantly babbling on about his intelligence and good looks. While I could admit that I could see where he'd be a charmer with his muscular build and naturally tan skin, it wasn't enough to make him attractive. And although he had warm brown hair accented by amazingly clear blue eyes, his looks were ruined when his personality took a shit on all of his favorable attributes.

As I stormed away, I overheard Lily making the introductions between the boys. And when I heard Finn's footsteps following behind me after he gave Hunter a curt 'hello', I groaned knowing he wasn't going to let this little charade go.

"El, wait up."

I stopped where I stood, knowing full well that Finn wouldn't drop it until I spoke with him.

"Babe? What was with the tackle maneuver? I kind of believe that he wasn't trying to hurt the dogs."

Spinning so that I could look Finn in the eye quickly, I reminded him, "I'm not your babe and I haven't been for over a year Finn, so just call me El if you need to talk to me."

I was even more annoyed now that Finn had attempted to call me by a pet name he'd used while we'd been dating. Ever since we broke up we remained friends but I could tell that he still carried one hell of a torch for me and it frustrated me that he hadn't moved on. We were best friends before we dated and I'd hoped that we could simply go back to that. No such luck. I couldn't understand it either. Finn was a good-looking guy with black hair, hazel eyes, and a thin muscular build. With his optimistic outlook and carefree personality, most women flocked to him. Yet, he still pined for me, even after a year-and-a-half long separation. I'd hoped to put some space between us after we split, but during the time we'd dated, he'd also struck up a friendship with Jake; therefore, I saw more of Finn around the house than I would have liked.

Holding up his hands in surrender, Finn cocked an eyebrow at me questioning my immediate defensive response. "*El*, I'm just trying to figure out why you got so mad — I'm just making sure you're okay."

The roll of my eyes was involuntary, but Finn was ever the peacekeeper and it was pointless continuing forward in my anger. "Finn, just drop it for it now, okay? I don't want to talk about it."

Storming towards the house, I threw open the door and dragged the dogs to the bathroom to wash the mud from their fur. When I'd accomplished bathing them, I went into the kitchen to feed them and grab a bowl of cereal for myself. While chewing the sugary rolled oat goodness, my mind drifted back to Hunter. I couldn't wrap my head around why any rational or sane person would lose it on a defenseless animal. Looking down at the two begging mutts at my feet, I smiled. Their fluffy faces turned up at me, tongues hanging low from their mouths, and the only thing I could see in their warm brown eyes was loyalty and love.

The front door slammed shut suddenly and the sound of Jake's footsteps preceded his entry into the kitchen. He smiled brightly, not even attempting to hide his delight in witnessing the impromptu mud-wrestling event in the front yard.

"Where's Finn?"

Jake used his thumb to motion over his shoulder when he answered, "Took off. Said something about you being in a 'Class-A' bitchy mood." Chuckling to himself, he opened the refrigerator door to pull out a cold beer. Leaning against the counter, he popped the cap and took a long sip before saying, "You might want to get yourself cleaned up and in more clothes before Dad gets homes. I don't think he'd appreciate finding out his baby girl was wrestling a strange man in the mud today." Another chuckle.

I looked down at my mud-covered body, thankful that my bathing suit had stayed in place during the event. Shrugging my shoulders, I said, "Alright, I'm getting a bath and going to bed. I'm heading out on the green trail tomorrow morning, so I won't be around when you wake up. Tell Daddy, I said goodnight when he gets home."

Jake nodded at me while taking another swig off his bottle and I left the kitchen to take a long shower and soak my ankle in hopes it would feel better in the morning.

~ ~ ~

The green trail is a 10-mile trail that winds its way through the nature preserve that's behind of my house. I had to cut a smaller path to reach it, but eventually, I made my own little private entrance into a secluded piece of paradise. That was a definite advantage to life in the middle of nowhere. Nature was not a great distance away and it was a quick journey for me to escape modern life when the need overtook me. My trek had started in the morning when it was cool, but by midafternoon the heat surged and I was sweating buckets by the time I made it back to the house. Walking between Lily's place and mine, I noticed that all the cars were missing from the houses, which was a pretty good sign that nobody was around. Since I was alone, I decided to wash off outside before tracking in dirt, leaves and other bits of the woods inside the house with me.

I always kept extra towels in a stowaway bench on the front porch, so I grabbed one and went around the side of the house to rinse off in the showerhead I'd rigged up the summer before. Stripping off my shirt and shorts, I stepped under the cool spray of water in only my underwear and a sports bra; and a sigh escaped my lips as the water washed away the sand and heat from my skin. After drenching my hair, I pushed it back out of my face and opened my eyes to the crystal blue shock in Hunter's eyes.

Jumping back, I fumbled for my towel while Hunter stood like a deer in headlights staring at my ... well ... headlights. His jaw hung open and he had a paint canister in each hand. Brown primer smeared down his shirt and was splattered over his legs. I held the towel up to cover my assets while using my hand to reach around and tuck it behind my body.

"Do you mind? Turning around would be the polite thing to do!" I huffed a lock of hair out of my face as I stepped off the concrete slab of the shower into my flip-flops. Hunter turned suddenly, paint sloshing out of the cans as he spun, his feet stumbling over themselves from the awkward weight of the liquid in motion at his sides.

"I'm sorry ... really ... sorry. I had no idea you were out here and I came around the corner, and, well ..."

"And well, what? You thought staring at a half-naked girl without alerting her to your presence was a smart idea? They have a word for that, you know."

His shoulders straightened allowing the thin material of his t-shirt to stick to his body with sweat. The material clung so closely, in fact, that every muscle that ran along his shoulders and down his spine was perfectly defined beneath the material. With his arms held out to his sides from holding the cans, I was able to see the perfect 'v' of his abdomen and it wasn't a bad package — until he opened his mouth.

"Look. I didn't intend to ogle you, but I came around the corner, you were just *there* and in my shock, I didn't react as fast as I should have. However, and in my defense, YOU are the one presently taking a shower in the front yard."

"I didn't think anybody was here! That's what I'm talking about. You had a voice to warn me of your presence and yet you chose not to use it!"

"Well, I thought I was alone as well! Maybe you should wear a bell or some shit so I'm alerted to your presence before I have the chance to walk in on you while you're naked in your front yard!"

I could not believe he'd just suggested that I wear a bell on my property. Who did he think he was?! And if I wanted to get naked on my property, I believe that I have that right without worrying about voyeurs lurking the grounds. There was no use in arguing, though ... so I had to get even.

"Turn around, Hunter."

"What?! No! You'll just call me a creep again!"

"Turn around." My face was straight and my tone of voice was even. I'd made my decision.

Hunter's body slowly rotated in my direction and his eyes shut to a point where the skin wrinkled at the sides. I laughed. I couldn't help it.

"I've been around you, in total, for less than an hour. Within that hour, all we've done is argue. So, I'm getting even, Hunter, and then we'll start from the beginning. Sound good?"

His eyes opened, shot to my chest momentarily, before immediately, and forcibly, shooting to my eyes. "Fine. What do you want?"

After securing the towel around my body, I smiled, took a few steps in his direction, before reaching out and taking the paint cans from his grip and placing them at his feet.

"I want you to strip."

Chapter Four

Hunter

She couldn't be serious. However, the expression on her face told me that under no uncertain terms, she was, in fact, serious.

"I'm not taking off my clothes. That's ridiculous!"

The expression on her face didn't change; except for the minute curl at the corner of her lips. "Strip. Then we will both have the advantage of knowing what the other looks like without clothes. It'll give us an even playing field."

I stood dumbfounded, not believing that she was telling me to take off my clothes. Since the moment I'd met her, she'd acted like a raging bull, tackling me over dogs and throwing out insults as fast as her tongue could form the sound. A spitting cat would have been more malleable than the headstrong blonde staring me down.

Her eyebrow was cocked teasingly over her eye and her mouth puckered up as she attempted to keep from laughing. Annoyance mixed thickly with my shock and I stood silent waiting for her to finally laugh and tell me she was joking.

She didn't.

Although the situation was odd, I couldn't help but inquire as to just how naked she wanted me. "You want me to take everything off?"

"No, just the pants and shirt. There's nobody here that's interested in seeing anything beyond that."

My ego took a small hit on that comment, but I pressed forward anyway. "So, let me get this straight. You decided to take a shower in your front yard after basically assaulting me yesterday over the fact that your dogs ruined my wall, and now you think that the only way we're going to be even is if I remove my clothes? I'm not exactly seeing how me being naked is going to solve anything."

Stepping back, she shook her head and finally let out the chuckle I knew she'd been holding in since the moment she told me to undress. "It's actually quite simple, Hunter. I feel embarrassed and ashamed that you've seen me practically naked and the only way I'm going to feel better about having been seen in that condition is to know that you feel equally as embarrassed to be seen that way as well. The dog incident has nothing to do with this, so that's just a dead issue."

She crossed her arms over her chest and her little foot popped out in front of her as she waited. Her words finally seeped their way through my shock and I noticed what she'd said.

"You think I'd be embarrassed to get naked in front of you?" I laughed. "Back home, I had hundreds of girls swooning over me daily. I work hard for the body I have."

Okay, not hard, because, thankfully, nature was kind and giving with my genetics.

"Well, yeah I think that." She walked towards me and motioned towards my shirt. "If you weren't embarrassed you'd have already taken off your clothes."

"I haven't taken off my clothes, because I think it's stupid!"

After tucking her towel into itself to ensure it wouldn't fall off, she stepped towards me and reached out to grip the bottom of my shirt. "Listen, I just want to get this asinine conversation over with, so take off the damn shirt and your pants and we'll call it even."

Her hands quickly pulled the sweat sodden material up my body and I stepped back in shock at her brazen behavior. Unfortunately, my foot caught on the paint can and I tumbled backwards, pulling Ellison down on top of me. Once again we found ourselves in a tangled mess of arms and legs and her wet hair fell down into my face, practically blinding me — which was unfortunate given the fact that the towel fell open and her barely covered chest and abdomen were front and center. I brushed the hair out of my face in time to see her wide-open blue eyes staring down at me just before she pushed herself up and fixed her towel.

Laughing, I said, "We've got to stop ending up like this."

She turned her face back toward mine and time stopped. I'm not kidding. I know it's the cheesiest way to describe what happened at that moment, but for a split second there, I was completely captivated by the beauty of the girl straddling my midsection. The sunlight peeked through the wet tangles of her golden hair and the glint in her eye sparkled ... just before she scowled.

"You know it's really creepy when you stare like that."

Standing up, she gripped the towel around herself tighter and walked towards her house. "Whatever, Hunter, I don't have all day to deal with you." She stopped and looked over her shoulder at me, just in time to catch me staring at her ass. A knowing expression fell over her face. "The way I figure it, you're too damn embarrassed to show some skin, so I'll leave you alone to deal with your insecurity issue. However, do me a favor and stop staring at me like some stalker. Let's just get through the summer and try to avoid each other from here on out."

My jaw dropped as she spun back towards her house and made her way inside. I could hear the two little fur balls barking as she entered and the distinct sound of the door slamming behind her. I stood motionless for a moment attempting to come to terms with meeting the strangest person I think I'd ever met in my life. I'm not sure how long I continued staring at her house, but at one point, the window curtain was pulled aside and her face came into view. She opened the window just enough so she could say, "See what I mean about you being creepy? Stop standing around staring at people and we might get along better." She closed the window and dramatically pulled the curtain back into place.

Sonofabitch! This girl was a nightmare.

I spent the rest of the afternoon painting primer on the exterior of the house. There may have been some choice expletives voiced the entire time I was *redoing* one side because that area of primer had been destroyed by Ellison's dogs. I was in shock that she didn't feel like she owed me anything for all those extra hours her mutts had cost me in doing this monotonous chore. I wanted to hate her. She'd done nothing but yell at me and call me "creepy" since the minute we'd met. But, unfortunately, every time I got close to convincing myself to forget her, my mind would reflect on that one

38

day: those piercing blue eyes and the view of her supple, barely dressed body under that showerhead ... those images flicker in my mind's eye and I've caught myself smiling a time or two.

I was coming around the corner after scraping the rest of the ruined primer off the wall and there she was: the sun glinted off the water that trailed down her tan skin. Her head was leaning back and her chest and stomach were the first things I saw. I didn't lie to her when I told her I'd been in shock. By the time my eyes had traveled down the full length of her legs and back up again, she was staring back at me like she wanted to murder me. I noticed that I'd started to run out of room in my pants from the view and I was nervous she would look down and see it too, so I turned around quick. Thankfully, she didn't and I was spared that train wreck of embarrassment. The time it took her to yell at me, and the disbelief I was feeling by what she was saying, helped my body calm down (quickly).

Squirt, Squirt, scrape, scrape ...

It was a mantra I repeated in my mind to cure the absolute boredom I had with the job I was doing. It was also a failed attempt at keeping thoughts of Ellison out of my head. Her body was insane and no matter what I did, or what I thought about, I couldn't keep the image of her smooth tanned skin from flashing itself in my mind. I wouldn't have minded considering her for a little summer fling if I could just find a way to keep her from talking and screwing up the mood.

Not able to stand the silence any longer, I stood up from my crouched position at the back of the house and went up onto the porch in search of a radio. Buried beneath all the greasy car parts and other odds and ends, I located a small radio and flicked it on before scrolling through countless country stations in search for some decent music. Eventually I found a station that was playing some industrial music and I carried the radio out with me to finish my job.

Having settled back into the routine, I picked up my speed and was finishing up the last part when I heard Ellison's front door open and the unmistakable sound of the little terrors being let outside. They instantly barked in appreciation and tore across the lot in my direction. I flinched immediately and stood up to protect the house at all costs.

"Sasha! Bear! You stop right there, you two!" Ellison's voice carried over the yard loudly and both dogs stopped instantly, kicking up little dust clouds with their feet. I looked up from the dogs to Ellison and she stared over at me with a crooked smile on her face. She patted her leg to call the dogs back to her. The dogs hesitated and looked at me, but eventually moved to stand at her feet.

"You got bacon in your pocket? They seem to like you — although I'm not sure why."

I smiled in response to her stab and responded, "I believe it's my shining disposition."

She laughed. "Somehow, I doubt that. Could you do me a favor and turn off the death metal? I can't even hear myself think."

I took her request as an affront. One of my favorite bands was playing at that moment and the way her expression soured when she heard it was insulting. I prided myself on my taste of music and her disapproval irritated me — although I couldn't immediately understand why.

Reaching over I flicked off the radio. "What's the matter? There's not enough twang to make it interesting to you country folk?" Okay — there was a little too much sarcasm in my tone on that comment, but Ellison seemed to bring it out in me.

"You must have an issue with silence. You know — that's a problem for a lot of people nowadays. They've always got to have something blasting in their ear or something to stare at. It's probably why so many of you are as miserable as you are. You don't know how to just enjoy the world around you."

I blinked up at her and it took me a second to absorb what she was saying. It must have taken me too long to respond because she spun on her heel and tapped against her leg to tell the dogs to follow. My eyes followed her as she walked towards a red, beat-up Jeep that I'd thought was broken down considering the terrible condition it was in. She turned to look at me again before climbing up into the driver's seat. The dogs happily climbed up into the Jeep with her and she placed them in the back. Looking over at me, she laughed.

"I've never known anybody who stares as much as you. Is there something on your mind that you need to say, or can you just not help yourself from looking at me?"

I blinked again and shook myself from my shocked silence. "No! You just keep saying weird shit and I'm not completely sure what to think about you."

"Then don't think about me. Just get back to your chore because it looks like it might take you a bit longer than you thought to finish it."

I turned to look back at the house to see what she was talking about. It looked perfect and all that I needed to do was let the primer dry before I painted it. Turning back to her, I asked, "Why do you say that?"

She smirked. "No reason."

After she turned away from me, the engine roared to life and smoke shot out of the muffler at the rear of the Jeep. She revved the engine a few times and pulled out quick enough to cause a cloud of dust and dirt to blow out from behind her. She looked at me in the rear view mirror as she drove off and raised her hand to wave out of the top before she turned and drove out of view. The cloud caused me to cough, but I still laughed and turned back to look at the house. Instantly I noticed that the dirt her Jeep had kicked up was now embedded in the tacky paint.

"Sonofabitch!"

She had to have known her Jeep would do that. Flicking my radio back on and turning it up louder, I marched over to fix the area her car had messed up and decided that when it came to Ellison James, the gloves were now off.

~ ~ ~

Well, she was correct. It did take me a few more hours to fix the area she'd messed up in her hasty departure and after scraping and re-priming again, I stood back to admire my work. I was packing up my tools when I heard a small bicycle bell chime behind me. Turning around I found Lily riding an old-fashioned blue bike that was equipped with a small brown basket in the front and streamers flying out the sides of the handles. I didn't even realize they made those for bikes large enough to be ridden by a person over the age of five.

"Hey, Cuz!" She stopped within feet of me and climbed off before kicking down the stand. "How's the painting going? Looks like you just finished."

One thing that amazed me about Lily was her ability to speak at least three times faster than any other human being I knew, but yet clearly pronounce each word with only the smallest amount of southern accent. Her blond hair bounced around her head as she approached me and I was instantly swept up into a large hug. Stepping back, she tucked her bangs behind her ears and smiled. "You did a good job; although, you could have been finished hours ago if you weren't such an obvious perfectionist. You do realize this is just primer, right?"

"It's the foundation for ...." I stopped before diving into my solid foundation speech and moved to continue gathering up the tools. "Never mind, but thanks. I would have been done a few hours ago if I didn't have to fix the front wall — AGAIN — after my run-in this afternoon with your friend."

I heard a small snicker behind me and I turned to glare at the little pixie of girl that she was. Her blue eyes were too big for her small head and her broad smile took up the rest of the room. Luckily, her nose was a perfect button and the combination gave her a cute innocent look.

"Ah ... you and Ellison had it out again, I presume. She's really not as bad as she seems, she's just extremely overprotective of animals, nature, friends, and family. As long as you don't litter, or try to hurt anything she cares about, she's an awesome person."

I laughed. "Well, does she have to be so irritatingly snarky all of the time? I believe she's called me a creepy stalker at least five times since I've been here. I'm starting to get a complex."

Lily looped her arm through mine and took one of the cans from me as we walked towards the back porch. "She must like you. If she really thought you were a jerk, she wouldn't give you the time of day. She's really good at not noticing someone if she doesn't want to."

"Well, I guess it's hard to ignore a person when he's staring at you taking a shower."

Lily stopped in her tracks and pulled me out of step with her. "What?"

I urged her to continue walking forward as I explained what happened between Ellison and me earlier that day. Lily laughed so hard when she heard the story that she snorted three times and her face was turning an interesting shade of blue. When she was finally able to breathe again, she removed her arm from mine and used it to slap me on the back.

"I can't believe you didn't just strip down. It would have saved you a few hours of re-priming this afternoon and, by my count, she still has to get even with you one more time. I hate to think what she'll come up with. I'd be nervous if I were you, Hunter." She climbed the steps giggling to herself after serving me her ominous warning.

I stopped at the base of the stairs watching her as she climbed up. "What is she capable of?"

Lily turned around and put her hands on her hip. After kicking a rock off the porch, she looked back at me and laughed.

"That's the thing with Ellison. You never really know."

"That girl is capable of anything."

Chapter Five

I spent the early part of the evening watching television with Lily and Uncle Bill. Every time I saw headlights coming down the dirt path that led to the houses, I peeked out the window to see if it was Ellison arriving home. I couldn't get her out of my head and I was a little annoyed that she'd gotten under my skin. By the time night had fallen, I'd gotten a good look at her freakishly large brother as he meandered home with an older gentleman I'd not met.

"That's El's daddy. He's never around during the day and leaves for work before the sun even comes up. You'll rarely see him around." Lily commented when she noticed how intently I was watching out the window.

Uncle Bill gave me a funny look. "Are you looking for anyone in particular, Hunter?"

Lilly laughed at his question and took the liberty of answering for me. "He and Ellison got into it again today. Apparently, he saw her in her skivvies when she was getting a shower after a hike."

"Oh dear. I wouldn't let her daddy find out about that. He'll remove your eyes if he knew you was looking at his little girl." Uncle Bill laughed and clapped me on the shoulder.

What was with these people and smacking me?

"It wasn't my fault! She was showering in the front yard for fuck's sake! How was I supposed to know she'd be naked out where anyone could see her? And from what I could see, she's not a *little* girl anymore."

Bill's face wrinkled from his scowl. "First off, son, there are rules in this house and one of them is to watch your language. I don't know about you kids these days, but when I was brought up, you'd get smacked upside the head for cussing in front of a lady. I'da thought your momma would have taught you better than that."

I smiled at the thought. In truth, my mother cussed like a sailor. Hell, she was the one that taught me the best words — most of the time, after I'd done something really stupid.

"And secondly, Ellison's not used to having extra people 'round here and normally she's got the place to herself during the day. Except for Lily, most of us are at work. I'm sure she realizes that now and will be more careful. What'd she do when you saw her?"

"She told me to strip so that we were even."

"Did you do it?"

"No! I see no reason why I had to remove my clothes just because I'd walked in on her. It wasn't my fault."

Bill laughed a deep belly laugh. "Well, son, if Ellison was trying to make you two square and you refused, you've got something coming. That girl will find a way to make sure she gets even. Her poor daddy had to put up with all sorts of pranks gone wrong between El and her brother through the years. Most of the time, it's entertaining as hell, just as long as you're not her intended target. I'd sleep with one eye open if I were you." He kept chuckling after giving me information that didn't really help out with the nagging obsession I was starting to have with her.

I stood up to stretch my legs and ran my hand through my hair. "Well, thanks for that. I'll be sure to avoid her as much as possible."

He looked up at me with a strange expression before busting out into another fit of laughter. "Good luck to you, son. I'd let her do what she's going to do so that you can get it over with as quickly as possible. It's kind of like ripping off a band aid.Band-Aid. Just let her do what she's going to do and eventually the sting will go away."

Lily bounced up from her chair and ran over to grab my arm. "I have an idea." Turning to Bill, she asked, "Daddy? Could Hunter and I take your truck for a little while? I'm going to take him into town and show him around."

"Well, sure, Lil — but you know the rules: No speeding and be home before midnight."

"Midnight, Daddy?! You can't be serious! I turned 18 *three weeks ago*. I should get an extended curfew now that I'm an adult!"

"Listen Darlin', the only thing 'round these parts that's open after midnight are the bars, and considering that you didn't turn 21 three weeks ago, you have no business being there. There ain't nothin' good that happens for kids your age after midnight and your curfew remains the same." Uncle Bill stated his case and by the tone of his voice, it was obvious he wouldn't budge from his decision.

Lily and I both groaned, but I was absolutely ecstatic with her suggestion that we get out of the house. I was never one to hang around one place for too long back home and I was starting to feel the effects of cabin fever after being holed up in this place for two days.

"Let me go change real quick, Lil, and I'll meet you outside." I quickly ran back to my room and changed into a clean pair of jeans and a button down black shirt. I wasn't sure where she was taking me, but I wanted to make a good impression in case we ran into any one worth noticing.

I guess now would be a good time to mention how unfaithful I'd been to Tiffany the entire time we dated. I know it will make you hate me and I'm sure you've been questioning my lack of thoughts towards her during my exile. To be honest, not having to deal with her was the only good part about having all my stuff taken away. I could imagine the battery in my phone was already dead from the amount of times she undoubtedly called and I was almost afraid to remotely check my voicemails for fear of hearing her shrill voice. I knew that when I returned home, I needed to man up and break up with her, but I just couldn't bring myself to do it when I thought about the hour of screaming I would endure after the deed had been done. I couldn't feel bad about hurting her though, because I knew she was the type to replace me within five minutes of splitting up.

I shook Tiffany from my thoughts and raced back out into the living room. Uncle Bill motioned for me to go outside without turning his attention away from the television. "Wheel of Fortune" was on and I grimaced when Bill started shouting out letters like the contestants could actually hear him. Quickly finding my way outside, I spotted Lily by Bill's truck talking to … well, shit … she was talking to Ellison.

As soon as I opened the door, the two devil mutts moved their little legs as fast as they could while cruising straight towards me. By the time they were by my side, drool dripped from their tongues and I reached down to pet them, only to come up with a disgusting mixture of dog spit and snot covering my palm. I looked at the black one and noticed that the front half of its body had long hair, and the back half had short hair. It was like someone cut two dogs in half and glued them back together, making it the most ugly and pathetic creature I'd ever seen. Oddly, it was so ugly, the little furball was cute. Ellison remained focused on her conversation with Lily and I took the opportunity to love on the dogs hoping to score some points and change El's mind about exacting revenge. From what I was told by Lily and Bill, Ellison had plenty of experience in the prank department and I wasn't looking forward to finding out just how creative she could get.

As I started down the rickety stairs, the dogs followed at my heels and Lily and Ellison looked over to watch me as I approached.

I ran my hand through my hair and then instantly regretted it after remembering the dog cocktail that had been left on my palm. "Uh ... hey girls." The dogs were jumping on my legs attempting to get my attention and I knelt down to lavish them with love. Ellison cocked an eyebrow in my direction and I smiled up at her in response. "Looks like the mutts have forgiven me for our less than stellar introduction."

Ellison smiled and patted her leg to call them to her. "Yeah, that's the thing about animals. They don't really hold grudges like people do."

Lily snorted out a laugh and Ellison looked over and smiled mischievously at her friend.

Shit ... apparently she didn't forgive as easily as her dogs.

"Well, I'm going to head inside, Lily, you two have fun tonight." Ellison waved as she began to walk off and Lily lunged forward and grabbed her hand.

49

"Come on Ellison. It's been weeks since we went out for some fun. Why don't you come with us tonight? We can hang at The Tavern and have a few beers. Please Ellie!" Lily followed behind Ellison as she made her way over to her house and once they were out of earshot, Ellison turned around and spoke to Lily.

Feeling awkward standing by the truck, I shoved my hands in my pockets and leaned against the passenger door looking anywhere but in the direction of the two girls. A sudden loud squeal grabbed my attention and when I looked in their direction I saw Lily jumping up and down excitedly. Ellison opened the front door of her house to let her dogs inside, then closed it and walked back towards Lily.

Great ... a night out with the girl who was out to get me ... should be interesting.

I plastered on a fake smile as they approached and Lily immediately ran around to jump in the driver's seat while El and I climbed into the passenger side. Ellison sat in the middle and when I squeezed in beside her, the smell of her hair wrapped itself around me. She smelled like coconuts and some flower I didn't recognize and I had to admit — it was intoxicating. The cabin of the truck was cramped and the heat from Ellison's body seeped into the side of my chest and leg. I trained my eyes out the window of the truck, but after a few minutes, I couldn't stand the uncomfortable silence in the truck.

"So, where are we going?"

Turning towards the girls, I smiled and waited for Lily to respond. It was apparent Ellison wasn't completely happy being in the truck and Lily didn't disappoint when she answered.

"We're going to The Tavern. It's a local hangout where my boyfriend, Ryan, is the bartender. He'll serve us, but only as long as the place isn't packed. It's a Thursday, so we should have no problems. Not many people do much at night when they have work the next morning."

Nodding my head, I responded, "Sweet. It's been two days since I've had any fun. I was wondering if there was anything around here besides trees." Things were looking up and I was excited to be getting back to the types of activities that I was used to. Partying, drinking and socializing were definitely things I knew how to do well.

We pulled up to The Tavern and I looked warily at a rundown building that looked like it could have been a bar back in its better days. The makeshift parking area was nothing more than loose stones and there were four dingy vehicles parked on either side of the front door. Lily pulled to a stop and hopped out of the truck to quickly dart inside. Ellison looked over at me after a few seconds. I hadn't noticed I'd taken to study the building.

"Not what you expected?" Ellison chuckled softly as she climbed out of the driver's side door. Opening my door, I stepped out of the truck and called out to Ellison as she moved towards the front door of the bar. "Hey, El! Wait up!" Picking up my pace, I ran to catch up with her and grabbed her arm.

She turned to me with wide blue eyes and a smirk peeked out at the corners of her enticing lips. I didn't know what was happening to me, but being this close to Ellison was causing my body to simmer with heat. "About this 'getting even' thing, I kind of just want to get past all the crap that happened today and start over. I think everything has just been a misunderstanding and I want to apologize for my part of it."

The smirk changed into a knowing smile. "Been talking to Lily or something? You seem a little nervous there, Hunter."

I laughed and rubbed at the back of my neck. I could feel the embarrassment of admitting defeat burn along my cheeks and I smiled down at the gorgeous girl in front of me. "Well, yeah, I spoke to her this afternoon and she warned me that you can be creative when you're mad. I just don't want any hard feelings between us. I think we got off on the wrong foot and both did and said things that were stupid."

My skin tingled when her eyes narrowed and she stepped back to look me up and down. After a few seconds she finally replied, "Yeah, I don't know about that, Hunter. From what I can see under that shirt, I might enjoy looking at you without clothes. You know, you can still strip down and we'll call this over."

I looked around. "What? Here?"

Laughing, she answered, "Yeah. Why not? I know the owner's son, he won't care, and he's the only one working tonight."

Holding my hands up, I stepped away from her. "No. That's insane. We're out in public and I'm not stripping down to my underwear in the middle of a bar parking lot. I think that's illegal anyway. There has to be some other way we can handle this."

She thought about it for a moment. "I tell you what ... why don't we head inside and have a few cold ones and I'll let you know later on what we can do to solve this. Sound good?"

I eyed her suspiciously. "Can I trust that you won't do something to embarrass me or in any way torture me?"

She walked towards the door, but stopped to look over her shoulder and responded, "Not really, but what other choice do you have?"

Dammit, she had a point.

I hurried to the door and reached around El to open it for her. She looked up at me and grinned, but didn't say anything as she moved inside. Walking in behind her, I immediately noticed that the smoke in the place was so thick you could barely see the back of the building from the front. Towards our right stood an old oak bar that took up the entire side of the room. Lily was on her knees on a barstool, leaned over the top with her arms around a guy that had the typical country look like my Uncle Bill. He broke from kissing her long enough to look over in our direction. Ellison waved and I followed her through the clusters of tables until she finally sat down in a booth on the left side of the room.

An old Southern Rock anthem blasted from the jukebox next to the bar and there was a couple in the middle of the room, drunkenly dancing to the song.

"What do you want to drink?"

I turned my attention away from the dancing couple and answered Ellison's question. "Doesn't matter. Why don't we order a pitcher of whatever you want?"

Ellison shrugged and waved over the waitress to order two pitchers. The waitress smacked her gum loudly while eyeing me, but then turned to go to the bar and fetch our order. I felt awkward sitting alone with Ellison and for the life of me I couldn't figure out a damn thing to say. It was weird. Never in my life had I been tongue-tied around a girl, but somehow her mere presence shut down my ability to formulate words. Her hair was windblown from the drive over and the look only made her hotter. The collar of her black shirt hung low enough that I could make out just a hint of cleavage, but it was enough to force memories of her mid-day shower back through my mind. I groaned at the imagery and forced myself to look away from her in search of Lily.

"So, did Lily bring us here just to ditch us or what?" I located my cousin sitting at the bar making googly eyes at the man I assumed was her boyfriend.

"Yep. That's why I tried to decline coming along tonight. Ever since she started seeing Ryan, she pretty much remains glued to those barstools every time we're here."

Great.

I turned back to Ellison. "So, this is it?"

"This is what?" Her expression remained blank, but the gleam in her eye let me know she knew exactly what I was asking.

"This is what people around here do for fun?"

"You could say that." She laughed. "I have other things I consider 'fun' but I come here for Lily's sake. Your uncle doesn't like Ryan too much. He was the bad boy of our high school class and hasn't been able to live down the string of women and wild parties of his past. He's calmed down, though, and he's been good to her, so I tag along to give her an excuse to come see him."

"So, what do you do for fun?" I couldn't help but inquire. I was intrigued to talk to a girl whose life didn't revolve around socializing and partying. Back

54

home, that's all the girls did and Tiffany was their ringleader.

"A lot of stuff. Mainly, hiking, but I also ride my bike through the trails sometimes and fishing, swimming, camping, stuff like that. I enjoy being outside if you couldn't tell by that list."

Crap. She was a nature lover. I'd already suspected, but to have her openly admit that she and my arch nemesis were tight? That put a kink in my sail. As I'd mentioned earlier, nature and I didn't get along. I'd attempted her aforementioned activities at least once in my life — each time returning home with scrapes and bruises, odd itchy rashes, and enough bug bites to drive any sane man mad. I wasn't sure how I was going to find anything in common with her, but I was too damn stubborn not to try.

"Sounds like a good time." Really it didn't, but I had to play along. Well, maybe fishing. I'd seen it on television once and it didn't look all that difficult. I mean, how much trouble could a fish give someone my size?

"I also read a lot, and play guitar ... stuff like that."

Okay, now we were getting somewhere. I continued my interrogation and about three pitchers later, I'd somehow agreed to go hiking with Ellison the following day. She mentioned something about starting me off on the "easy" trail, but I had to act like a badass and insist on taking whatever trail it was that she normally walked. There was too much alcohol in my system to concern myself with what that would entail, but I had a sneaking suspicion I would be kicking myself for it the next morning.

Ellison and I didn't have much to talk about and I was putting away tall ones faster than I wanted to admit. With the liquid courage running through my system, I decided to break up the boredom by asking Ellison to dance. Lily was still sitting with Ryan and I was dying to get up and move around. Ellison accepted my offer and we made our way out onto the dance floor.

"I have to warn you that I don't dance all that well. I can get through the basic steps but I wouldn't attempt anything fancy." Her cheeks reddened with her admission and I couldn't help but grin.

"You don't dance? How is that even possible? Pretty girl like you, I'm shocked you don't have guys hanging all over you."

"You can stop with the cheesy lines, and, no, I don't dance. As for guys, I've only really dated Finn and we've been off and on for a little over two years."

I stopped moving almost instantly. "Wait, Finn? That guy with your brother yesterday was your boyfriend?" I wasn't quite sure why I was so bothered by it. I was only going to know this girl for the summer and then I was heading back to real life — but for some damn reason I had the overwhelming urge to escort Finn to a boat and send him on his way to his own little island in the Caribbean — far away from Ellison.

She shook her head. "No. We broke up over a year ago, but he still hangs around because of his friendship with my brother." She rolled her eyes and I chuckled at the look of dismay plastered across her face.

"Judging by the look he was giving me yesterday, things aren't completely over between you and him — at least in his head, it isn't. He looked like he wanted to smash my face in after he caught us down in the mud."

Ellison laughed a deep belly laugh and her head fell backwards. My eyes ran down the smooth stretched skin on her neck and then lower to her chest before lifting again to catch her twinkling blue eyes as she straightened. I couldn't help but smile and I knew the two dimples on my cheeks were standing front and center due to my beaming grin. Her laughter was infectious.

"Finn? Smash your face in? Hardly. He may be a redneck, but he's not a hot head. If anything, he would diffuse a fight before he would join one. That's what I liked about him at first. He didn't feel the need to puff out his chest at every insult. He just let shit roll off his back and kept doing his thing."

She looked up at me and the light bounced off her golden hair, making it look like she was glowing. I should have been paying attention as she sized up the competition for me, but I was too damn distracted by the beauty of the woman in my arms. My hands brushed down her back and I instinctively pulled her closer in to me. I stared down at her silently and my eyes focused on the pout of her lips and the way the lip-gloss she wore glistened. I wanted nothing more but to reach down and taste her lips to find out what flavor she'd chosen. Her eyebrow cocked over her eye in question after I'd been staring for too long and she placed her hands on my chest to push me away.

"Think we've danced enough, big guy. You want to split another pitcher?"

"Sure do." I wanted to get her drunk. I know it's awful and, under normal circumstances, I wouldn't attempt to get a girl wasted, but Ellison seemed to have opened up some and I figured it had to do with the alcohol. I wasn't planning on doing anything with her; I just wanted to keep her talking.

And that's when I realized that something was definitely the fuck wrong with me. Never before had I given a shit what a girl had to say. Typically, I would lose interest after the first few sentences they uttered and focus my attention on what their body could offer me. But Ellison was different. She didn't talk about normal shit like clothes and celebrities and the next opportunity she had to get fucked up. We were on opposite sides of the line when it came to our lifestyles, but I was damn interested to find out more about her.

We made our way to the booth and I sat down hoping she would slide in beside me. My body already missed the heat I felt rolling off of her when we'd been dancing. My feet were killing me because she was right — she was a horrible dancer. Every time we rotated, her heel found the arch of my foot and I wondered how it was possible for her to hit the same spot every single time. But I didn't care. If she'd been kicking me in the shins, I would have bit my tongue and endured it just to hold her for a few minutes longer.

El slid in the seat facing me and waved over at the waitress to indicate we needed a refill. Looking towards me, she smiled. "How much can you drink, big guy?"

I smiled. Now we were in my area of expertise: Drinking, partying and drugs. I'd built up quite a tolerance through the years and I chuckled to myself when she appeared to be challenging me to a drinking contest.

"You think you can drink more than me?"

She smiled. "No. Drinking contests are dangerous. You can poison yourself that way. I just want to make sure you walk out of here with a pretty good buzz."

I returned her smile because I liked where this was going. Clenching my cheeks to present my dimples, I pulled out all the stops to attract her attention. Girls always loved my dimples and I wasn't ashamed to admit I used them to my advantage. "Why? Do you want me buzzed?"

She looked over to the bar and grinned as she considered some inner thought. Turning back to me she winked when she said, "No reason."

Oh yeah. This was going to be a good night

Chapter Six

"Boy! Can you explain to me why, exactly, you are laid up in my driveway naked as a jaybird?"

I felt a boot kick me softly in the side and I startled instantly. My eyes peeked open and I saw a strange man standing above me. I sat up quickly, but instantly regretted it when a headache started pounding against my skull. Holding my head in my hands, I attempted to block out the floodlights that were glaring down at me from the porch of Ellison's house.

What the fuck?!

Laughter erupted behind me, just before another voice said, "Holy shit! What the fuck is wrong with you, man? You are covered head to toe in mosquito bites. That shit is going to suck as soon as you start moving around." When I turned to look behind me, I spied Ellison's brother standing there.

"Like I asked, boy, what are you doing naked in front of my house? Who the hell are you? Why I shouldn't shoot you for being naked outside of my little girl's window."

That got my attention.

I looked down to see just how naked I was and I breathed a sigh of relief to find that I still had boxers covering my nether regions. Looking up at who I presumed was Ellison's father, I opened my mouth to talk, but was interrupted by Jake.

"This is Lily's cousin from up north. He's staying with her and Bill for the summer."

El's dad eyed me warily. I sat up straighter, groaning from the blood pounding through my head, and pulled my legs up to my chest. My skin started itching like a motherfucker and I tried desperately to remember how I ended up naked in the dirt. The last thing I remembered was drinking with El at the bar and ... fuck.

Ellison. I knew she had something to do with this.

Holding my hands up in surrender, I looked up at Mr. James. "I'm really, really sorry, sir, but I have no fucking clue how I ended up here. I went out with Lil last night and I don't remember much of what happened. If it's okay, I'd like to just stand up and go inside and we can talk about this when I have some clothes on."

Speaking of which — where the fuck were my clothes?

Mr. James snorted in response. "Well, yeah, we'll be talking about this all right. Just as soon as Bill is up, I'll be having some words with him about ya. I don't much appreciate strange naked men lurking around my daughter." He uncocked the gun I hadn't notice he'd been holding and replaced it in a holster at his side. "Now get inside before I change my mind and take care of your sorry ass myself."

He didn't have to tell me twice. I was still stuck on the fact that the man had been holding a gun and I almost pissed myself wondering what could have happened if Jake hadn't been around to identify me. Pushing up from the ground, I resisted the temptation to move quickly and start itching the shit out of the

61

bites on my chest and legs. I didn't know if this guy had a quick trigger finger when it came to his daughter and I sure as hell didn't want to stick around much longer to find out.

Not even bothering to brush the dirt off the back of me, I backed up to my uncle's house — slowly — while still holding my hands out in surrender. "I'm just going to go inside now and get dressed and talk to Lil, I'm sure there's a perfectly reasonable explanation as to why I'm sleeping in the driveway naked. I'll be happy to explain it to you once she tells me what happened last night."

Mr. James scowled and took a step toward me. "Boy! It is two o'clock in the fucking morning. Don't you dare go waking that girl up in the middle of the night! Now, get your sorry ass inside, put on some clothes and crawl your ass underneath your blankets. I'll talk to Lily myself when I return home this evening."

"Yes sir." I nodded my head while continuing to slowly back away. When my foot finally hit the stairs to the front door, I turned quickly and hoofed up three steps at a time just to get away. Quickly opening the door, entering and slamming it behind me, I groaned when the entire house shook and hoped I didn't wake up Bill and Lily. No lights turned on and I figured they'd slept through it. I made my way to the bathroom and grimaced when I caught sight of myself in the mirror. I was c-o-v-e-r-e-d in mosquito bites. My skin looked like I'd just gotten over a bad case of chicken pox and my skin itched so badly, I wanted to rip it off my body. I flung open the toiletry closet and located a bottle of calamine lotion. I looked between the bottle and the tub and when I determined it wasn't enough to fill the tub for me to soak in the shit, I opened it and start pouring it over my skin. By the time I emptied the bottle, I looked like I'd been thrown up on by a bottle of Pepto-Bismol. Pink was not my color, but the itching had stopped and I was going to have to sleep in this shit.

Finally hightailing it to my room, I carefully shut the door climbed beneath the covers. I laid on my back for a few minutes completely freaked out over what had transpired and annoyed as shit that I didn't remember how I'd ended up naked in the front yard. I knew Ellison did this and I kicked myself for having trusted her at the bar. I made a mental note that when Ellison James uttered the words "no reason," I needed to get the hell out of Dodge before she had the chance to follow that phrase up with whatever *fuckedupery* she was planning.

But damned if I wasn't impressed with her execution. I had no fucking clue it was coming even after Lily and Uncle Bill had warned me. All that girl had to do was smile and wink and I was putty in her hands. The realization was unnerving. She'd somehow crawled under my skin and implanted herself in my head and the only thing I could think about was how I was going to plant myself in hers.

~ ~ ~

The mattress dipping down at my feet woke me up later in the morning. I peeled my eyes open to find a smiling Lily at the foot of my bed. Her hand reached out and tugged the covers down off my chest. After looking me over, the corners of her mouth curled and she snorted while trying not to laugh. She gave up the fight within seconds and started laughing her ass off at the sight of me.

"What the fuck, Lil? It isn't funny."

She was balled over herself and I could see her back shaking from her laughter. Finally looking up, she laughed again, but then wiped the tears from her eyes as she said, "I knew I shouldn't have left you alone with El in the driveway last night."

"Yeah! About that! What the hell happened?!" I didn't mean to sound as pissed off as I was feeling, but my anger was boiling out of me.

"Calm down, pink boy, the bites have probably already stopped itching considering you slept in a blanket of calamine." She smiled brightly at me and I turned my attention to the window. It was still dark outside.

"What the hell time is it, anyway?" I sat up straight and the blankets puddled around my hips revealing even more of the pink shit smeared down my abdomen.

Lily giggled when she looked at me. "It's five in the morning."

"What the fuck?! Do any of you sleep?" I was annoyed that the sun hadn't even come up and I was being awoken yet again. My circadian rhythm was taking a beating and I was seriously fucking exhausted.

"What do you mean any of us? I was just waking you up because you told El you'd be hiking with her today and she usually leaves just before the sun comes up. I wanted to give you time to get a shower and get dressed. If you're not ready by the time she heads out, she'll leave you behind."

I groaned at her reminder that I'd acted like a bad ass and signed up for a hike, which I was sure would count as military training.

"But, seriously, what do you mean 'any of us'?"

I scowled at her. "Well, at TWO o'clock this morning I woke up NAKED in the driveway with El's dad and her brother standing over me."

Lily bust out laughing again.

"It isn't funny! Her dad had a gun. He'd could've shot me if it wasn't for Jake telling him that I wasn't some freak." My jaw dropped as I watched her work diligently to get herself back under control. By the time she looked back up at me, her eyes were bloodshot from laughing tears.

"I'm sorry, Hunter. El must have left you out there. I told you to be careful with that girl. She's real serious about getting even." Her words were broken up by her continued chortles.

Balking at the fact that she was blaming me, I let out a resigned sigh. "Can you just tell me what happened and how I ended up ALONE with a girl who was out to get me? We're family, you should have looked out for me better than that."

Lily's eyes grew wide. "I tried. When we left the bar, you were shitfaced and Ryan had to help El and I drag you to the truck. We rode home and all you kept doing is telling El how *beautiful* she was and calling her an angel. By the time we made it home, you begged me to leave you in the driveway with her so you could *continue to work your love magic*." She made the little air quote signs with her hands as she spoke.

"I didn't really say that, did I?" Oh God. I was dying inside. Absolutely, 100 percent dying if I really said those things to El.

"Uh, yeah, you did. You're so damn big, I couldn't just drag your drunk ass in and Daddy would have killed me if I stayed outside much longer. I had no choice but to leave you."

I couldn't believe it. I had not been able to drink to the point of blacking out for the last few years. How did it happen last night? I didn't understand how I got so drunk splitting a couple of pitchers with Ellison. "Was Ellison drunk too?"

Lily snickered. "No. She doesn't drink that much so she takes it easy when we go out. She was pretty much normal by the time we left the bar. I don't know what she did to you after I went inside. You're going to have to ask her that yourself."

"Lily! You up?!" Uncle Bill's voice boomed through the house and the volume did nothing for the massive hangover headache that was creeping back into my skull.

Lily turned towards the door. "Yeah, Daddy, I'll be out there in a second!"

I cradled my pounding head in my hands and tried to cover my ears to mute the volume of her voice.

"I gotta go check on Daddy. You should get ready. El will be heading out within the next 20 minutes or so. She said she'd stop by before leaving." Lily stood up to head into the hallway, but turned back to me. "If you want, I can whip you up some breakfast. Might help you with that hangover you're sporting."

My burning eyes peered out at her through my fingers. "Is it that obvious?"

"Just a little." She had a sympathetic look on her face for about a split second before it was replaced with a smile. "I'd wash off all that lotion if I were you. Pink is not your color."

I flipped her off and she laughed while walking out towards the living room. Peeling myself off the mattress, I immediately made my way into the bathroom and washed off the inch thick layer of lotion I had over my skin. When the water finally ran clear again, I climbed out, dried off and threw on a pair of shorts and a t-shirt. Walking into the living room, I smelled eggs and bacon being fried up in the kitchen and my mouth watered. My stomach growled loudly and I sat down next to Uncle Bill at the kitchen table and watched Lily cook up the goods. Uncle Bill folded down the newspaper and eyed me suspiciously.

"What's this I hear about you streaking in our front yard? I received a voicemail from a really pissed off Henry this morning letting me know he found you sprawled out in the driveway, naked and smelling like you'd just returned home from a brewery. I know you're not legal drinking age, son, so I think you need to give me a really good explanation that doesn't cause me to whip your ass from here to next Wednesday." He was yelling at me as Ellison entered through the front door. My eyes immediately went to hers and she chuckled to see how miserable I was at that moment.

"Hey, all! How's everyone doin' this mornin'?" Ellison waltzed in looking absolutely stunning in a pair of khaki shorts and a black tank top. Her hair was pulled back in a braid and she held several bags in her hands. The little furry demons followed in at her heels. They must have smelled the bacon, because within seconds, they were at Lily's feet *sitting pretty* as they begged for the food. Lily smiled down at them and threw them each a small piece of bacon.

"Now, Lily, don't you be feeding those mutts before the human members of this family have had a chance to eat," Uncle Bill scolded.

Lily nodded, but then rolled her eyes and kept feeding them when Bill wasn't looking — which was when his eyes had returned to me. "So, are you going to tell me what happened, Hunter?"

"Oh! That was my fault, Bill." Ellison spoke up quickly when Bill started giving me the third degree. "It was just a harmless prank and I'll explain everything to Daddy when he gets home tonight. No worries." She smiled sweetly and I could literally see Bill melt. I had to admit: the girl had charm.

"Well, okay, Ellison, but you know you three shouldn't be out drinking. I have a real problem with that and you know why. I don't see the need to get into it now, but cut out the bullshit until you're legal, at least. Maybe by then, you'll have enough sense to stay away from alcohol."

We ate breakfast in silence and every once in a while the three of them would crack up after getting a good look at the bites along my arms. I was itching like a madman and I resembled a hyperactive toddler with the amount of squirming I was doing in my chair. I eyed Ellison across the table and I was balling my hands up trying to keep from demanding she tell me what happened the night before. It wasn't a conversation I wanted to have in front of Bill, so it took everything I had not to grab her and force the information out of her right where she sat. She must have known what I thinking too, because the whole damn time we were eating, she kept smiling at me across the table just before laughing at some unshared thought. After we'd finally finished eating, Ellison stood up and walked to the front door.

"You ready, Hunter? It's not going to get any cooler out there, so it's best that we start now." She picked up the bags from the floor and threw two of them at me when I approached her. "You've got a camel pack and a regular pack for food and water. I've filled up both, so you should have no problem walking the trail with me."

I stopped in my tracks. "How far a hike is this trail? Two miles — five? Why do we need provisions?" I had a sinking feeling in my stomach that I really should NOT have agreed to this. Why did I not just agree to the easy trail? I hate it when my testosterone and need to show off ended up putting me in fucked up situations.

Nonchalantly, she answered, "It's about 20 miles, give or take. We should be able to complete it in a little less than seven hours if we really hoof it. No biggie."

My jaw dropped. I was so fucking tired already that I couldn't even close my mouth without pushing up on my chin with my hand. And this girl wanted me to walk 20 miles in the Florida summer heat?! Uh-huh. No way was this happening. She was crazy.

"I don't think so, Ellison. That sounds like suicide."

She smirked at me and reached to take the packs from my hand. "That's fine, Hunter. It's decent of you to admit you can't handle it before going out there with me and slowing me down. I'm sure I'll see you around when I get back." It was a hit to my ego and then she did it again. That thing she does that drives me crazy and makes a certain part of me want to stand at attention: She winked.

Dammit. I was going to do this.

"Fine. Whatever. I can do this. I was just worried about you having the energy to handle it given the fact that you didn't get much sleep last night. Oh, wait! That was me."

A smile escaped her parting lips and her eyes twinkled with humor. "I can imagine sleeping outside in a swamp is a bad idea ... especially while naked. I'm surprised you got any sleep at all."

And with that, she opened the door and walked outside.

Chapter Seven

The sun was just starting to come up over the horizon and if there's anything to be said about Florida, it was that the sky was so beautiful at times; it looked like it had been painted by a master artist. Pinks, reds, yellows and oranges streaked across the skies, casting a brilliant light on the trees and plant life surrounding us. Ellison and I navigated our way through a small path that was cut into the dense vegetation, and the two fuzzballs were following fast on our heels.

"Are you sure the little guys will make the trip? Seems like they have to move their legs four times as fast to keep up with us." The two dogs were panting heavily behind me and I almost felt the need to pick them up and carry them.

Ellison glanced behind her to look at the mutts. "Don't let them fool you. They've made this trip with me several times already. Plus, there are plenty of places to take a break and cool down, so it won't be a problem for them. They're tougher than they look." She smiled at me before returning her attention to the trail.

We walked in silence for a short while until I couldn't hold my curiosity any longer. "So, are you going to tell me what happened last night?" I couldn't help the fact that while I asked that question, I was also hungrily staring at the perfection of her ass in the hiking shorts she was wearing.

She stopped and bent over to place her hands on her knees when she laughed loudly at my question. I was instantly hard from the sight of it, not even caring that she was in the middle of laughing at my pain. When she straightened and turned suddenly, I shifted the position of my body to try to hide my excitement.

She walked towards me seductively which contrasted sharply with the innocent smile she had on her face. "Well, first you told me repeatedly about how beautiful I am. I mean, really, the whole drive home, all you did was praise me. It was very flattering to say the least."

My entire body froze.

"And then after we finally arrived back, you begged me to sleep in your bed because — and I quote — *you wouldn't be able to sleep without the scent of me wrapped around your body.*"

That was it. My internal organs were all shutting down and I was dying from embarrassment. Never, and I repeat NEVER had I ever acted like such a douche because of a female. She had to have slipped something into my drink. Although, come to think of it, the scent of her wrapped around my body was actually a really good idea on the part of my drunken alter ego. I gave him a mental high five for that.

"I didn't actually say that, did I?"

She smiled. "Oh, yes … yes, you did. Apparently, my shampoo smells as good as a tropical island, which, by the way, was actually the sun lotion I'd put on earlier that day. But thanks anyway." Again, she winked. This girl was trying to destroy me where I stood and she was doing a damn good job of it.

When she reached me, she ran her finger down my chest and stomach. Every muscle she touched flinched as the pad of her finger brushed over it. Her eyes sparkled when she looked up at me.

"But my favorite part was when you started taking off your clothes. Since I wouldn't go in your house with you, you decided that we should sleep outside and that is when you decided to strip down. You laid down on the ground and refused to get up, so I sat there and let you fall asleep. I thought about waking you before I went in but then I remembered I had to get even with you one more time. I knew daddy would wake up and leave early so you would only be out there for an hour or so." She chuckled softly while holding my stare.

"You do realize your father almost killed me when he found me, right? And what if I'd been allergic to mosquitos? I could have gone into anaphylactic shock right there. I would have died and you would have felt really bad." I wanted so badly to be mad at her, but she was adorable when she was gloating. I was shocked at how awesome it was to hang out with a girl who could best me — and to a certain extent, it was a breath of fresh air.

"Well, of course you're allergic to mosquitos, that's why you itch where they bite you. The real problem is if you get West Nile Virus or some other nasty disease that they carry. Let's hope that didn't happen. In fact ... " Placing her hand on my forehead she grinned, "How are you feeling right now?"

The laughter rolled out of me and I pushed her hand away. "You're a bitch, you know that"

"I prefer that you call me 'Evil Princess Bitch,' thank you very much. Show some respect." It was at that moment that I realized her smile was absolutely perfect. As the sun rose higher in the sky, the light it cast was magic. Every detail of her face was perfectly outlined in light and Ellison's smile beamed up at me with full lips and white teeth, and I was going crazy controlling myself from touching her.

We stared at each other and it felt like electrical currents were shooting between our bodies. My mouth ached to explore hers and I couldn't help myself when I leaned down to try to kiss her. She took a step back and I groaned at the distance she put between us while my cheeks burned from embarrassment of having been refused.

"We should get going if we're going to make it home at a decent time." Spinning on her heel, she turned back to the trail and we continued our path. After a few minutes, my curiosity got to me again.

"So, how is it I got so drunk and you were sober when we left the bar? We were drinking those pitchers together."

Her shoulders shook with laughter. "Well, I drank two beers, but you were slamming them back. After a while, when I was 'going to the bathroom', I was actually going to the water fountain when I got thirsty. You kept drinking without noticing you were taking the pitchers out by yourself. After a while, I had a soda in my hand and you were oblivious to the fact I wasn't drinking. It was kind of funny, actually."

"But why did you want me to get drunk?"

She stopped and turned to me. Shrugging her shoulders, she said, "No reason."

Oh shit.

~   ~   ~

I'd never been happier to sit down than I was at that moment. We reached a small clearing by a spring and while the dogs were happily lapping up the cool water, I took a seat at a small picnic table that the state park had graciously placed here for weary hikers. The Florida sun beat down heavily on my skin and it felt like a fucking sauna. Rain clouds gathered lazily in the sky and I prayed that they'd let loose just to cool down my body. The muscles in my legs were burning and I immediately unstrapped the bags from my back and placed them down so that I could lay flat across the top of the table. Ellison looked over at me from the edge of the spring and chuckled.

"Not used to walking? Come on now, you've been doing it since you were a baby, I presume. You should have more in you than that." Pulling her GPS from her bag, she looked at me and said, "We've only gone seven miles at this point."

Seven miles. Seven fucking miles. Which meant there were 13 more fucking miles to go. I saw my life flash before my eyes and I knew there was no way I was going to make it out of here alive. And, once again, she was laughing at me.

"I'm really happy you can take so much pleasure in my pain. It makes me feel good to know you'll be entertained thoroughly while I'm down here for the summer. That is, if I live through the rest of it." My words were coming out in choppy huffs as I attempted to regulate my breathing. The headache from my hangover had subsided around mile four, but now the rest of my body was in absolute revolt against the continued activity.

"Stop being so dramatic. With a physique like yours, I would have sworn you were in better shape than that."

Wait a second. I think she just admitted she liked my body. Suddenly, my energy levels elevated back up to an almost normal level, but not quite. Laying there for another few minutes with my eyes closed, I finally decided to move again when I pushed myself up into a sitting position and heard a splash. Looking over towards the spring, El was nowhere to be seen and the dogs stood back from the water whining as they looked around for her.

"El?!" Fuck! I knew Florida was the land of crazy reptiles and I jumped down from the table and ran to the spring's edge. El's shirt and shorts lay in a pile with her bags on a rock off to the side. Was she wearing a bathing suit under her clothes? My eyes flicked back over the glassy surface of the water and I noticed bubbles moving out deeper into the water. "Ellison!" I was nervous but eventually she popped up and I openly gawked when her hands came up to smooth her wet hair back. She opened her eyes and the sunlight bounced off of them, making it appear as if they generated light all on their own. It was mesmerizing to say the least.

"What in the hell are you doing? I thought you fell in or got dragged in my some large animal that I had no intention of saving you from!"

She smiled. "You should come in. The water feels great."

"I don't have a suit."

"So?" She shrugged her shoulders and laid flat along the surface of the water, happily floating with her face turned up into the heat of the sun. "You don't need a suit. Nobody will come around here. Just strip down and jump in."

"Are you naked under there?" My eyes squinted in a desperate attempt to see under the water. I shouldn't have been trying so hard, but, dammit, I was a guy and there was a smoking hot body under there without anything to cover it.

Laughing, she righted herself and was treading water. "I'm not naked, Hunter. So stop trying to sneak a peek. You are such a perv."

"Am not!" Okay, I'll admit that was an elementary school response, but the thought of Ellison in nothing more than her underwear was enough to cause short circuits in the old gray matter. "Why is it every time I'm near you, you're trying to get me naked?" It was a valid question.

"Get over yourself, Hunter. I won't look if that's what you're afraid of. Isn't it possible for two people to go swimming without you trying to turn it into something sexual?"

No. No, it was not possible — and the sudden tight fit of my pants was proof of that fact.

The sun was beating down on my head and back and the water looked oh so enticing. I kicked off my sneakers and socks and waded ankle deep into the water. "Holy shit! That's cold!"

"Well, yeah. It's a spring." She pointed over to a darker area where more bubbles were breaking up at the surface. "This water is fed from underground, so the temperature remains cool, even during the hot summer months. Just jump in and you'll adjust to it in no time. Stop being such a sissy."

Walking back to shore, I pulled off my shirt and turned to notice that Ellison was watching intently as I stripped down. Her cheeks reddened when I caught her looking. "It's okay. You can look if you want to. I'm not shy." I winked at her. Two could play this game.

She shook her head and dove back under the water. When she resurfaced, she said, "It's not like I haven't seen a naked man before, Hunter. Don't get all big headed about it."

"Yeah, but you haven't seen ME naked. I promise you it's like nothing you've ever experienced before." I couldn't tell, but I swore she rolled her eyes at that comment. My ego was taking hits left and right with this girl.

Swimming farther out, she called back, "We can't stay here all day, so either shut up and get in, or just shut up."

Stripping down to my boxers, I attempted to walk into the water slowly. The water was so cold, it felt like ice against my heated skin. My balls instantly retreated into my body and my manhood, well, let's just say, I'm sure it wasn't looking all that impressive at the moment. I hesitated and instinctively wrapped my arms around my chest as if that would somehow warm the chill now shooting through my body.

"Just jump in, Hunter! You'll torture yourself if you walk in slowly. Trust me, once you get past the initial sting, you'll thank me for suggesting it." She was even farther out and all I could see was her head floating above the surface of the water.

"This sucks!" I screamed out before quickly lowering my body into the water. A cry escaped my lips almost instantly, but within seconds, my skin adapted to the frigid temperature and my muscles relaxed as a heavenly feeling crept through me.

Ellison swam in my direction and took my hands before pulling me out deeper. Just below the surface, I could make out the fact that she was in her bra and panties and I prayed that little Hunter wouldn't make an appearance outside of the thin material covering him. Okay — not *little* Hunter, it was far larger than that, but you know what I mean.

"Come on out to where it's deeper. I want to show you something." I hoped she meant something that involved more of her skin but when she swam me out to where the bottom appeared to drop out and when I looked down in the crystal clear water, I saw schools of fish swimming below us. "You can swim down there with them if you had a mask and snorkel. It's magical when you get in the middle of them and watch the sun reflecting off their bodies; kind of like mini rainbows springing out in all directions around you."

We stayed there for a few minutes watching as the school of fish swirled beneath us, swimming in one direction before being disturbed by some unseen force only to swirl over themselves and head like a wave in the opposite direction. It was disturbingly silent and the only thing I could hear was the light swish of water from where we were swimming and the occasional bird song from the trees. Other than that, there was — nothing. No honking cars, no distant radios, no mumbled conversations, nothing. It was disturbing to say the least. I had to break up the silence.

"So, how long before we have to get going again"

She looked up from the fish and smiled. "Can't take it, can you?" She started to swim farther away from me, but kept her sparkling blue eyes trained to mine. "For some reason, I thought you'd be different. What a shame." Then she went under.

I had no idea what the hell she was talking about and the two minutes it took her to resurface drove me mad. When she finally popped up, my words flew. "What do you mean, I can't take it? I'm in the water, I'm hiking this crazy death march with you, what can I not take?"

Her smile was nothing more than a small curl to her lips. I knew that smile. It was a judging smile — and she was really good at it. "You can't take the silence. It gives you too much time to think. It's like I said, people are comfortable when they are surrounded by outside stimulation. It's safe, they don't have to pay attention to their thoughts or feelings." Swimming closer, she reached out and took my hands, our feet kicking in unison as we worked to keep our heads above the water. My eyes kept flicking down to sneak looks at her body and she watched me intently until I gave up. Stupid water was distorting the view.

"That's my favorite part of being out here. The silence. It allows me to think through things. To take a moment of introspection and figure out what's important in my life — and what has no meaning. I don't want to be one of those people who, at the end of their lives, look back and realize they missed it." She pulled me closer to her and our feet brushed across each other from their movement. I knew she was trying to help me understand what she was saying, but the proximity of her body was distracting me.

"I know what's important to me already, El. I don't need silence to think about it."

"So, what's important?"

Well, damn, after being put on the spot, I had no idea how to answer that, so I turned the question around on her. "You're the one who's had all the time to think. What's important to you?"

A small laugh floated across her lips. "Nice deflection. But we were talking about you."

The silence returned and I stared into the eyes of a girl that was nothing like I'd ever met before.

"Okay. Having fun. That's important to me. And, well, having fun." Damn. Actually having to articulate my feelings, I determined quickly I'd never really put a lot of thought into the subject. It was unnerving.

"So, what's fun for you?" Her hands slid along mine while she toyed with my fingers and the touch was almost intimate, even in its innocence.

"Going out, hanging with my friends." It was lame. I know. But, dammit if she wasn't right; I'd never really thought about it. I was too busy with ... with the mundane, the normal activities of a 19-year-old man.

I pulled her to me, forcing the water to swirl over our skin and the heat from our bodies to mingle in the water. Her mouth opened slightly and her eyes widened. She was extraordinary. A beautiful girl who thought strange deep shit, and at least to me, did strange things. But there was something about her and I wanted to know more.

"What about you, Ellison? What's important to you?"

"Are you trying to deflect again?" Her voice was breathy and brushed over my senses awakening every nerve ending in my skin.

"No." I smiled. "Just trying to get to know you." I may have forced the dimples out again and I desperately hoped my blue eyes were as impressive to her as hers were to me. I would have never guessed it, but out here, surrounded by nothing but plants and animals, water and dirt, I suddenly felt connected to Ellison, completely absorbed in a shared moment that belonged to nobody but ourselves.

She forced herself away from me again and it felt like we were dancing — like some inherent mating dance where she teased and I chased. If it had been any other girl, I would've thought she was playing hard to get even though she had every intention to get in my pants. However, I didn't know with El. She seemed honest in her behavior. I didn't think she was simply playing games.

"A lot of things are important." Her words snapped me back to the conversation. "Family, friends, my future, my sense of self." She kicked out farther away from shore — and from me. So I chased. I eventually caught her and, in the spirit of the game, I pulled her against me. Her chest and thighs pressed up against mine and our skin slid against each other. It was incredibly hot despite the cool temperature of the water. I knew little Hunter was about to emerge, but I didn't care. I would never have believed I would be thinking this — but nature was a fucking godsend at that exact moment. There was nobody to interrupt us, nothing to distract us from the moment. I had to kiss her, to taste her. Every sense in my body wanted to explore her: sight, taste, smell, touch and sound. All five were brought to life around her and I wanted more.

Lowering my head, I kept my eyes locked to hers. There was no expression on her face and the golden tan of her skin was lightly brushed pink over her cheeks. My heart pounded in my chest as I leaned in. I'd expected her to move, but when she didn't pull away my lips brushed against hers and she closed her eyes. I moved in to deepen the kiss and just as my tongue flicked out to seek entrance to her mouth, she raised a hand out of the water and placed a single finger between our mouths.

"Stop, Hunter." Her eyes popped open and she pushed away, completely disengaging from me. Disappointment set heavily on my shoulders and I didn't chase her again as she placed distance between us. She turned around and after a few long strokes of her arms, she moved back towards the shore. When she reached a point where she could stand, she turned back to me. We were quiet for a moment, just staring at each other and I couldn't get past the fact that she was an absolute knockout. Her hair was plastered to her skin and she didn't have a lick of makeup on, and yet she outshone any girl I'd been with in the past. It was remarkable — magical even — to find myself alone with this girl in a place I could finally admit was breathtaking.

"You're only going to be here for a couple of months and then you are heading back to your home. We can be friends, Hunter, but I don't think we should be getting any more involved than that. I don't know about you, but I don't like to risk my heart when I know something won't work out in the end. I'm not a fling. I'm not some girl that's okay with having fun just for the sake of the moment. Plus, I don't know anything about you, like what you do with your time, what you want to do when you get older — or even if you have a girlfriend." She turned and walked completely out of the water. The water glistened as it rolled down her skin and my hands clenched when I forced myself to show some respect and look away. When I finally turned back, she was laid flat over the table, still in nothing more than a bra and panties. She appeared to have no shame when it came to nudity.

"Are you going to get dressed or what?" I called out.

Her head popped up to look at me and she had a confused expression on her face. "You've already seen me like this. What do I have to hide? Plus, it's no different than a bathing suit."

She laid back down, and I treaded water while trying to come up with something to say. She was right. The deafening silence was pounding against my head and I felt these weird thoughts and feelings bubbling up inside my head. The constant activity of my life, mixed with the numbing effects of alcohol and drugs had suppressed them, shoving them so far inside that I could feel them pushing their way back into my head. It was almost painful. Thoughts of my parents, school, my friends — Tiffany; all of it started to swell up and I was instantly saddened to think that none of it really mattered to me. I'd been going through the motions of life, developing a routine that acted as nothing more than a distraction. What the fuck was I going to do when I got older? I had no interest in college, even less in actually going to a job every day. It seemed like it would be so monotonous: getting up at the same time, arriving at the same place at the same time, leaving that place at the same time, only to go home at the same time. Add in a wife and children and what was left?

And what the fuck just happened?!

"What in the hell are you doing to me, El?" I called out to her and she sat up to look out over the water at me. The sunlight bounced off the waves of the water and it looked like a small light show was swirling all over her body.

"I don't know what you're talking about." She smiled. She knew exactly what I was talking about.

I powered through the water towards shore. Climbing out, I was thankful for the button in the front of my boxers as I walked practically naked in her direction. Her eyes traveled over my chest and legs and I wanted to growl in appreciation of the blush to her cheeks and the desire I was sure I saw in her eyes. So yes, even though I was having this enlightening experience with a girl I barely knew, sex was still part of the equation. I was 19 years old and sex was important. It was natural. It was something I wasn't ashamed to admit: I wanted to have sex with the blond sitting on a picnic table in the middle of the woods. I wanted to run my tongue all along the smooth skin of her body and just taste her — *experience* her. This girl was already better than any drug I'd taken and I hadn't even done anything with her yet.

When I finally reached her, I sat down on one of the seats. She turned to me and placed her feet on the seat beside me, her wet braid hanging loosely over one shoulder and her eyes alight with humor. I grabbed the backs of her calves and fought hard not to spread her legs and pull her down on my lap.

In a moment of absolute honesty that I had no idea where it came from, I confessed, "I don't know what I'm going to do later in life. All I know is that I'm supposed to go to college, and I'm supposed to get a job after that. Once that's accomplished, I'm sure I'm supposed to get married and have kids and grow old and shit. And to be completely fucking honest with you, I don't actually *want* to do any of it. It's so boring. There's no challenge to it. Everybody does it."

She looked surprised to hear my confession. "So then, don't do that. Pick something else. What are you interested in? You could do something where you have to travel, where you get to explore the world. Take the image of what you think your life should be and make it a reality. Travel the world until you figure it out, live life like a pirate if you want."

I laughed. "Like a pirate? You're kidding, right?"

She shrugged. "Yeah. But you know what I mean."

"What are you going to do?" It was weird, but I really wanted to know. She was fascinating.

She motioned around at our surroundings. "Well, we're kind of doing it now. I want to be a forest ranger, I want to help take care of the environment. I want to make a difference. It won't be a huge one, but it'll be something. I start college at the end of the summer and Finn and I both are majoring in forestry."

Finn. My heart sank and a lump formed in my throat at the mention of her on again off again boyfriend.

"So, you and Finn will be seeing each other every day? Won't that be rough if you don't want to be with him?" There was a little bit of jealousy in my voice. I didn't intend it, but it happened.

Thankfully, if she noticed, she didn't act like it. "Finn and I can be friends again. That's how we started. He'll move on at some point because he has no problem attracting women. I refuse to let a failed relationship destroy what we had before it happened. Maybe it's stupid of me, but I think it's a shame when two people can't put aside their differences and still remain in each other's lives. He's a good guy. He understands me. It's rare for me to be able to find someone like that."

"Then why don't you just stay with him?"

She let out a humorless laugh. "My dad would like that. He thinks Finn would be the perfect husband. But I just don't feel those things for him. There are no butterflies when he's around, there's no electricity. When he touches me or kisses me, I feel nothing." Her eyes caught mine at that moment and my breath was stolen from my chest. "I love Finn, but I'm not *in love* with him. Do you know what I mean?"

I didn't. I had no idea what she meant because I wasn't even sure I knew the difference between *like* and *love* … much less *love* and *in love*. I didn't know what love was. I knew what it was to want a girl, but that was pretty much where it ended. I also knew the basic definition of love, but I had never actually felt it.

I looked up at her. I wanted to lie, to tell her I knew exactly what she was talking about, but, somehow, I knew she'd see right through me.

"No. I hate to admit it, but I am clueless when it comes to that concept."

Chapter Eight

Ellison

I was shocked, to say the least. His brown hair hung haphazardly in his face, tempting me to brush it away, and his dark blue eyes swirled when he admitted he didn't know what love was. It was a brave response, honest, and my heart skipped at his confession. Everybody should know what love is. If a person had a family, they should know love. But, that wasn't true, was it? Sure, there were the kids who were abandoned, and the people who were deserted that had an excuse for not knowing, but Hunter wasn't one of those people. He had parents, he had friends — he had a home. He, of all people, should know.

"How is that even possible? You have your mom and your dad. Don't you know what love is because of them?" My voice was whisper soft and my insides grew tense while I waited for his answer. His smile faded and his eyes looked away from me.

"If you call the once a month lecture and access to their credit accounts love, then yes." He looked back up and I was momentarily shocked by the honesty in his eyes. "My parents worked constantly. My dad went to his job for long hours and my mom did — well, whatever my mom did. I was left to deal with myself and they judged me by my grades and judged themselves by the things they were able to give me. We didn't spend much time together." He shrugged it off suddenly. "It doesn't matter, though. I had the life every kid wants; money at my disposal and no parents to breathe down my neck."

"I don't want that." It was an immediate response and one that appeared to shock him. "If I could have just one minute more with my mom, I'd do anything for it — anything. To see her smile, or hear her laugh, or even to feel the warmth of her palm against my cheek." A tear threatened my eye, but I kept it from falling. I didn't want to get emotional in front of him.

His hands idly rubbed up and down my calves. Even though I didn't want to admit it, his touch was doing funny things to my body and I enjoyed the contact. It felt normal, natural. I hadn't known Hunter for very long but my soul recognized him and it was easy to fall in step with him - to feel like I'd known him forever.

"What happened to your mom?" He was curious. I couldn't fault him for that, but talking about her was hard even though it had been 10 years since I last saw her.

I wrapped my arms around my waist when I answered, "She died. Ten years ago from a car accident. A drunk driver swerved into her lane, killing her and Lily's mom. That's how we ended up living next to each other. Our dads relied on each other for help raising us kids.

His face fell and I felt terrible. I didn't want to talk about sad things and it seemed that our conversation had turned from one of hope to one of despair. I grieved the loss of my mother, and he grieved never having had one to begin with.

When it grew quiet between us, I stood up and stepped down off the table. My underwear had dried from the heat outside and I could put the rest of my clothes back on. Hunter stood up and followed behind me and we dressed without speaking.

The rest of the hike was tedious. Hunter was pretty strong up until the last two miles or so, but he dragged ass that last little bit, dramatically falling to the ground by the time we reached the front yard of my house.

"Oh thank God! We made it. I can't feel my legs, but I'm alive."

I scowled down at him and laughed. "It wasn't that bad. It's obvious you spend way too much town sitting around. You know, beyond TV and video games, there's a whole world out there waiting to be explored."

His brilliant blues found mine and he smiled that dimpled grin of his that made me melt every time I saw it. "I know. I've seen that world on the TV. And it didn't destroy my legs in the process."

When he winked, my heart skipped and I had to restrain myself from dropping to my knees so I could kiss him. His lips were soft. I knew that from our encounter at the spring and I'd been a strong woman to be able to pull away from it. A chill ran across my skin and I blamed the summer winds so that I wouldn't have to admit to myself that it was his presence that was affecting me.

"I'd better get the dogs inside. They need water and sleep. After a walk like that, they are usually down for the majority of the night."

Hunter rolled over and failed to push himself up. "Crap! I'm too tired to move. You'll have to go on without me, El. Save yourself."

My laughter rolled out of me. "Stop being so damn dramatic. You'll feel better when we do it again tomorrow. It gets easier."

Rolling on his back, he opened one eye at me. "No. No way. I have a house to paint and I'm not even sure I'll be able to pull that off. Hell! I'll be lucky to make it to my bed. It's too far away." He opened both eyes and looked over at my bedroom window. "But, yours is closer. I might be able to make it to that one." Another wink.

I couldn't stop the grin that spread across my face and I could feel the heat reddening my cheeks. "That's not going to happen, Hunter."

He looked pained to be turned down. Reaching one arm up, he said, "You can at least help me up, considering it was your treachery that did this to me."

He was such a big baby. I reached down to help him, but as soon as his large hand wrapped around my wrist, I was pulled down on top of him, our bodies colliding with each other and my legs falling open on either side of him as I straddled his abdomen. I pushed up and moved the hair from my face to find an odd expression on his.

His grin was crooked and charming when he said, "If you keep ending up on top of me Miss James, I'm going to start believing you like me."

And then I did something that completely went against my character. I looked him directly in the eye, never letting go of his stare as I lowered my body down and brushed my lips against his. It was heaven, like silk across my lips and I opened my mouth, allowing his tongue to run across mine, allowing his taste to fill me, and his musky, woodsy scent to wrap itself completely around me. I felt his hands move up my back just before his fingers tangled themselves into my hair, pulling gently but trapping me against him. It was like being pressed up against a wall of rock and I loved the feel of him underneath me. It didn't seem like he would ever let go, and I wasn't sure I wanted him to — until I heard a throat clearing behind us.

I jumped off Hunter and my butt hit the ground with a thud. Slowly turning, I spotted a grimy pair of work boots attached to a dirty pair of legs and even farther up I saw the murderous expression on my father's face.

"Hi, Daddy."

Hunter was frozen in place. His eyes glued on my father.

"Ellison. You need to go inside sweetheart and we'll talk about this in a minute. I'd like to have a word with Hunter, man to man, if you don't mind.

This wasn't good. In fact, this was really bad. My daddy still thought of me like I was 10 years old and he wasn't too pleased when he saw a man brush up against me, much less, me straddling a man in the front yard. "Daddy, this isn't what this looks like. We were just playing around." I stood up quickly and tried to move so that I was blocking my father's view of Hunter.

My father's hands landed on my shoulders and his tired brown eyes met mine. "Baby Girl, you need to head inside. I'm not going to kill the boy, so stop looking like you're trying to prevent a murder. I'm only going to talk to him."

I was scared, but I knew I had no choice but to go. I looked at Hunter apologetically as I gathered the packs we'd thrown on the ground and called the dogs to follow me inside. Once I was in the house, I wanted to peek out the window to see what was going on, but I was afraid it would only piss off my father more to see me spying.

Doing whatever I could to keep my mind off of it, I gave the dogs food and water and watched them as they finished up their lunch and wandered over to their doggy beds to pass out. I grabbed a shower and after I'd dressed and dried my hair I returned to the living room to find my father sitting on the couch laughing to himself about something.

"Hey, daddy. Is Hunter still breathing?"

"Yeah, he is. He's probably at Bill's right now cleaning the shit out of his shorts after what I had to say to him." He chuckled and it shook it shoulders.

"Daddy! It wasn't his fault ... "

"Ellison James, I found that young man outside your bedroom window at two o'clock in the morning, naked. I warned him then to stay away from my little girl and then, to come home and find him holding you on top of him? Hell! You were lucky I didn't kill the boy right there. And what the hell are you thinking acting like that anyway? I raised you better than that and I know you've got a level head on those shoulders of yours. Don't go losing it because of some cute boy that will only be around for the summer. I'm glad it was me that found you and not Finn. It would have broken that boy's heart to see you that way."

Finn. I was so sick of hearing about Finn. I didn't know what was wrong with the men in my life but they'd all decided that I was marrying Finn and there was nothing I could do about it. "What did you say to Hunter?"

"That's between Hunter and me, baby girl. It was a talk between men and there's nothing that was said that needs to be repeated." His mouth shrank to a thin line and I could tell he wasn't going to budge in this conversation. There was no use fighting it and I didn't want to upset him further.

"Did you make it to your appointment today?" Sitting down beside him on the couch, I snuggled into his side waiting for his response.

"I did." He grew quiet for a second and it worried me. "They need to send me off for some tests. Said it's normal and I shouldn't worry about it."

"So then why do they need tests?" My father hadn't been feeling like himself for a few months and it was almost impossible to convince him to go get a check up. Daddy hated doctors. He always said that if you go to a doctor, they'll tell you you're dying and then you die. In his screwed up logic, he argued that if you didn't find out you were dying in the first place, you might have lived ... so he didn't go. But I fought him hard and he eventually relented to getting a quick checkup to ease my concerns.

Knowing they wanted to do more tests, however? Now, I was absolutely terrified. I'd already lost my mom, I didn't know what I'd do if I lost my dad too.

"I'm getting old, Ellison. They need to do extra stuff to check me out. It's completely normal and nothing to worry about. I'll still be around to keep an eye on you for the next 50 years. You can count on that." He wrapped his arm around me and pulled me closer to his side. "I love you, baby girl, and even though I'm ready to go be with your mother on the other side, I'm not willing to leave you here alone just yet. At least, not until your brother has grown up some more and I can trust him to take care of you."

"I can take care of myself, Daddy."

"I know. I made sure of it when I raised you, but it never hurts to have someone to help pick you up when you fall. And it's bound to happen. You can't live life thinking you won't screw up every now and then. The mistakes are just as important as the successes. You wouldn't be who you are without both of them. So when those mistakes happen, it's good to have people around who can push you through them."

He must have known my mind went instantly to thoughts of Hunter, because he added, "And, Ellison, that boy, Hunter, is not the person you need to tie your life to. Did Lily tell you why he was sent down here? That boy is shoulder deep in a lifestyle of partying and drugs and he's nothing like you. He'll only drag you down with him if you give him your heart."

I opened my mouth to argue but he held his hand up to silence me. "Don't argue with me, Ellison. You're a smart girl and a beautiful girl on top of that. You've got your whole life ahead of you to make a difference in this world and the last thing you need is someone holding you back. I want you to be happy, El. And I know you've got a heart the size of this state and will take in any stray that looks like it needs help; but attaching yourself to a boy like him will only hurt you. You won't find happiness until you find your equal. And unfortunately for the male population, you are a difficult person to compete against."

He kissed me on top of the head before standing up. "I'm going to go lay down and I'll be up in time for supper. Do me a favor and stay away from that boy. If you want to be friends, I trust you to make that decision, but don't let it go farther than that. You're better than he is, Ellison."

I watched his back as he walked from the living room into his bedroom. I was scared for him. He'd not been himself for months and he was always tired. I couldn't stand the thought of something happening to him and the fear only added to the aggravating feelings I was having for Hunter at that moment. When the door finally closed, frustrated tears fell from my eyes and I smacked them away angrily. I didn't even know why I was mad because there was no way Hunter and I would end up together anyway. He didn't live here. After a few months, he'd return to his life and I'd never see him again. But that thought didn't make my heart feel any better. I knew he was bad news, but there was something else, something deeper inside him and I'd seen a small glimpse of it near the spring. His words surprised me, but I felt like they were only a small trickle of information that hinted to the real flood hidden within him.

Chapter Nine

Hunter

Henry James was probably the scariest SOB I'd ever met in my life. When he told me he could come up with 50 ways to kill me and hide my body without going outside a mile of his house, I paid attention. I knew it didn't look good. First, he found me practically naked outside of Ellison's window and then, he found me with my tongue shoved as far down her throat as I could get it. But, dammit, I'd do it again. She was amazing. Everything about her. The way she looked. The way she smelled. The way she talked and those crazy, ridiculous ideas she had. But her taste, holy shit, her taste ... it was like nothing I'd ever experienced. It was the perfect mixture of sugar and spice and I was addicted to it after only tasting it one time. Her scent was all over me when I dragged ass up the stairs and into my uncle's house — and I loved it. My fucking legs felt like they were on fire and my balls shriveled considerably after Henry told me what he had planned for them if he caught me touching his daughter again — but I didn't fucking care. All I could think about was the feel of her lips on mine and the feel of her silken hair wrapped around my fingers. I was thankful as shit that Henry didn't notice how rock hard I was when Ellison first crawled off my body. It would have made for a much more awkward conversation in the long run.

I quickly showered and laid down on my bed sighing in relief to take the weight of my body off my legs. My heart was hammering with thoughts of Ellison and I reached down to grab my crotch in an effort to relieve myself of the ache I'd had since she'd been sitting on top of me. My hand wasn't enough; I needed her ... wrapped around me ... intimately. I knew I shouldn't do it. I was somehow completely obsessed with her and it had only been three days. If I was this addicted already, I couldn't imagine what I would feel like if things ever went farther between us. I had to remember, I didn't live here. I was going home to my friends, to college — to my life without her. The thought was depressing and I beat the shit out of my brain trying to come up with a way to convince her to go with me. But I knew she'd never leave her family and she'd never leave Lily. This was her home and mine was over a thousand miles away.

I fell asleep for a few hours and woke again when Lily came in my room. "Dinner's ready. Thought you might be hungry after walking the red trail with Ellison today. I've made that trip before and I know it's brutal.

"Lil, I'm starving, but I don't think my legs work anymore. I seriously can't feel them right now."

She pinched me on the thigh ... hard.

"Ow! Sonofabitch!"

Laughing, she pushed herself up off the bed. "See? You can still feel them. Now, stop being such a baby and get your ass in the kitchen. El and I are building a bonfire tonight in a clearing not too far from here. Some other kids in town are going to meet us out there and you'll miss out if you don't go."

Ellison. That was the magic word. Suddenly I didn't care if I my legs would fall off if I used them again. I was getting up and I was going to that bonfire.

When I sprung up, Lily gave me a funny look. "I'm starting to think you have a thing for Ellie. I haven't seen you move that fast since you've been here. Did something happen on your walk today that I don't know about?"

I rubbed my eyes into focus and looked up at her. "Have you talked to her since we've been back?"

"No."

"Then I will leave that information to the girl talk. I'm going to treat Ellison right and do the gentlemanly thing by not talking." I winked and Lily laughed. "Hey, Lil, before you go. Can I borrow your phone? I want to check in at home."

"Sure! But go easy on the minutes. It's a cheap phone and I can't afford too many for the month." She grabbed her phone from her back pocket and tossed it in my direction.

"Thanks." After she'd left the room, I checked my voicemails and cringed to hear Tiffany's voice.

Fifty. There were 50 messages total and in each one, her voice got louder and more annoying. I didn't listen to more than the first three words of each message, but it was pretty clear by her tone of voice that she was mad. Real mad. And I wondered if she'd bothered to go by my parents' house to find out what happened to me.

I wanted to move forward with Ellison. I knew it was wrong, I knew that we didn't have that much time to be together, but I was willing to risk my heart for just the memory of her. Three days and she'd already touched a part inside me I didn't even know existed. But if I was going to do this, I was going to be honorable about it, and there was baggage back home that I needed to unload.

Quickly, I dialed Tiffany's number and pumped my fist in the air when it went to her voicemail. This was a cheap move. I knew that; but it had to count for more than a text message, right?

"Hey Tiff. Listen, I'm in Florida for the summer and I've been thinking a lot about things. I think we should split up and I don't have a lot of time to explain, but I wanted to let you know so you could hopefully move on while I'm away. If you want, we can talk more about it when I get home. Sorry to break up over voicemail, but I've been stripped of my phone and everything, so this is the only chance I have to tell you."

I hung up. It was done and it was done without several hours of screaming and crying. My exile was the best thing that could have happened ... I ditched Tiff without drama and it would give her time to move on before I returned. But, more importantly, I'd met Ellison James and I knew that just knowing the girl was going to change my life forever.

~   ~   ~

When Lily said 'bonfire', what she really meant to say was 'tower of flame that had to be illegal in most states and the heat from which would melt your plastic solo cup if you got too close.' It was impressive. I couldn't imagine how long it'd taken these guys to construct the monstrosity, but I was slightly afraid that the entire fucking forest was about to go up in flame. However, looking around, I appeared to be the only person with any concern. I'll admit the space that was cleared out was large and we were nowhere near trees or other vegetation, but if the wind picked up the wrong way, we were going to be in some definite trouble.

Lily tugged on my arm. "You look like you're about to shit your pants. Is it the bonfire that's scaring you or was it Ellison's driving?"

Let me stop here to explain what happens when a person rides with Ellison James. First, you must understand that she drives around in a 1979 Jeep that is practically held together with duct tape and electrical tape. She has the engine tuned just enough that it only blasts out one incredibly large puff of smoke when it starts; but for most of the journey, she's not creating holes in the ozone around the areas she travels. The Jeep had no doors, no roof and the floor had holes in it. If a person was brave enough to climb into the hunk of metal after taking a good look at it first, then the rest of the ride they had coming to them. Ellison took off fast, she drove fast, she stopped fast, and she turned fast. Sometimes the car was on the road, and sometimes it was on the shoulder. That didn't appear to faze Ellison, she just ignored the flying rocks and dirt her tires kicked up and she bounced in the driver's seat happily singing along to ... and you'll want to brace yourself for this ... Kenny Rogers' *The Gambler*. I kid you not. While Ellison was off in la-la land having warm thoughts about poker games and whiskey, Lily and I were holding on for dear life. I'm not a religious man, but I prayed more during that trip than I'd done my entire life. And there were a good number of praying incidents in my past — mostly when cops were involved.

"A little of both, I think. Are you sure we're not going to start a forest fire with this thing?" I pointed at the fire but then quickly pulled my hand back to my body when a few of my arm hairs sizzled. Holy shit that thing was hot.

There were people everywhere; spread out on blankets, sitting on trailers beds and just laid out in the grass or lawn chairs. It was high energy and people were having a good time. Music blasted out of the speakers of a few of the cars and I enjoyed watching people laughing and joking around with one another. When we'd arrived, Ellison had grabbed a guitar case from the back of her Jeep and had taken off so fast; I'd lost sight of her. She was acting really weird towards me since the incident with her father and I didn't want to push the issue. But I was pissed. The only reason I was at the party was for her and in the 30 minutes we'd been here, I hadn't spotted her once. There were a couple of kegs near the trucks. I'd already had two beers and I was working my way towards another refill when a hand fell on my shoulder.

"Hey, Hunter. I'm surprised to see you out tonight. Did you know Ellison's here?"

I turned around to find Finn standing behind me. He was dressed casually in jeans, a black shirt and cowboy boots. He wore a straw cowboy hat on his head and I rolled my eyes at the typical 'southern' look he was going for. But then, what did I know? From what Ellison told me, he was the typical 'southern' guy, so I guess it fit.

"Uh, yeah, I rode over with her."

He smiled. "And you're standing upright already? First ride in Ellison's Jeep and I was kissing the ground for a solid two hours when it ended just because I was thankful to be alive." He walked up to the keg with me and we both filled our cups. "She didn't tell me she brought you along. I thought you two hated each other or something after the incident with the dogs. But if you've made up, I guess you should come over and sit with us."

Two things occurred to me at that moment. The first was that I hated the fact that Ellison hadn't mentioned she'd brought me when she apparently immediately went out and found her ex; and second, I hated that this guy was as nice as he seemed to be. I wanted to hate him. I wanted to not want to hate him. I wanted to not care about Ellison the way that I was.

"Are you sure that's cool?"

"Well, hell yeah. Your cousin and her man are sitting with us and you've met El's brother, Jake." His smile was genuine — and I wanted to smack it off his face. That was shitty of me, I know.

We arrived at the blanket and Lily was curled up with Ryan, Jake had some girl I didn't recognize tucked into his side and El was sitting up, holding a guitar in her lap. She was strumming softly and humming a song so low, I could barely hear it over the music from the cars. Finn immediately took a seat beside her and I was stuck sitting on the outskirts of the circle.

Third wheel — table for one.

Damn if this wasn't awkward.

Finn sat back and his arm went behind Ellison close enough that it was brushing up against her back. She looked beautiful illuminated by the firelight and the shadows danced along her body and hair; making it appear that she was swaying to the music. She looked up at me for a moment when I sat down, but her eyes shifted back to her guitar quickly. The next half hour was pretty quiet while the two couples did their thing and the three of us took our time absorbing our surroundings. Finn was the first to talk.

"So, what are you doing down here for the summer, Hunter? Jake tells me you're Lily's cousin, but that's all I know. Is there any reason in particular why you came down, or is it just a family reunion type thing?"

"I need a beer." Ellison pushed up suddenly, handed her guitar to Finn after she'd stood and she walked in the direction of the kegs. Finn had an odd expression on his face when she walked away, but he seemed to shake it off by the time he looked back over to me. He started to strum the guitar while he waited for me to answer and he played well.

Of course. Fucking, of course, he's the sensitive guitar-playing guy!

I was more annoyed than ever.

I cleared my throat. "Well, uh, my parents sent me down because I pissed them off. I'm going back at the end of the summer to attend Harvard. I got a full ride for academics, so I have to make sure I return for that." It was cheap, and I was *puffing out my chest* like El would say, but I had to show this asshole up. The fucked up part was that he probably hadn't intended to show off with the guitar, making me the real asshole.

He laughed softly. "What'd you do to piss them off?"

"I parked my car at the bottom of their pool."

Finn's eyes grew wide and he whistled. "Well, damn, yeah, I can see where that would piss a person off. Were you in the car when it went for a swim?"

"No. I was sleeping when it happened. I think. I don't know, I was pretty trashed and it could have gone for a dip as soon as I stepped out of it and I wouldn't have noticed."

His eyes searched me after I said that. He was sizing me up and, judging by the look on his face, he wasn't too impressed with his competition — if he even knew I was competition. "You must party hard to get that fucked up."

"I have," I admitted. There wasn't any point lying about it. I'm sure Bill told Henry and Henry told El. It might have been the reason she'd been acting strange.

Ellison returned with a solo cup in her hand. She gulped down the beer and I raised my eyebrow to see her drink as quickly as she was. I knew she didn't like to get fucked up. I mean, this was the same girl who'd stayed sober while drinking pitchers the night before for fuck's sake. Why was she now drinking like a fucking fish?"

When she'd finished, she set her cup aside and grabbed the guitar from Finn before asking him to get her another drink. When he left, she started playing a song, but I interrupted.

"Everything okay, Ellison?"

Her eyes shot to mine, but the clear blue was covered by shadow. "Yeah. Why?"

I tried to search her face, but she was doing a good job concealing her thoughts. "Because you're drinking pretty heavily. Is something up?"

She shook her head, the effects of the beer she'd just downed already apparent in her movements.

"Are you driving home tonight?"

Shaking her head again, she used her thumb to motion in the direction Finn had walked. "Finn can drive if I drink too much. I just feel like relaxing tonight. Really, nothing's up." Her words were slightly slurred and I looked around to see if she'd had any other beers before I'd arrived to the blanket. I didn't see any, but she could have been using the same cup.

Finn returned and Ellison turned her attention back to her guitar. He didn't restart his previous interrogation of me and I was glad for that. The last thing I needed at the moment was to be judged by a really nice guy who I would feel horrible for punching in the face; but I couldn't help it, that's all I wanted to do to the guy. Hours passed and at some point I got up from the blanket to walk around and socialize. There was a group of hot blondes giggling off to the side at one point and one brave girl made her way over to me. She smiled the sweetest grin that was curled unevenly to the side indicating that she'd had one too many of the wine coolers she was holding in her hand.

"Hi, I'm Amber. I haven't seen you around here before. Are you new to town or somethin'?"

Her southern accent was divine and the dog in me started moving front and center. I flashed the million dollar dimpled grin and my stance instantly went into one of interest. I swaggered up closer beside her. "I'm from New York. I've been down for a few days. I didn't move, I'm just staying for the summer."

Her eyelashes batted over her large brown eyes. "Where you stayin'?"

"With my cousin, Lily McCormick." I held out my hand. "My name's Hunter."

She took my hand and I surprised her by pulling it to my lips. I was in full dog mode and I could tell the girl was quickly becoming putty in my hands. Her lips curled more and a small dimple popped out on her left cheek. It was a girl after my own heart. Letting go, I took another swig of my beer.

"With Lily, huh? I live about two miles south of you. We should meet up while you're in town."

I didn't want to be talking to her. I wanted to be sitting next to Ellison where I should have been if Mr. Sensitive-Guitar-Playing-Nice-as-Hell-Nature-Guy didn't already occupy the spot! Feeling rejected and hurt, I turned on the boyish charm with Amber. "And what would we do?" My voice may have dropped to a seductive tone when I asked that, but what can I say? It came natural to me.

She smiled brighter and her eyelids hooded over the brown. Bingo. Right where I wanted her. "I dunno. I'm sure we could come up with something. There's a bunch of parties farther into the city. They're a hell of a lot more wild than what goes on 'round here."

Tiffany. All I could see was Tiffany standing before me: the hair, the clothes, the fingernails, the makeup, the jewelry and the personality. It was her — just in a non-wealthy, southern form. My first instinct was to brush her off and avoid that complication, but, despite my intelligence, I didn't seem to have any common sense when it came to girls or getting fucked up. My heart was hurting because of a certain blonde singing to her ex on a blanket not more than 20 feet away from where I stood. I needed something to numb it. Plus, it wasn't like Ellison wanted anything to do with me anyway. If she did, she'd be by my side where she should be. I needed to forget about her.

Amber and I launched into a flirtatious conversation. I wasn't holding back. First it started with talking, then it moved on to talking with little touches on the arms, then it progressed forward to where she leaned up to kiss me. But, the feel of her lips on mine did nothing for me. It wasn't Ellison. It didn't smell like Ellison. It didn't taste like Ellison. And it pissed me off.

I pulled away from Amber and she scowled in response. I looked up just in time to catch Ellison's blue eyes. She was staring right at me — and she looked hurt or mad or ... *fuck!* I didn't know. But she didn't look normal.

She was standing near the kegs and as soon as I looked up at her, she turned and strode quickly in the direction of the distant woods. I looked to the blanket, only to watch Finn get up and chase after her. When they'd disappeared into the tree line, I excused myself from Amber's company and I went in search of them. I didn't care that I took the chance of walking into something I didn't want to see and I knew Ellison said there was nothing between them — but I had to see for myself. I hoped they'd do something to prove they weren't as *over* as she'd claimed and I could get over these annoying fucking feelings I had for her. But at the same time, I was afraid to see it; afraid I'd want to rip her away from him, throw her over my shoulder and run like hell. It was stupid. I knew that, but I went after them anyway.

Making my way into the woods, I was ambushed by a large spider web that wrapped itself tightly around my face. I wanted to vomit. I immediately freaked out — as quietly as possible — and I pulled the little bits and pieces off of me, hoping and praying there wasn't some gargantuan eight-legged creature currently crawling its way down my back. When I felt satisfied that I'd done all I could to deal with that obstacle, I pushed further into the woods — and instantly tripped over a large root and went down like a stone. See what I told you? Nature and me didn't mix. I'm not sure why it was being kind when I was with Ellison but I decided that her being in tune with the bastard must have somehow rubbed off on me when I was in her company. Now that I was alone, nature was coming at me at full strength.

After a few more embarrassing incidents that would most likely end in a couple good bruises, I located El and Finn talking in a small clearing. Ellison sat on top of a large rock and Finn knelt down beside her. She was crying softly and it broke my heart.

"He might be sick, Finn. I don't want you telling anybody, but I can't be afraid like this on my own. Please, PLEASE, don't say anything, especially to Jake or Lil. That's for daddy to tell and he's not worried, but I am." Ellison whispered as she spoke, but her voice still carried to where I could hear it.

"I won't say anything. But, it's too soon for you to freak out, in fact, besides him being tired, there is nothing to freak out about. They always want to run tests, that's what doctors do." His hand reached up to rub along her back and I wanted to break his fingers off. But I refrained.

A slight smiled creased her lips. "I know. It's just a bad feeling I have. I'm sure it's nothing."

"Why'd you run off into the woods, El?"

She shrugged her shoulders. "Same reason I'm drinking, I guess. I'm just worried." I don't know how I knew it, but I knew she was lying. I could just tell.

Finn nodded his head. He stood up and reached down to grab her hands and help her stand up. And then it happened. He leaned over and he kissed her. My hands instantly fisted and I could feel blood rushing through my veins, but I just stood there like some fucking voyeur ... watching. Damn if Ellison wasn't right. I was a creepy stalker.

She pushed him away suddenly. Lifting her arm to wipe off her mouth, she glared at him. "What the fuck, Finn?! I can't believe you just fucking did that. I'm confiding in you as a FRIEND and you take advantage of that by kissing me?"

Finn held his hands up. "Babe, I'm sorry, I just thought … "

"Just thought what? I should kick your ass for this! I'm already fucked up emotionally and you go and add to it? And I'm not your 'babe'! Stop referring to me like we are anything more than friends. Please! I just want to go back, Finn. I just want things to be like they were. You were my best friend; we got along like that. But we do not work as anything more. Get that through your thick fucking skull!"

I was glad I'd spilled my beer on that first fall in the woods. I needed to get sober and I needed to do it fast. There was no way I was letting that guy drive her home.

"Ellison, just come back to the fire with me."

"No Finn." She sat back down. "Please, just go and give me a minute. I'll go back in a little bit, but I just want to be alone right now."

Finn stood silent for a few seconds, but eventually he turned and left the woods. I stood watching her. She'd stopped crying and she had her elbows braced on her knees and her head cradled in her hands.

And then a twig snapped under my foot and my cover was blown.

Ellison looked up and I stepped out from behind the shrubs where I'd been hiding. I felt like an idiot. Once again, I was acting like a little punk bitch and this girl was the one doing it to me.

"Hunter? What the hell is wrong with you guys? First Finn and now you're pulling the creeper, stalking act again? Fuck!" She threw her hands up and stood up from the rock. "Did you hear everything?"

I nodded. I was ashamed, but I wouldn't lie to her.

"Great. Just fucking great. Don't say anything to Lily or Bill, Hunter. I don't know if I'm not freaking out over nothing and I don't need the whole family getting upset."

"I won't say anything, Ellison. I promise you. That's not why I'm out here. I just wanted to know what was up with you ... and Finn."

Her eyes shot to mine. "Why do you care, Hunter? I told you before; I'm not a fling. What happened this afternoon, it was a mistake. I'm not going to say I hated it or anything, or that I'm mad about it, but it was a mistake, nonetheless."

The words sliced through my heart. I was eviscerated and I was broken and I didn't know why. This was ridiculous. She was right, I knew she was right, I knew this could be nothing, but my heart didn't know it. I didn't even know why my heart was getting such a strong vote when it came to my thoughts on the matter. It had never said anything to me before Ellison and I was annoyed that it wouldn't shut up now.

"I know, but I ... I don't know, El. I just want to be around you and I have no idea why. I've only known you for three days, most of which we spent arguing or screwing with each other, but I can't stop thinking about you." The alcohol had apparently helped loosen my lips and I was confessing things to her that I didn't want to admit to her, much less, myself.

She frowned and looked away without responding.

"Why did you get so mad when you saw that girl kiss me? You were staring right at me and then you ran off. I was worried about you."

She huffed out a breath. "I don't know. I'm not worried about it. But I'd watch it with Amber, if I were you. She's been around and there are rumors about certain health issues she might have. I'm not one to spread the rumors, but I don't want you going home with a permanent reminder of your stay, if you know what I mean."

I nodded again when she added, "And be careful with drugs, Hunter. I don't agree with your lifestyle and I think it's stupid considering how smart you are, but it's your choice. Amber's big into some heavy stuff at times, so just don't go doing something stupid." She looked up at me. "Lily says you're smart. I haven't seen it yet, but I imagine she must be telling the truth for some reason. There's not many people who can make that claim. You should do something useful with it rather than flushing it down the toilet with drugs. It's your life, Hunter and you don't have to listen to what I say — but I still have to say it. So, there; I said it."

At that moment, I realized I was right. She did know why I was down here, she hated me for it, and I felt ashamed by it. I'd never apologized for my lifestyle before, but she was somehow changing that in me. She made me feel like it made me a bad person

I approached her and we stood nose-to-nose and chest-to-chest because I'd walked up so close. She craned her neck to look up at me and I raised my hands to smooth down her arms. But I couldn't touch her. I held my hands at her shoulders and I looked down at her longingly, but I just couldn't push past the thin, invisible force that seemed to surround her. I didn't want to be like Finn. I didn't want to push myself on her when she was already upset about something else. It wasn't fair to her. The energy from her body brushed across my palms and I felt twisted up inside that I couldn't actually touch her.

Her eyes blinked slowly and the blue was shining in contrast with her red-rimmed eyes. I could smell the beer on her and she swayed slightly. "Please don't, Hunter. Please don't make this harder." Her voice was a breathy whisper and I closed my eyes in reaction to it. I wanted to do more than touch her. I wanted to sweep her up in my arms and cradle her to me. I wanted to hold her until all the pain and worry left her body. I wanted to tell her I'd take care of her, that I'd cherish her, that I'd ... that, in reality, I'd end up leaving her.

I'd never felt pain before like I did at that moment. It tore at me. Physical fucking jolts shot through my body and my chest tightened. But I pulled my hands back to myself. I protected her heart by not touching her.

For once, I was trying not to be the selfish bastard I knew I was.

She sniffled after I pulled my hands away; but then she nodded her head once and looked up like she'd just fought the same battle as me. "We're friends, Hunter. I like you and, if I need anything right now, it's a friend. I need someone I can talk to that's not part of all this, who isn't involved."

"We can do that. I can be that friend." I was resolute in my offer and she smiled at the sound of it. She pushed up on her tiptoes and lightly kissed me on the cheek. Reaching up to wipe away the tears under her eyes, she said, "Well, now that I'm done acting stupid, we should probably get back."

We walked out of the woods and just before we approached the bonfire, I grabbed her arm and turned her to me. "I'm driving you home tonight, El. I won't drink anymore and I'll be okay to drive once we leave. I don't want to hear any argument about it, so just know that I'll be the one driving you home tonight. Okay?"

She didn't answer for a few seconds while she stood there and stared at me. "Fine. You can drive me home."

I smiled

Chapter Ten

Up down, up down, dip …

Up down, up down, dip …

Holy shit, this sucked. Painting the exterior of a house is probably the most monotonous and grueling task a person can perform at the beginning of the Florida summer. With sweat dripping down my head, I was finishing up the last walls of the house. After I finished this, all I had left was the trim and the house would be done. There was a light at the end of my 105-degree tunnel and I was happy to finally have it in sight.

And I was proud

After the primer provided a solid foundation, I'd painted on the next layer; the outside skin, the beauty that would project the personality of its occupants, and the part that every person would see. It was the outward reflection of the stability and strength of the job. And, to me at least, it had to be perfect.

I'm not going to explain to you why that is important, but I will say that if you missed the significance, then you haven't been paying attention to the story.

It had been a week since the bonfire. As I'd demanded, I'd driven El home that night. Lily had opted to ride with Ryan, and Finn had grudgingly accepted a ride with Jake. That left El and me alone for a long and awkward ride back to our houses. Not much was said between us, except for the occasional directions and warnings about an animal in the road. There were a lot of them, by the way. It was like playing a game of "Frogger" the entire way back. Luckily, we didn't hit anything and that was a blessing considering how upset I knew Ellison would have become.

I didn't go on the hike Ellison and I had planned for the following day. I woke up early as usual, thanks to Lily and Bill, but I went to work painting the house instead. When everybody had left the property, I'd reached for the radio at one point — but I couldn't turn it on when I'd tried. I just couldn't hit the button. Ellison's words about silence played in my head and I made a choice to endure my thoughts for several hours rather than having angry, angst-filled ballads blasted in my ears.

That sucked as well. Thinking. It really was a form of torture I was inflicting on myself. But, I think it might have done me some good after all. It was actually quite disturbing to discover I really didn't care about anything. Nothing was important to me — but me. And now, Ellison was as well. I couldn't ignore that annoying fact, but the epiphany was still the same. I was wasting my life. I was filling it up with pointless distractions and I was partying to cover up the boredom and pain I was suffering. And I felt like a pathetic little bitch to admit it.

Ellison had said to find something that interested me, something that I wanted to explore. There was nothing. I didn't have an emotional connection to anything and I worried that I'd end up laid out on some shrink's couch because something needed to be fixed in my head. I needed to find that connection to something and for the week it took me to paint the house, I'd scoured my brain in search of it. But no matter how hard I tried, I couldn't find it.

"It's looking really good, Hunter."

Ellison. I knew her voice. It was imprinted in my thoughts and seared into my memory. It was musical. It was a sound I would never be able to hear enough. I was seriously starting to lose it and it was driving me fucking mad. It had to be an infection of some sort. I had to be sick. Because there was no other reason why I should be feeling what I was for this girl.

Turning towards her, I reached up to wipe some sweat from my forehead. She laughed and pointed.

"You just smeared paint all over your head. The light blue looks good on you."

Well, shit, it's better than the pink calamine lotion ...

She was dressed in her hiking gear and her bags hung off her shoulders. The two devil beasts were at her feet, but luckily, they were too tired from the hike to mess up the job I'd just finished. I had to thank nature for that small favor.

My lips curled into a grin. "Thanks. Just have to finish the trim and it's done. Bill says I can take a break after that for a day or two before starting on the porch."

Ellison made a point to look around my shoulder at the porch in question. When she returned her eyes to me, she laughed and commented, "That should take you the rest of the summer to complete. Good luck to you."

I couldn't help the laugh that escaped me. I knew she was joking — but not really. The porch was bad, real bad, and there was no telling what types of dangerous booby traps were hidden within the piles of crap that covered it.

"What are you planning on doing during your break?"

I watched a bead of sweat slide down from her temple to her cheek. It shone against her sun kissed skin and I suddenly remembered the salty taste of her. It was a thought I shouldn't have been thinking, but I was thinking it anyway. Nature fucked me again when a gust of wind blew across us and her scent blanketed me. My body shuddered and my mouth watered. My tongue flicked out to lick along my lip and her eyes followed the motion. This was the hardest thing I'd ever done: keeping myself from kissing her was next to impossible.

"I don't have any plans yet." I should have come up with something ... lied ... not opened myself up for the invitation I knew was coming.

"Well, you're welcome to come along with me on the trails. We could take a shorter one tomorrow and do some fishing. I think you'd have fun. I'll invite Lily to come along, but she's been at Ryan's a lot lately and she probably won't come with us."

She was lonely without Lily. I could see that and it wasn't a good time for her to have nobody. She was hurting. It was obvious in her demeanor and I wondered if they received some of the test results about her father.

"Yeah. That would be cool. Do I have to get up at the butt crack of dawn this time?"

She laughed. "Nope. Although the fish will be biting better in the early morning than they would at midday. If you actually want to catch something, it's best we go early."

I wanted to catch something. It just wasn't a damn fish.

"Sounds good. Do I need to bring anything, like a bathing suit?" I winked and the dimples flew. I couldn't help it. It was an instinctual behavior that surfaced whenever Ellison was near me.

The pink that instantly flamed on her cheeks was so fucking adorable. I never knew why people always wanted to pinch the cheeks of chubby little poop monsters in the past, but looking down at Ellison now — I completely understood. When something that adorable is staring a person in the face, there's nothing you can do but reach over and touch it.

"That's probably a good idea. I'll bring one as well."

"That is entirely up to you. If you're more comfortable in the buff, I won't complain." I shrugged. "Seriously, it's your call."

Her smile was brilliant. "You've never seen me in the complete buff, Hunter — unless of course there's something your creepy stalker ass isn't telling me."

It was comfortable. Our encounter. Even though there'd been distant tension in the past week, we were immediately able to fall back into step with one another. And I was fucking ecstatic about it.

"Well, see you tomorrow, then. I'll come by in the morning to grab you around six. Or is that too early?"

I shook my head. She could have picked me up at three in the morning and it wouldn't have made a difference. If she was going somewhere and she wanted me to tag along, there wasn't a damn thing on this planet that would stop me.

~   ~   ~

I'm not going to get into the details of what happened on that first fishing trip. Let's just say it ended in a couple of stitches in my back from where'd I caught my skin with the hook I was trying to cast. It wasn't a pretty picture and it makes me look like a punk, so I'm not going to talk about it. One thing was for sure, television had lied and fishing was not as fun as it looked.

After that craptacular adventure, Ellison decided it would be best that I was introduced to her leisure activities slowly and easily. Hiking took up the majority of our time. It was a simple activity that didn't require the use of pointy objects. It's not that I was a klutz by any means, but Ellison finally realized my issues with nature and all the things it had to offer. The walks were good. It was rare that I did anything stupid and after the first few times, I was able to pace her with no problem. We talked a lot during those walks — about life, about love, and about things I'd never discussed with another person. Her ability to pull information out of me was astounding and I learned more about myself in those hours with her than I had the entire 19 years I'd been alive. She had a simple outlook on life. There were no complications or strings when it came to what she considered was happiness. She told me numerous times that I had to find what mattered. That I had to keep looking and keep exploring, but that I shouldn't stop experiencing life while I searched for it. It killed me at times to be around her. She didn't have much in life and she'd been dealt a pretty crappy hand when it came to what happened to her mother. But she never stopped smiling and she wouldn't stop trying to rescue me from something I didn't even know was threatening me to begin with. At times, I thought she knew me better than I knew myself, and I was entirely thankful for her insight.

"It's been a month. I'm surprised Bill hasn't gotten on to you about getting that porch finished." She walked in front of me as usual and my eyes were following the highlighted pieces of blonde that wound through her braid. Everything about her amazed me — even the color of her hair.

"Yeah, well he said something about the hikes being good for me so he hasn't made it much of an issue. I'm sure he'd be less giving if I was just sitting around doing nothing all day."

Bill encouraged my friendship with Ellison, and Lily did as well. But they were the only ones. Finn was still nice when he saw me around, and Jake was too oblivious to care, but Henry still gave me the evil eye every time he spotted me. He hadn't threatened me again and I was thankful for that, but I'd hoped he would warm up to me after seeing that I had no ill intentions towards his daughter. He didn't. But he didn't come between us either and I could respect him for that. He was letting Ellison choose for herself and I appreciated that he wasn't trying to tell her what to do like her brother and ex-boyfriend seemed to do often.

"Here we are! Thank god, because it's really hot today." Ellison ran towards the spring, while stripping off her shirt and shorts and she jumped immediately into the water. I could imagine the shock of the cold water against her skin, and I hated the fact I'd have to experience it as well, but I knew eventually I'd be happy to be cooled down. My clothes were soaked with sweat and the sun shone down without any cloud cover to give us shade. But it was a beautiful day and I was spending it with a beautiful girl. You wouldn't catch me complaining.

She splashed through the water in a tiny blue bikini and the light colored straw hat she'd been wearing on the hike. A thin necklace of beads hung around her neck and they bounced over her breasts from her movement through the water. My attraction to Ellison didn't decrease with the amount of time we'd been spending together — it only increased — and just the sight of her was enough to light a fire under my skin that was painful to endure. I kept to my word though and I never tried to push the line of friendship that she'd asked for the night of the bonfire.

Stripping my shirt and shorts off, I stepped into the water wearing the bathing suit I'd worn underneath my clothes. Ellison looked up at me for a moment, but then turned to swim farther out to watch the fish I knew she loved. We'd brought snorkels with us a couple of times and I had to admit: it was magical to swim within the school and to watch the waves of their brightly colored bodies edge in around us. It was like existing in an entirely different world and I was glad to share it with her. It was our world that summer; it was our moment together.

Swimming out to her, I floated beside her and we watched the fish swirl beneath us. Every once in a while, you'd see a turtle swim through the herd and Ellison would gasp each time — even though she'd seen it a million times before. Her innocent excitement was compelling, it was attractive, and it was something I'd never known I'd been missing in other people.

"That was a big one, huh? Makes you wonder how they swim around as easily as they do with that giant shell on their back. Guess the webbed toes help."

I didn't answer right away and she reached out to grab my hand. "Everything okay?" Her touch sent electric pulses shooting up my arms and I flinched in response to how sudden she'd done it. Turning to her, I squeezed her hand in mine and pulled her quickly to wrap her in a hug.

"Yeah. Everything's more than okay. I'm just enjoying the day."

She grew quiet, but smiled shyly and returned her attention to the fish, her back was pressed to my chest, my arms were wrapped around her stomach, and our legs brushed against each other as we kicked in the water. The scent of her hair sat just below my nose and I breathed deeper just to have her close by.

"Some of the test results came back."

My arms tightened around her.

"And? Were they normal?"

"No."

I sighed and rested the side of my head against hers. "What's the diagnosis?" I didn't want to hear the answer to the question because I somehow knew that whatever it was, it wasn't good. The thought of Ellison losing her father scared me. But the thought of her losing him when I couldn't stick around to take care of her terrified me more than anything else. She was a strong girl, I knew that, but she needed a shoulder to lean on every once in a while. She shouldn't have to do it all on her own.

"They don't know yet; but something's not right. They just said that he'd have to undergo more tests. You know how doctors are; even if they suspect what it is, they won't say something until they know for sure."

I didn't want to be the one to bring it up, but I had to know. "What if it's really bad, El? What are you going to do?"

She fidgeted in my arms, but she didn't pull away. "I don't know. I guess I'll keep going. He'd kick my ass if I didn't. I'll be angry. That's for sure. I don't think it's fair that my mother was taken from me, and my father after that. Most people get to keep at least one parent until they're older. Fate would have to be a cruel thing to take both of them from me.

However, fate could be cruel. I'd realized that over the time I'd known her. What I'd once thought was an awesome childhood full of freedom and carefree days, I now understood was a missing piece in my life. My parents' inattention bothered me. I could admit it when I was around her. I didn't have fond memories of just sitting around and laughing with them. There were never times that I could remember just being myself and enjoying my time in their company. Even holidays were spent trying to impress their friends and business associates during the endless parties and social gatherings. We'd never traveled to spend time with family, and never bothered to invite that family to spend time with us. I suspected that his brother embarrassed my father. However, after spending time with Bill, I realized that he had more to him than my father ever would. He'd raised a child on his own and he'd loved her despite the difficulty of his life. He was a good man and I was angry with my dad for never having allowed me to get to know him growing up.

She turned in my arms. "I'm afraid, Hunter."

It was a confession voiced so quietly it was barely voiced at all. But it was enough to awaken every protective bone I had in my body. I didn't think I'd ever be able to let her go.

"Are you afraid of being alone?

Her eyes watered and I didn't brush away the tears that fell from them because it meant that I would have to let her go to do so.

She nodded. "It's not that I'm afraid of being alone because I'll have no one. I can manage on my own. I have no doubt of that. But to be alone would mean that I lost every person that I cared for. That's what scares me, Hunter. Knowing that they'd be gone — and that I could never have them back."

My heart ripped apart and I pulled her in to me even tighter. Our faces were so close that I could feel her breath roll over my skin and the scent of her strawberry lip-gloss mixed with the tropical scent of her body and hair: sugar and spice — it was a heady and intoxicating combination.

"I promise you El, somehow, I'll find a way to be there for you. Even with a thousand miles between us, you'll always have me if you need me."

The brim of her hat shaded her face, but her eyes still danced from the light reflected up from the water. Birds sang in the distance and every so often a chorus of cicadas would belt out over the land as a gentle breeze brushed across our skin. Paradise could never be more perfect than the place where we were at that moment.

My heart beat soundly against my chest and her chest heaved as her breathing quickened. We stared into each other's eyes for God knows how long. The tension of the moment was almost too much to bear, but I wanted to give her strength, to really be there for her when she needed me, and I wasn't going to look away.

And it was a damn good thing I didn't.

The next thing I knew, Ellison James raised her arms out of the water and wrapped them around my shoulders. The perfect pout of her mouth came up to brush across my lips and I closed my eyes when a shudder rolled through me. She placed delicate kisses on my lips — they were soft, they were light and there was no need to rush them. I enjoyed the moment and I worried that she'd realize what she was doing and stop.

But she didn't.

Her fingers curled into the hair at the back of my head and she pulled away long enough to say, "I know that I asked for us to just be friends, and I know that anything more with you would be like shooting myself in the foot. But I can't help what I feel about you, Hunter. So maybe ... maybe if I choose to make the mistake myself, maybe if you're not the one who started things between us in the first place — maybe I could just own that mistake and not hate you for it in the end." She laughed quietly. "Whatever happens between us will be a mistake. But which would be bigger? The mistake of having been with you ... or the mistake of never having allowed myself to love you when I had the chance?"

My resolve snapped and my mouth crashed against hers just as she opened her lips so I could deepen the kiss. The skin of our bodies slid against each other while my tongue slid along hers. Her touch, her taste, her smell, every part of her that I could experience, I was taking at that moment. The gentleman in me told me to stop, but then her words repeated in my head, and I decided that, mistake or not, she was correct and it was something that had to happen. We'd denied each other for too long and this moment could be the only chance we had to correct it.

Chapter Eleven

My body was tight against her and, even though she was tall, she still felt tiny in my arms. My fingers found their way to her head and I slipped the little tie from her hair and shook out her braid. I'd imagined wrapping my fingers in the silken strands for a long time and I was using them to pull her closer to me and hold her in place. I wanted to devour her; to taste and touch every inch of her skin. I'd wanted it since the first time I seen her pissed off and covered in mud — and I was going to have it.

Our legs kicked lazily below us even though the top half was moving with a lustful frenzy. With one hand still wrapped in her hair, I pulled her head to the side so I could explore the skin of her neck with my mouth. She gasped when I nipped at her earlobe and I felt her muscles relax against the arm that I still had wrapped around her.

Goose bumps raced across her skin and I prayed that it was my touch causing that reaction in her rather than the cold as fuck water that surrounded us. Her arms tightened around my shoulders and I took advantage of the added support to remove my arm from her waist. She moaned when I ran my hand along the side of her body and the small sound aroused something feral within me. My thumb brushed across her breast just as my chest rumbled with a growl. An actual fucking growl. This girl was doing things to me that I never knew were possible. Her fingernails trailed down my back and my hand gripped around her hip, securing her body against mine. I wanted to take her right there, but I didn't want the distraction of remaining above water to distract from the experience.

Letting go of her hair, I used that hand to explore her body. I found her thigh first, running my hand up the side of it, making a point to rub my thumb along the inside and up along the sensitive skin between. Her stomach was a work of art — not too hard and not too soft. It was perfectly round where it should have been and a primitive instinct flickered within me to touch her there. When my hand found her breast, I paused waiting for a rejection — one that never occurred. I cupped the weight of it in my palm and I used my thumb to rub along the tip that was now hard beneath the thin covering of the triangle top of her suit. The movement of the cold water between us only added to the sensuality of the moment — and the silence, holy fuck, the silence — it let me hear every little sound she made and it kept me there, right fucking there, with her. I was connected to nothing but her. It was something I'd never experienced before and knew I could never experience again with another girl. Nobody would ever compare to Ellison James.

I pulled the tiny scrap of her top aside and shivered when the heat of her breast warmed my palm. Her head fell back and my lips trailed over her neck. I wanted to take the peak into my mouth, but the fucking water would have drowned me in the process. There's nothing sexy about not being able to breathe — not when it's not intended, anyway. I was hard as a fucking rock and I knew she could feel the length of me on her thigh. If she noticed — and trust me, she had to have noticed — she didn't care. Releasing her breast, I ran my hand back down her body and my fingers dared to reach between her thighs. I wanted her to stop me ... I silently begged for it, because I knew that by taking anything beyond this point I'd be giving this girl not only my body - I'd be giving her my fucking heart.

She didn't stop me.

My fingers smoothed over her bathing suit and her body trembled against me. Her mouth slid over mine and we molded to each other like two pieces of a puzzle that had finally found their match. Emotions tore through me that I'd never felt before and I was absolutely lost to her. Nothing would distract me from her. A nuclear bomb could have gone off beside us and I wouldn't have paid attention.

When my fingers slid below the fabric of her suit and rested over the entrance to her body, she pulled from my kiss, while at the same time, her fingernails dug into my back.

"Oh god, Hunter."

My name rolled off her kiss swollen lips like it had belonged there our entire lives. I loved the way she said it, and I pushed my finger into the heat of her body only to bring my mouth back to her shoulder and bite down. Her thighs tightened against each other when she moaned and I suddenly needed her out of the fucking water.

It took everything I had to pull away from her, but when I did, I looked deep into her eyes and the chemistry between us was certain. Neither of us could handle it if we stopped and there was no way in hell I was going to let the water get in between us. I swam towards shore and she followed behind me. When we got to a point where we could stand up, I picked her up quickly and threw her over my shoulder. She laughed loudly and squeezed the cheeks of my ass in her hands. When her nails dug into the skin, I growled again.

"You're really pushing for it, aren't you, woman?"

She slapped me hard against a cheek and it shoved me over the edge from modern man to caveman. I powered my feet through the water as I walked to shore and laid her down in a bed of grass off to the side of the clearing. I wanted a secluded spot for her, even though nobody had ever been around when we'd been out here. It was our own little piece of the world and I was intent on christening it at that moment.

Laying my body on top of hers, I was greedy to immediately take her mouth with mine. Her hands explored my chest and shoulders, but then slipped down along my abdomen. I could feel every muscle clench as she brushed across it and when she reached between my legs and wrapped her palm around the length of me, my body bucked against her. My teeth instantly found her bottom lip and I bit down into the swollen flesh softly, but desperate for more at the same time. My bathing suit had become a fucking nuisance and I wanted to rip it off, but I didn't want her to think I was going to rush this.

Because I wasn't ...

I was going to take my time memorizing every inch of her body. If there was something to be seen, I was going to see it — and if my mouth could go there, she was going to feel my kiss. I didn't know if this was the only shot I had to be with her and I wasn't going to move it along any faster than I had to.

I pulled her up off the ground just enough so I could reach behind her and release the strings of her bikini. Tossing her top aside, I looked back to see that the thin beads of her necklace were laid out beautifully between her breasts — and they were absolutely fantastic breasts.

Finally — fucking f-i-n-a-l-l-y — I was able to take the tip of her breast into my mouth and when the salt of her skin met my tongue, I almost lost it right there. She arched her chest up when my tongue smoothed over the tight peak and my hand went beneath her so I could hold her to tight to my mouth. I worked on one breast for what felt like forever before I moved over to start on the other. The sound of her little mewls, gasps and moans was driving the blood through my veins even faster and it felt like I would explode at any second. I bit down into the sensitive skin of her breast and her fingers found my hair, wrapping into it so tightly, it pulled at my skull adding a delightful element of pain to the intense pleasure that was consuming me.

"Fuck. Oh god. Hunter, I need … I need … "

It was all she had to say. I knew what she 'needed' and I was going to deliver.

My mouth released her breast and I worked my way down, kissing along the curve of her stomach, making sure to tickle her over the belly button before pushing myself up over her. The bottom to her suit was tied at the sides and all I had to do was pull on those strings and I would finally be admitted into the only kind of heaven I ever wanted to know. Who needed a happy white fluffy fucking cloud to float on when they could have Ellison James naked and writhing beneath them? Certainly, not me. If Heaven actually existed, it was in the arms of this woman and she was waiting to give me everything I could ever need.

I pulled at those strings and removed the last bit of fabric from her body. She was laid out beneath me, gloriously naked and the sun shone off her skin as if it wanted to kiss her as much as I did. She was perfection, she was the definition of beauty, and she was the epitome of every good thing a woman had to offer. I didn't just love her body, I didn't just love her perfectly kiss swollen mouth, I loved the words that came out of that mouth and the crazy thoughts hidden behind the blue eyes that sparkled up at me from where she lay.

I lowered my head down and flicked my tongue between the slick skin at the apex of her thighs. Her taste was like ambrosia. Holy shit! My organs were twisting over themselves as I licked and kissed and nipped along every single part of her. Her body wiggled beneath me and her hands massaged her breasts as I watched her from where I was positioned. I was lost in what I was doing to her — in what she was doing to herself — but at the same time I couldn't take my eyes off of her. There were no words to describe the view of her body. It was beauty in motion — art brought to life. I was an absolute cheeseball for even thinking those thoughts but there was no better way to describe what I was watching.

She reached down with her hands and tangled them in my hair forcing me against her and I gladly flicked out my tongue and used it to push inside her. My hand came up to join the actions of my mouth and the moans that rolled through her vibrated along my body. Giving her what she wanted was enough to get me off, but I wouldn't allow the release until I was buried as deep inside her as I could get. Moving so that I could suck on the bundle of nerves I knew needed attention, I crooked my finger so that I hit that magic spot inside her and she lost it. Her fingers gripped so tightly in my hair that it caused me to hiss in reaction. The pain was exquisite because I knew that it meant she was taking me along for whatever ride she was experiencing. And I'd done that to her — for her. When I heard my name shouted from her mouth, I had to physically stop myself from ripping off my shorts and mounting her. Her inner muscles clenched at my fingers and all I could imagine was the feeling of being inside her.

When her body calmed and all that was left were the small aftershocks and tremors from her fall back to Earth, I slowly moved up her body, paying special attention to her stomach and breasts on my way. My mouth crashed into hers once more and I could feel her chest brush across me from the excited pants that were quickly escaping her. She reached down to grasp me through my shorts, but then she moved to pull the material off my body. Helping her, I forced the shorts down and kicked them off my legs, my bare ass now on display for any person who happened to walk by.

I didn't care.

I didn't fucking care if there was an audience of 50 people standing around, taking fucking pictures, or cheering us on while peanuts and beer were being sold off on the sidelines, I was going to have Ellison James and there was nothing that would stop me.

"Shit. Hunter? Do you have a condom?"

Except that.

That would stop me.

FUCK!

I dropped down on top of her and buried my face into the perfection of her breasts. "No, no, no, no, no, no, no, no! NO! This is not fucking happening."

She laughed at my pain. What else was new?

Of course, I didn't have a fucking condom. Who the fuck thinks *oh hey, I'm going hiking with my buddy, I'd better be sure to bring along a rain jacket, just in case?* Not me. That's who.

"Hunter ... "

I held up a hand without lifting my face from her chest. "I know." The words were muffled. "You don't have to say it. Trust me, I know."

Sonofabitch!

A myriad of reasons of why I HAD to stop plowed through my head. Actual tears threatened my eyes when I realized that not using protection could lead to some real complications that would potentially ruin both of our lives. We had a future to work towards and a baby was not in the cards for at least another seven to 10 years — for her. Not me. I decided to reach in and pull out that baby card from my deck just before tearing it in shreds and setting it on fire. But I knew Ellison would become a mother someday. It would be an absolute crime against nature if she didn't.

"I could ... "

"No." I reached up to place my hand over her mouth. "Don't say it. My entire world just shattered around me and there's nothing that can be done that would make it any better. It's best we let junior calm down and then maybe I can just work through the blue balls during the 13 miles we have left to go on the hike." The sarcasm in my voice was intended on that comment.

She giggled. "Junior?" Running her fingernails along my back, she whispered, "You don't have to be so dramatic, you big baby. There's always next time."

I didn't know why I said 'no'. If any other woman had offered that, I would have shoved her down so fast she wouldn't have known what hit her. But not Ellison. Nope. I wanted the grand finale and after having it cruelly and mercilessly ripped from my grasp, the opening credits could never make up for it. Once again, I'd made a decision that was so unlike me.

And I realized it was official ...

Ellison James was a wizard.

~ ~ ~

The rest of the hike was a nightmare. After discovering that a big stop sign had been placed in between us, we'd gotten dressed and made our merry way up the trail. My balls were being assholes and painful shocks erupted as the blood in my groin worked its way back into my body. It was a nice 13-mile reminder of the roadblock with which I'd just had a head on collision. It wasn't her fault and I didn't hold it against her. I was pissed at myself for not having thought of that problem before taking things as far as we had.

Ellison looked at me with sympathy every time she noticed I was hobbling and the expression did nothing for my ego. I brushed it off and replaced it with thoughts of 'next time.' Ellison had said those words and I was holding her to them — and I was doing so armed with a brand spanking new box of condoms. There was nothing that was going to stop me again. There was going to be a 'next time.' It was the mantra that pushed me through the rest of the trip — the ONLY thing that pushed me through the rest of the trip.

"So, there's another bonfire tonight, if you want to go."

We were climbing through the small path that El had cut between the trail and our houses. It was single file only and she had to turn around and look over her shoulder when she mentioned the bonfire.

"Sounds good. Do we get to hang with Sensitive-Guitar-Guy again? Because it's so much fun." I smiled my megawatt grin to let her know I was joking and she laughed in response. I knew it was the dimples that made her grin like that. They were magic.

"Finn will probably be there, but we'll do our best to avoid him. He really is a good guy, Hunter, he just has to get used to seeing me with other men." She turned back to continue down the path.

I inwardly gloated about that fact until I realized that after I returned home, I would have to get used to seeing her with other men as well. It was the wonder of the social networking phenomena: endless reminders of people who were in your life, who you wanted out of your life, and who you would most likely never have in your life again. It sucked.

Staring at the back of her head, I admitted, "I don't think he likes me very much. I mean, he's nice and all, but he knows why I came down here.

"Because of your car and your parents' pool? Yeah, he told me all about that."

My body tensed. I wanted to destroy him.

"But none of it really matters to me and I told him how I felt. It doesn't matter why you came down here in the first place. All that matters is what you're doing now." She turned to face me after saying those beautiful forgiving words. My eyes burned into hers and I took two broad steps before grasping her head in my hands and crashing my mouth to hers. We were still far enough out that nobody would see us from the houses and I wasn't going to give up the last opportunity I had to show her exactly how I felt about her. I was still banking on 'next time', but I wasn't about to give up what I could have 'this time.'

I pulled away only when I had to breathe. Her cheeks were flushed and she was slightly unsteady on her feet. The previous hit to my ego was soothed.

Her lips pulled up into an adorable smile. "Was it something I said?"

"It's everything you've said, since the first day I fucking met you."

Her eyebrow arched.

"Okay, maybe the second day. But still ... "

She stared up at me with an odd expression on her face. Finally she laughed. "Okay, freak, whatever you say."

I growled at her and she laughed again before turning to walk the rest of the path. We broke out of the woods between the two houses and I saw a car I didn't recognize in the driveway. Lily stood by it when she turned to look at El and me. She waved quickly, however, her expression was anything but friendly.

"Who's that?" Ellison looked at me. "Think Ryan bought a new car?"

I shrugged my shoulders. "I don't know."

We crossed the yard quickly and I couldn't see who was sitting in the driver's seat of the car because of the tint to the windows. Whoever it was had money because the car had to have been worth more than $50,000. Lily shot me a murderous glare when I approached and the driver's side door of the vehicle opened so they could climb out.

My eyes flicked over and the smile fell from my face.

No.

This was not happening.

This was not fucking possible.

Ellison looked between the woman who'd stepped out of the car and me. She gave me a strange smile but then walked over to offer her hand. "Hey, I'm Ellison James. Are you a friend of Lily's?"

"Hi. Uh, no." She smirked at me when she talked to Ellison. "I'm Tiffany. I'm Hunter's girlfriend." She stressed that last word, by the way. On purpose.

Ellison's jaw dropped and my eyes were glued to every expression that sped across her beautiful face; each one taking a piece of my heart with it. She looked back up at me and that's when I saw something in her eyes that caused my shoulders to drop and what was left of my heart to sink into my stomach.

It was shock.

It was anger.

It was pain.

And it was the absolute and complete annihilation of 'next time.'

Chapter Twelve

Ellison

I didn't know what to say or what to do. This woman stood in front of me saying words that didn't make sense. Or maybe they did.

Come to think of it, I'd never directly asked Hunter if he had a girlfriend back home.

Wanting to make a quick exit to avoid shedding angry tears in front of Hunter's girlfriend, I plastered on a fake bright smile and said, "Well, it's nice to meet you, Tiffany. I'm sure you want some time alone with Hunter considering it's been a while since you've seen him. I'm just going to head to the house and get a shower. Maybe I'll see you around later."

I didn't know what else to say. It wasn't like I could be mean to her, she'd done nothing wrong. It was Hunter who I wanted to strangle. I was a little shocked to see the type of girl he dated back home, but then I remembered he was a different person when he'd first arrived. And judging by the fact that he'd neglected to mention his girlfriend, he was probably still that same type of person. I'd been stupid enough to fall for his charm and I was damned sure I wouldn't be making that mistake again.

I tried not to look at him when I strode quickly away towards the house. Lily was fast on my heels and I was both aggravated and comforted to know she'd be joining me inside. I wasn't in the mood for 20 questions and I knew she'd be unloading them as soon as the front door slammed shut behind us. My heart was pounding painfully against my ribs and my knees shook as I made my way back to the house.

By the time we were safely outside of sight of Hunter and his girlfriend, I lost it. My eyes shed angry and hurt tears and my fists balled up in desperate need to impact with Hunter's face. Since he wasn't available at that moment, I hit the wall instead — and immediately regretted it.

"Ow!"

Cradling my hand to my chest, I bit down on my lip to try and keep from screaming. Lily ran to my side and pulled me towards the kitchen before plopping me down in a chair at the table. Moving to the freezer, she quickly gathered up a few cubes of ice. After wrapping them in a towel, she sat down beside me and placed the makeshift ice pack to my hand.

"Well, that was surprising."

"Surprising?" I laughed like an idiot. "No, Lily. Winning the lottery is surprising ... that was absolutely heartbreaking. I opened my burning eyes to look over at her. "How long has she been here?"

"She drove up about 15 minutes before y'all got back. I'd just come home from Ryan's house and was heading inside to get ready for tonight when I saw her. Judging by the car she was driving, I thought it was Hunter's parents comin' down to check on him. I didn't expect to be met with brunette Barbie when I approached."

"She is beautiful, isn't she?"

Lily sighed. "Well, yeah, if you like the fake and plastic look, I guess a person could say she is."

I could rely on many things with Lily and the most important was her honesty. Lying to me and telling me that Tiffany wasn't beautiful would have only made me feel worse to know she was saying those things to make me feel better — and that would have been pathetic.

My thoughts immediately went back to what Hunter and I had almost done. For a split second I was thankful it hadn't gone as far as it could have and I regretted not having kicked him between the legs as he hobbled home. I'd felt sorry for him then — but now I was thinking he'd gotten off too easily. Well, not 'off off', but you know what I mean.

"She was perfect; her hair, her clothes, her makeup, her nails. There wasn't a single part of that woman that wasn't put together. I can't compete with that, Lily. I don't know the first fucking thing about most of it." I was babbling because of my anger. Normally girls like Tiffany didn't bother me and I usually felt sorry for them because they spent more time looking at themselves in a mirror than they did looking at the world around them. It had to get depressing spending day in and day out watching yourself get older. But that was beside the point and this girl was different. I'd opened myself up to Hunter, I'd exposed my heart, and I'd had it ripped from my chest with nothing more than a stupid expression written across his face.

"Her boobs were fake. Your boobs are much better, if you ask my opinion." It was Lily's weak attempt at consoling me. Oddly, it did kinda help.

"Thanks." I looked down at my chest and remembered all the things Hunter had been doing to it only a few hours before. God, I hated him — although he was really good at what he was doing to it. I can admit that. And it just made the situation that much more sucktastic.

"So, did she say if she's staying? How much longer do we have to deal with her being around?"

Lily shook her head and shrugged her shoulders. "I don't know. She didn't really say much. She just kept stressing that she was Hunter's girl and she wanted to see him. I was as shocked as you. I take it Hunter never mentioned her."

I folded my arms on the table and laid my head on top of them. "No, of course not. If I'd known, I wouldn't have … "

Her eyes bugged out. "Wouldn't have what? Oh shit, Ellie, did you have sex with Hunter? I mean, I knew you two were hanging out and all, but I didn't think it was that serious."

Burying my head even farther beneath my crossed arms, I attempted to hide the shame reddening my cheeks. "Almost."

Lily sighed, but then reached out to rub my head. "Well, almost ain't all the way, so you shouldn't be hidin' your shame just yet."

She knew me so well.

Looking up again, I held the ice closer to my throbbing hand. "It might as well have been all the way. There wasn't an inch of me he didn't see or touch." We sat in silence for a few moments while I gathered myself together. It wasn't the end of the world. Hunter was never going to be anything more than a summer love and I was more mad at myself for having fallen for someone who'd be leaving. This was the same, just earlier than expected. Whether it was the end of summer or the arrival of Tiffany, Hunter McCormick was going to leave my life. But, it was also knowing that we'd done things just a few hours before while he knew full well he had a girl back home — that enraged me and I thought maybe her arrival was a blessing in disguise. My heart would still grieve, but it would be an angry grievance, the kind I could push past me. It wouldn't be the longing grievance — one where I was angry that fate had been cruel and made it impossible for me to be with someone I loved.

"Are you still going to the bonfire tonight? I can have Ryan pick me up if you aren't feeling up to it … or I could just stay here and take out a few gallons of ice cream with you until you're better."

I looked up into the kind eyes of my friend and decided that I didn't want to be one of those women wallowing around in misery. "I'm still going, Lil. Hunter is a lesson learned and nothing more than that. Can't stop moving forward because of an arrogant asshole that crossed my path. I'm sure there will be plenty more of them by the time we finally start back at school. I might as well learn to get past it now."

"That's my girl. Okay — I'm going to go next door and start getting ready." She eyed me. "You should probably get a shower. You've got grass and dirt all over you. What were you doing? Rolling around in the … " Her eyes got wide. "Oh."

I wanted to smack her. Gently, of course.

"Okay, well, I'm leaving." She bounced out of her chair, leaned down to give me a quick hug, and then bounced her little butt right out the front door. Sasha and Bear came up to me after she left and gave me little sympathy licks on my legs. I reached down to pet them and then pushed myself up from the table to feed them. I didn't really feel like going to a bonfire, but I figured it was safer to hang out there than to stick around and risk running into Hunter and his girl.

~   ~   ~

I'd showered and dressed, paying particular attention to drying my hair into loose waves and throwing on the tiniest amount of makeup. I was upset, but I wasn't dead and there was no reason to go out in public looking like someone had just run over my puppy.

Stepping into the living room, I found my dad sitting in a chair at the table in the adjacent dining room. He was looking over paperwork and his facial expression screamed fear and frustration.

"Daddy? Why are you home so soon from work?" It was only six in the evening and normally he wouldn't arrive back for another hour or so.

"Hey, Ellie baby. You should probably take a seat. I need to tell you something'."

I didn't like the defeated tone to his voice, but I slowly made my way over to him and sat down. "Everything, okay? Did you get news from the doctors?" Looking down, I noticed that the papers in his hands were bills and financial ledgers. I didn't see anything medical within them and that made me feel better about his mood. If it was money problems, those could be solved. They weren't something that would crush me.

"Baby." He paused and sighed. Placing his hand on mine, he continued, "Baby, the doctors are sayin' that I have prostate cancer. It's at an early stage and they think it's operable and I'll be fine — but they want to run a few more tests to make sure that it isn't anywhere else. They said my heart and lungs are good, so that's a good sign."

"Okay." My throat closed up suddenly with fear and I choked back some tears that were threatening the back of my eyes. The doctors said they could fix it — and I had to rely on that. "So, when I are they running the next tests?"

"Tomorrow. I know you kids have plans tonight, but I was wondering if you could be sure to come home early enough that you can drive me to the hospital in the morning. I'd ask your brother, but I don't want this getting out and worrying people until we know more. I hate to worry you, but I know you've got the best head on your shoulders than any of the other clowns in this family and you'll take it in stride." He pinched my cheek.

My father's health was more important than a stupid party and I made the instant decision to stay home and take care of him rather than go out. "I'll stay home. I don't want to chance not being able to take you."

His expression softened and he squeezed my hand. "Baby girl, you're young and it's the summer before college. There's no reason for you to be sitting around here worrying over an old man. Go out tonight, have fun … just not too much. I'll be sitting here for a few more hours figuring out the medical bills and making sure I can still put you through college. You got a bright future ahead of you and I'll be damned to let my illness get in the way of that."

It was just like daddy. He'd spent his entire adult life putting his problems aside to raise his kids. And even now, when he was facing a potentially fatal disease, he was still only concerned for his kids. The man would work himself to death if it meant giving his children what they needed and it broke my heart to think about it. Someone needed to be worrying about him as much as he was worrying about us.

"Are you sure, Daddy? I don't mind stayin'. We could hang out and watch a movie or something'. Tell you what ... I'll even sit through a black-and-white war movie without complaining if that'll make you feel better."

He chuckled and ruffled my hair with his hand. "There's no need to torture yourself like that right now, baby girl. Your old man isn't dying tonight. I'd prefer you go out and have a good time. Keep an eye on your brother for me. That would make me feel better."

I nodded just as someone knocked on the door. Lily entered without waiting for a response. "Hey, El and Mr. James." She bounced over to the table and took a seat by daddy. Giving him a quick hug, her big blue eyes next turned to me. "You ready? ... "

The funny expression on her face told me something was up.

"'Cause I kinda mentioned the bonfire in front of Hunter and his girl and she's dragging him out to it. You shoulda seen the fit she threw. Poor guy didn't hear the end of it for almost two hours. I had to throw on some headphones just so I could get a break. She's got some lungs on her, that's for sure."

And an annoying fucking voice — I remembered that much from the little bit she said at the car. "Serves him right. Hopefully, she's still blasting him now that you left. What was she yelling at him about it, I thought he wanted to go even before she got here."

"He doesn't want to now. He kept trying to convince her to go back home. Claimed he broke up with her over a voicemail, but she wasn't hearin' it. He'd just broke down and agreed to go around the time I left. But, I promise you, that boy didn't want to get her anywhere near the bonfire tonight. Thank goodness Dad wasn't around 'cause he would have thrown a fit over the fighting they were doing."

Daddy looked between Lily and me. "What's it matter if that boy has a girl back home?" His eyes locked to mine. "Especially, considering he's nothing more than a friend to you, right?"

"Right." I hated lying to my dad, but there was no point bringing up mistakes that wouldn't happen again. "We should get going, Lil. Finn, Ryan and Jake will be looking for us once they help get the fire built."

"Well, you two girls have fun. Be sure to act like ladies. I know those kids are drinking and carrying on down there and you'd better act like you've been raised better than that. I trust you girls to make your own decisions, but don't think I'm not aware of what's going on at those parties. Hear me?"

"Yes daddy."

"Yes Mr. James."

I hugged my father and dragged my feet as we walked towards the front door. Taking a deep breath, I called the dogs to follow me, I opened that door and I stepped out into what would end up being an emotionally exhausting night.

Chapter Thirteen

Hunter

Tiffany.

Of all the people that could have pulled up and invaded my little piece of paradise, it would be Tiffany. It could have been my parents and it could have been my friends. But, no! It had to be a girl I felt obligated to! Even though I couldn't stand to be in her presence.

"Want another line before we go. I just need to fix my makeup real quick and brush my hair." She fished around in one of the countless suitcases she'd dragged inside. "I can't wait to get to a hotel tonight. This place is a fucking dump." She pulled out a pair of fuck me heels from the suitcase she was searching. "I'm going to change my shoes as well. Can't go to a party looking like a slob."

She winked, but it didn't do the same things to me that it did when Ellison was winking.

Almost immediately after she'd arrived, she'd pulled out a couple of grams of coke she'd brought along for the trip. She must have flown down on her parents' private plane because there was no way in hell she'd snuck that past security at a regular airline. She'd offered it to me before Lily arrived back at the house and I'd sucked it up into my nose as quickly as I could get the dollar bill rolled up. I felt guilty as shit for doing it, but I needed it to help numb me.

I couldn't stop imagining what Ellison was doing at her house. I'd seen that look on her face when Tiffany'd introduced herself. It was a look of sadness and anger mixed into one. It was desolation and it was betrayal. It was everything she'd thought I'd done to her. And somehow I knew, it would be a fight to get her to give me the chance to explain. Ellison was the type of girl who gave you one chance — and if you fucked it up, you might as well pack your shit and move along. And I'd fucked it up. Big time.

However, even knowing that, I was still determined to explain.

I didn't want to take Tiffany to the bonfire. I wanted her out of Florida and out of sight of Ellison. I could handle waiting it out for Tiffany to leave before making Ellison understand, but having to drag Tiffany around Ellison, and not having had the chance to explain, that was a recipe for disaster. I could have kicked Lily for even mentioning it in Tiffany's presence. I was about 10 seconds away from convincing Tiffany to stay the night in a hotel and go home ... but then Lily had to go and open her big mouth. I didn't even know why Tiffany was interested.

"You do realize that this party is out in the woods right? Like with grass and trees and shit. Those shoes are going to suck if you wear them, Tiff. Plus, I don't even think you'll have a good time. It's just a bunch of rednecks drinking beer out of plastic cups." I yelled at her across the house praying that she'd change her fucking mind and drive us into town.

"No way, Hunter! I want to see what you've been doing all this time — or who you've been doing. There has to be some reason you felt the need to break up with me over voicemail. It's a good thing I came down here to show you that you didn't really want that. Distance is hard so I forgive you."

Fuck, she was stupid. I'd tried everything I could besides throwing her out on her ass to convince her that things were over. She wouldn't believe me. She kept arguing that it was because we weren't around each other and that a night out would show me how much I'd missed her. Three hours in her presence and I knew for a fact that I hadn't missed her at all.

"Ready to go? Let's get our party on!"

"Yeah, let me finish up what I've got laid out." I quickly snorted five lines.

"Jesus, Hunter. You're acting like a junkie who hasn't had his fix." She knelt down between my knees where my legs hung over the bed. Spreading them apart with her hands she smiled before licking her lips and smacking them together. "I bet I know something you've missed." She reached up to unbuckle my belt and open my pants. Her hands immediately were on my cock and it hardened at her touch.

That's the thing about coke. It might numb the soul, but it made the nerve endings hypersensitive. Sex was amazing on it. I hadn't forgotten that and neither had Hunter Junior.

She freed me from my underwear and immediately wrapped her mouth around me. The wet heat felt so fucking good that I moaned and allowed my head to fall back. I didn't want to see the girl that was sucking me off. I wanted it be Ellison — and despite how good it felt, I had to stop it.

"Tiff stop."

She reached up and worked her hand and mouth on me at the same time. Holy fuck, it felt good.

"Tiff. Fucking stop."

She didn't listen.

I grabbed her hair and tugged her off of me. "Tiff! I said to fucking stop."

"Ow! What the fuck, Hunter?!" Standing up, she reached back to smooth down her hair. "What the fuck is your problem?"

My hands worked quickly to shove everything back into my pants. "I don't want a fucking blow job, okay? Let's just get going so we can get through this fucking night."

. . .

The drive to the bonfire was an exercise in self-control. I can't tell you how many times I had the overwhelming urge to pull the car over and dump Tiffany on the side. But, it was her car and luckily, that left me with no choice but to refrain from ditching her.

"I don't see why you didn't just run their fury little asses over. It's our road. They deserve to get hit if they are stupid enough to sit around on it."

I hated her.

She bitched the entire drive over. I'd demanded to drive just because of the type of rental she had, and I'd played the usual game of Frogger on the way out. Tiffany was annoyed that the car kept coming to sudden stops. She yelled at me each time I did it and she about lost it when I stopped the car for something as small as a lizard at one point. It didn't matter if it was a raccoon, an opossum, a squirrel or a duck ... if it was on the road Tiffany believed it deserved death for being stupid.

"Just drop it, Tiffany. We're here now and there's no point in hashing it out. Try to have some fun or just shut up or something."

"Whatever; where's the beer? If I have to party with hillbillies, I may as well see what it's all about." She started to walk in the direction of the kegs but the heels of her shoes kept sinking into the dirt. "Fuck! Haven't these people ever fucking heard of cement or pavers?! Seriously, they are living like fucking homeless people or ... well ... hillbillies."

She took off her shoes and bare-hoofed it to the kegs. I raised a brow at that maneuver and gave the girl some credit for not be afraid to get her feet dirty.

But I still hated her.

My body rotated around while I searched out El. I didn't see her in the same area she'd been at the last bonfire and I wondered if her and Lil were running late. Or maybe Lil had told her that I was bringing Tiffany, and Ellison decided to skip it all together. I was giving up hope when, in the distance, I saw Ellison walk by carrying her guitar with Finn following closely behind with a blanket in his hands. So much for avoiding him like she'd said, but I guess circumstances had changed since the afternoon.

She looked beautiful. She had on a short dress, her cowboy boots and her straw hat and it felt like someone had shot me in the chest to see it. Her blond hair blew out behind her in soft waves and she had a smile on her face that burned brighter than the large bonfire ever would when it was finally lit. It was still light outside and the brilliant sunlight shone off her skin as she laughed and talked to Finn who'd caught up to walk beside her. The dogs followed at their heels. They looked one big happy family. And I hated it.

I started to move in her direction. I had to talk to her. She didn't seem upset, but I knew she was good at hiding her emotions when she didn't want a person to know what she was thinking. The blow I'd done before coming here wasn't helping my thought process either. It would have been best for me to leave her alone, but I couldn't. I just fucking couldn't. I had to explain.

I started to run, but my arm was suddenly grabbed and I was jerked back. "Where are you going? You're not bringing me out here just to ditch me with a bunch of redneck idiots." She took a swig out of the solo cup and made a disgusted face. "Least they could do is have imported beer."

I rolled my eyes. "I didn't want to bring you out here in the first place. I have someone I need to talk to. Just stand around and look pretty until I get back."

If there was ever a time where I felt like I'd been cut a break, it was at that moment. Lily and Ryan walked past us on their way to the kegs and I grabbed Lily around the arm. Pulling her to me so I could whisper, I begged, "Please, please, please, fucking, puh-lease, will you distract Tiffany for a second? I need to to talk to Ellison."

Lily looked up at me with an angry expression. "Hell no you don't. I think you've done enough to that girl, Hunter. I haven't had a chance yet to get you alone and away from your raging bitch of a girlfriend, but you can bet that when I do, I'm ripping you a new one for what you've done!"

"Fine ... rip me a new one, rip me a few new ones, but only after I've had a chance to talk to Ellison.

Lily, this isn't what it looks like. I broke up with Tiffany when I came down. I didn't think she'd show up. I need to explain it to El."

Lily eyed me suspiciously. "You broke up with her before you left New York?"

"No. I broke up with her three days after coming down. The night of the last bonfire. I left her a voicemail."

"Are you fucking kidding me Hunter? You broke up with the girl over voicemail and you expected her to be okay with that? I know you're smart and all, but you sure as hell don't act like it."

"Whatever, Lil! That's not the point at the moment. Please distract her so I can find El."

"You want a bump, baby?" My eyes met the cocaine tipped key Tiffany was holding at the exact same time Lily saw it.

"What's wrong with you?!" Lily turned so that she was nose to nose with Tiffany. "Don't bring drugs and shit around here, Hunter's trying to quit. That's the whole point of him coming down."

Tiffany laughed. "Quit? Why? Everyone's doing it. Plus, he's already finished off about ten lines since I've been here, so I highly doubt another bump is going to hurt him."

Fuuuuuuuuuuck ….

Lily turned her blue eyes back to me. Her face was red with anger and I flinched knowing that I was about to hear it.

But then she surprised me.

154

Plastering a sweet smile on her face, she angled her head toward her shoulder when she said, "Hunter, why don't you go deal with what you need to deal with for a moment, okay? I'd like to have a little girl talk with Tiffany."

Tiffany rolled her eyes.

I didn't wait around long enough to let Tiffany object. I looked around the clearing and eventually found Ellison sitting with Finn on a blanket out near the tree line. I had no idea why they were sitting so far away, but I didn't have time to concern myself with the details. I just ran in their direction. By the time I reached her, she was bent over her guitar strumming out a slow song.

"Hey, Hunter! Is your girlfriend having a good time at the bonfire?" Finn smiled up at me.

This guy was really starting to piss me off with the friendly act ...

"Uh, she's not my girlfriend ... "

Ellison snorted.

"Hey, Ellie. Can I talk to you? Privately, please?"

She looked up at me and the smile I'd seen earlier was completely gone. "What do we have to talk about, Hunter? I think you've had plenty of time to talk to me over the past weeks and you had nothing to say then. Why now?"

Finn looked between us with a suspicious look on his face. "Look, Hunter, maybe you should just take your girl- ... "

"She's not my fucking girlfriend! Say it again and I'll beat your fucking face in, asshole!"

155

Okay — so, the blow was definitely not doing good things for my thought process.

Ellison stood up and the guitar swung on its strap to her back. "Whoa! Hunter, calm down! If you want to talk to me so bad, then fine, we can go for a walk. It's obvious you've got more in you than anger at the moment and walking it off might do you some good."

She knew. I didn't know how she could always see right through me, but, somehow, she knew.

She walked towards the road and Bear followed behind her. Sasha chose to stay on the blanket with Finn and I eyed the dog. *Traitor.* Ellison was moving fast and I jogged to catch up to her.

"Ellison, listen, this is so not what it looks like. I broke up with Tiffany. She's my ex-girlfriend — EX. Just like you and Finn. She hasn't accepted the split, but that's not my fault, El. You have to see that." I was babbling, but I was so freaked out, I couldn't formulate an intelligent statement to save my life.

She didn't bother to turn around when she asked, "When did you break up with her, Hunter?"

"On the night of the last bonfire. I borrowed Lily's phone and called Tiffany to end things."

"Did you talk to her?"

"No ... but I don't see why that matters."

Ellison stopped suddenly and turned around. The brim of her hat shaded her face as the sun set beautifully in the distance behind her.

"Because it's the respectful thing to do. When are you going to learn that? You can't just go around doing things that are right for you without considering how it affects other people. I believe that you probably broke up with the girl, but not in a way that would give her any kind of closure. I'm not surprised she showed up. I mean, it's a little bit crazy for her to travel all that way, but still. She has a right to know what happened. And you disrespected me by never saying anything to me about her. You could've mentioned you'd just broken up with your girlfriend. I don't want to be the branch you use to swing away from her. Take some time to be alone before jumping from one bed to another. But, dammit, Hunter, if you can't learn to respect yourself, you'll never learn to respect other people — which is obvious given your current state. How long did it take for you to go back to drugs since she's been here? Five minutes? Ten?"

I looked down at my clothes. Everything was clean and in place. How did she know? "I've got to ask how you know, El. It amazes me that you can see right through me. How the fuck do you do it?"

She sighed and crossed her arms over her chest before uncrossing them and pointing at me. "You're all fidgety, Hunter, and you're sniffling like you have a cold. Plus, your eyes are dilated and shifty. It doesn't take a rocket scientist to figure out what that kind of behavior means. Not to mention you threatened Finn when all he was doing was trying to get you to leave me alone."

El wasn't psychic. She was just observant.

"I ... fuck ... I know I shouldn't have done the lines and I won't do it again. Not while I'm around you ..."

"It shouldn't be about whether or not you're around me. It should be about the fact that you want to care about yourself and you don't want to end up a fucking loser who is too damn stupid to do something meaningful with his life. Especially you. You're a special person, Hunter, and it's a damn shame you don't see it! All I heard about before you came down here is how smart you are. I was really excited to meet you because I thought you'd be a great person to be around. But all that you've shown me since you've been here is that the only thing you're good at is making bad decisions. I have no problem with alcohol, Hunter, when it's used in moderation. Hell, I don't even have a problem when people smoke pot around me. But you're an addict and you don't need to be around it at all. You can't handle it."

I held up my hands at the 'a' word. "I'm not an addict, El. I was sent here to change my lifestyle, not to attend rehab!" I was yelling again and I tried to calm myself down.

She walked up to me and craned her neck so she could look me in the eyes. Poking her finger into my chest, she said, "When it gets to a point where you are parking your car in a pool, Hunter, you have a problem. There isn't anything you can tell me that would convince me otherwise. Withdrawal symptoms or not … you're an addict."

I grabbed her around the shoulders. She was so close to me that the heat from her body rolled over and intensified my own. Her scent permeated everything — it was the only thing I could smell. I didn't want her to move away, I would fucking die if she moved away. I was a stupid bastard at that moment and I leaned down to kiss her.

"Ow! You fucking bit me!" My hands released their grip and I pulled away from her and brought my hand to my mouth. It stung like a bitch and when I looked at my hand, I noticed a speckle of blood.

Her finger was pointed in my face when she warned, "You try anything like that again and I'll take your lip off the next time. You can forget about kissing me, Hunter. I won't be making that mistake again."

She turned around and I watched her as she walked down the street into the setting sun. I didn't know where she was going and I wanted to stop her. But I knew she'd only yell at me if I tried. Bear followed at her heels and her guitar was held to her side. I wanted to fucking puke and I wanted to cry like a bitch while I watched her walk away, but I couldn't do anything but stand there.

I was defeated in that moment — absolutely and completely. I'd finally met someone who I could connect with and my dumb shit decisions were screwing it up.

I was an idiot.

I was a fool.

And I was the man who was letting Ellison James walk out of my life.

Chapter Fourteen

"Bitch! Let go of my fucking extensions! Those cost more money than your entire fucking outfit!"

"Oh?! Of course, your hair is fucking fake as well! Is there anything about you that's real or are you 100 percent plastic?! I bet if I check your ass, there's an imprint there that says 'Made in China'!"

My eyes bugged out of my head when I witnessed the girl fight that was going on between Lily and Tiffany. Ryan was doing his best to pull the little rabid beast that was my cousin off of Tiff.

"Why don't you just take your Louboutin-wearing-Mercedes-driving-coke-snorting ass right back to the state where you came from?! Nobody wants you around here!"

Breaking into a fast sprint, I reached them within seconds and helped Ryan pull the two girls apart.

Lily looked like she was giving Ryan a run for his money, but he whispered something in her ear and she calmed down. With her chest heaving out in front of her, she demanded, "Hunter, love you to death, Cuz; but you're going to need to take that THING away from this party before I throw her fake ass into the fire."

Tiffany scoffed, but I just grabbed her arm and dragged her in the direction of her car. "Let's go Tiff, it looks like your not making many friends tonight."

"Like I'd want to be friends with these people! They're all a bunch of poorly-bred lunatics!"

I shoved Tiffany in the passenger side of the car and walked around to take my seat behind the wheel. As we drove down the road, I saw Ellison walking up the shoulder on her way back to the party. Her face was tear streaked and red and she looked absolutely alone and miserable. My foot hit the brake pedal to slow down, but when she looked over to the car, she fake smiled and waved, and I knew that stopping wouldn't do me any good.

"I mean, just look at the people you've been hanging around. Take that bitch for instance. Who the fuck wears a dress with cowboy gear? Add in the guitar and the dog and you've got the poster child for backwoods. Mark my words, Hunter: that girl will be barefoot and pregnant before the night's even finished. No class. None of them."

My hands gripped painfully around the steering wheel while I kept myself from doing something stupid like hitting her. I remained quiet and stepped down on the gas pedal. Even traveling at 80 miles per hour wasn't fast enough and luckily, there were no animals in the road to slow me down.

By the time we'd reached the hotel, Tiffany had shut up. It only took 20 minutes of me not responding to her snide comments and annoying babble for her to realize I wasn't interested in talking. I helped her carry her suitcases to the room and she immediately jumped on the bed and assumed a seductive position.

"It's about time we get alone in a place where I don't have to worry about bugs and rats and shit. Why don't you come over here so we can make up? I've been missing the shit out of you since you've been gone." She reached over to her purse and pulled out the rest of the coke. Dangling it in front of her, she smiled and said, "I've got the goods baby. We can still have some fun tonight."

She licked her lips and I walked over to the bed. I sat down and she immediately moved to crawl over to me. She went for my pants without hesitation.

Grabbing her hands, I stopped what she was doing. "Tiffany, we need to talk."

Looking up at me she pouted. "Baby, we can talk all we want later. My man hasn't ridden me in over a month and I'm needing it. You know I'm obsessed with that body of yours." She worked her way up and went to kiss me. I placed a hand between us.

"Tiffany, I'm serious."

"Fuck! Whatever! Just say whatever it is you need to say so we can get back to our lives and forget all about this bullshit trip of yours. You need to call your parents. I convinced them to let you come home early. That's why I'm here — to pick you up."

I let out a loud breath and my head dropped down. When her hands went to massage my shoulders, I forced her arms away and looked her dead in the eye. "We aren't going anywhere, Tiffany. You are getting on your plane tomorrow and going home. I'm staying here to finish fixing up my uncle's house. He needs the help and I'm going to finish the job before I return."

She rolled her eyes and I resisted the urge to get up and leave without saying what I needed to say. Ellison was right when she said I'd been disrespectful to people. I lived for myself and made decisions that would benefit only me regardless of the needs of any other person. I was hurting people and I was hurting myself in the process.

"I shouldn't have broken up with you over voicemail. I get that. But what I said was the truth. I don't want to be with you anymore, Tiffany. I want to move on with my life and change some things and I can't do that and remain around people who only care about getting off and getting high. You have a whole group of men who want you back home and I suggest you go choose one of them. I'm not boyfriend material anymore — not for you anyway."

Her mouth opened and the shrill quality to her grating voice as she screamed at me was enough to chase me out of that motel room. When I heard something hit the door after I'd closed it behind me, I knew she was most likely destroying the room. But that wasn't my problem and it wouldn't be my problem ever again. She was a grown woman. If she wanted to act like a spoiled brat, she'd have to suffer the consequences all on her own.

. . .

I walked around the porch attempting to mentally survey the damage and come up with a game plan on how it needed to be fixed. The piles of miscellaneous car parts and chemicals would have to go first. Once I could get the area cleared out, I'd be in a better position to determine what needed to be done to the structure itself in order to repair it.

The porch had been neglected for too many years and I was sure once I removed all the excess baggage I would find a weak shell underneath. But, just like any good thing that's been neglected in life, all it took was a little TLC to make it functional again — unless it's neglected for too long. In those instances, the only thing you can do is tear it down and start all over again. Regardless of what you had to do, there was always a way to pick up and fix it. It just took some desire, will power and elbow grease and a person could always turn things around. I was looking forward to this part of the job. At that time in my life, the mundane task of clearing out the garbage, fixing the loose boards and slapping on a new coat of paint would be rewarding. It was a type of meditation I could understand — one where I could force myself to work through things and one where I could be alone with my thoughts.

Lily stepped up behind me and huffed out a breath. "I'm surprised to see you up so early. What time did you make it home last night?"

"Late. It was a four-hour walk back from the hotel. I didn't sleep well so I've been out here since about six."

"You weren't trying to catch Ellison before she went on her hike, were ya? She left with her daddy real early in the morning. I don't know where she was taking him, but she said she wouldn't be around here today."

Crap. After all the other drama that happened yesterday, I'd completely forgotten about what El was going through with her dad. I hoped they'd taken the day to have some fun and it wasn't something having to do with his health. She didn't need that shit on her shoulders and I felt like a dick for having made things worse for her. I was also pissed to realize that I'd been hoping to see her. I wouldn't have admitted it to myself if it wasn't for what Lily said, but now that I recognized it, the fact that I wouldn't see her added disappointment to the load of crappy emotions I was already experiencing.

Lily followed me as I walked around the perimeter of the porch.

"Well, it's going to need new screening, that's for sure." She pointed a spot at the base of the structure. "Looks like you've got a snake living around here as well. That's definitely a burrow of some sort."

I looked down where she was pointing and looked up at the bent and busted rain gutters that ran along the top. "I don't think so. I think the rain has just been beating the hell out of the ground. It probably drops heavily right there where the gutter is broken."

Lily cocked an eyebrow at me. "If you say so, Hunter — but I've been living in Florida long enough to know that when you see a hole like that, you've got critter problems. And that one there is a snake hole. I'd bet money on it."

I shivered. One of the things you didn't run into very often in the city was a snake. Sure, they could be found in the state parks and even the city parks on occasion, but not too often. Most of the time, it was too damn cold for snakes in New York to be out in the open where you could see them. And that was a good thing — because I hated snakes. Reptiles that could chase you on four legs were scary enough; it just got weird when they could chase you on no legs at all.

I walked back up to the porch and picked around in the piles of junk. A lot of it was garbage and I would need several boxes of contractor bags to get rid of it. Lily stood silently on the steps watching me complete my task. The silence between us was killing me and I couldn't get past my urge to ask her more about Ellison.

"Did Ellie say anything to you after I left last night?"

Lily nodded and smiled. "Yep. She high-fived me for kicking your girlfriend's ass. It wasn't that she cared about Tiffany being with you or anything; she just didn't like the fact that the girl was carrying cocaine around with her. El's got a real problem with drugs like that."

I stopped and looked at her. "Did she say anything about me?"

She sighed and slowly moved up the steps to stand beside me. "Hunter, listen — you hurt Ellison pretty bad by not telling her about Tiffany. I understand that you are a man and that instantly makes you an idiot, but still ... you should have known better than to keep from telling her about a girl you had just stopped dating. It's important when you're trying to date someone new."

Turning to her so I could look her in the eyes, I argued, "That's just the thing, Lil. I wasn't trying to date Ellison. I mean, sure, I've been into her since I laid eyes on her, I'd be blind and stupid if I didn't want her — but after she asked that we remain friends only, I respected her request. She's the one that ... well, you know what — I'm not going to be the one to tell you what happened. Just know that she wanted things to change and I didn't have much time between that occurrence and Tiffany arriving to tell Ellison about my previous love life. It all kind of happened at once."

The understanding look in Lily's eye made me feel better because I thought, for once, someone was listening to what I was trying to tell them. Ever since I'd left El on that road, I was pissed off at myself for not having chased her down to make her listen. Sure, it wouldn't have worked and, in fact, it would have just pissed her off more; but at least I would have tried, at least she would have known my side of the story — my *complete* side of the story. But like a pathetic bitch, I let her walk away and I may have lost the opportunity to repair what needed to be fixed between us.

"Well, I think El should hear that. But, she's not at a point where you should approach her on it, Hunter. Something's been going on with Ellison — even more than this thing with you. She hasn't been herself lately. She's sad, or scared, or I don't know … she's serious. All the time. I don't know what's bothering her, but I can't let you push yourself on her. You're going to have to give her time to come to you."

I looked over towards Ellison's bedroom window. I hadn't been able to sleep for shit last night. All I could think about was the fact that the girl of my dreams was sleeping within a thousand feet of where I lay. I couldn't stand that I wasn't lying beside her. I fantasized about getting up, sneaking over to her window, breaking in and telling her everything I wanted her to know. There were even two occasions where I physically got up from my bed and got dressed to go over there. But, I didn't go. Even with the picture of what her face looked like when she walked down that road playing in my head, I couldn't go to her. I was too scared. Both times I lay back down and hugged the pillow to my chest. I imagined she was sleeping beside me and fell asleep with the imaginary Ellison by my side.

"I know what you're saying, Lily, and I'll be patient." Reaching out, I hugged her to me. I turned around to start clearing the porch and I picked up a pile of towels that had been thrown down near the stairs. "Are these trash or what?"

"Yeah, I think Daddy just used those for cleaning up chemicals. You should probably throw them out."

Tossing the sodden pile of towels on the grass I reached down and picked up the remaining towel. Something thick was beneath the towel and I turned it over to investigate. My eyes set on what looked like black tubing …

That was — until the head popped up.

"Holy fucking shit!"

I'll admit it. I screamed like a little girl at that moment and I dropped that towel like it was on fire. My flight down the stairs wasn't too graceful either, because my foot went through the rotting wood of the first step and launched me face first across the lawn. I didn't let the grass burn across my cheek faze me and I popped back up and ran like hell until I thought I was far enough away that the little fucker couldn't slither after me. I had no shame either. I was fully aware that I'd left Lily alone — but we were talking about a snake and that made it every man for himself.

Lily's laughter gave away the fact that she wasn't too scared of being on the porch with the incredibly large, most likely poisonous snake. "I told you there was a snake!" I could barely understand what she was saying because she couldn't stop laughing. "Yep, I recall saying 'oh look, there's a burrow'. But noooooo, Mr. City Boy knew better than me."

She kept babbling her inane nonsense as she stood up to grab a broom. Bending over, she lifted the towel and threw it in the pile on the grass. I couldn't see exactly what was going on because of the low wall of the porch, but Lily looked like she was poking at the beast with the broom. I finally saw the snake slither along the porch while Lily pushed at it and eventually the damn thing stood up at least three feet in the fucking air.

Okay. I'm going to do it. I'm going to man up and admit that another girlish scream may have escaped me at that moment. Don't judge. You would have screamed too.

"Watch out, Lily, that thing's about to fucking eat you!" Lily looked over at me like I was an idiot and continued pushing at the snake with the broom. Eventually, it lowered itself back to the ground and disappeared under the house where Lily had found that hole.

"You can come back now, Hunter. It's safe." When I finally returned, she explained, "It's called a racer. It's perfectly fucking harmless. When it raises up like that it's just trying to move along faster." She chuckled again and grabbed one of the garbage bags out of the box. She was still laughing at me an hour later when we'd finished clearing out a good portion of the junk.

"Whatever, Lily, it's not funny anymore."

She giggled. "Oh ... no. You're wrong there. It's still pretty fucking funny."

I was embarrassed as shit and I was pissed off.

And I fucking despised nature.

Chapter Fifteen

Ellison

"I'm sorry to tell you this, Ms. James, but your father is a very sick man. The scans that we performed indicated that his cancer is metastatic; meaning, it's traveled to other places in his body. He's developed some tumors in his bones."

My mind refused to process what the doctor was telling me.

"Well, okay, so what do we do? Does he need surgery, or chemo or radiation or what? I mean, whatever it is that'll fix this, just go ahead and sign him up and tell me when to have him here."

The doctor's expression never changed. It was all business all the time with this guy and his face wasn't giving away anything that he was thinking. I waited for what felt like forever for him to smile and tell me there was some ridiculously expensive medical procedure that would save my father's life. I knew he would worry that I wouldn't have the money, and I'd convince him that no matter what, I'd make sure the bill was paid. He was then supposed to smile and tell me that it was a common surgery and that any bonehead doctor could perform it because it was so simple, and I was supposed to breathe out a sigh of relief and know that my father was going to be okay. That's how this was supposed to happen.

"I'm sorry Ms. James, but you're father only has a short time to live. We could attempt to extend that time with a combination of chemotherapy and radiation, but it would only be an extension — not a cure."

That was not how this was supposed to happen.

"What? So, there's nothing we can do? You're saying that my dad is going to die — no matter what? I just want to be perfectly clear on what you're saying, because that's what it sounded like you just said and there's no way you can be saying that. It's … you have to be wrong, right? There are other tests to make sure that we haven't done yet, right? There has to be."

I was begging. There was no other way to describe what I was doing at that point but to say I was begging. I could have dropped on my knees at his feet and it wouldn't have made what I was saying any more like begging. That's how much I was begging him with the questions I asked.

"I'm sorry, Ms. James. We haven't told your father the diagnosis as of yet. He's just now coming out of a mild anesthesia so you can go see him. You're welcome to be the one to tell him what we found, or if you prefer, I can be there in a few moments to explain.

"No." I shook my head. "I'll tell him. It should be me that tells him."

The doctor nodded and walked off leaving me standing in a waiting room with an audience of sympathetic family members of other patients looking up at me. I didn't get angry with them for staring, though. I knew that they were only worried that they'd be receiving the same results as well.

Not that I'd imagined it often, but I had imagined how I would react when I was told that I was losing my remaining parent. Losing my mom had been hard enough, but I still didn't feel like I'd been abandoned. I knew my father was there. I knew there was still someone who was wiser than me, stronger than me and willing to be there for me. So, of course, when I imagined receiving that type of news, I thought I'd be crying — hysterically. I imagined I'd be balled up in the corner of a room somewhere rocking and shaking. What I didn't imagine would happen is that I would go completely numb; that I wouldn't feel anything at all; that some switch in my brain would be thrown; that I'd turn into a pragmatic machine incapable of pain or sorrow. I didn't imagine that I would be broken.

I steeled my spine and breathed out a large breath to calm myself. I didn't want daddy seeing me sad. I didn't want him to know I was scared. I didn't want him to know I'd gone numb. I wanted him to be in as much peace as he could with the news I was about to give him. I had to be strong — for him.

Walking into the room, I was met with a jovial grin on my father's face. He was sitting up in bed and waving his hand around in front of him.

"How're you feeling, Daddy?"

His laughter was unexpected. "Feeling great, baby girl. I don't know what they gave me, but this shit is great!"

A smile cracked on my lips.

"Well, I have some news for you. I'm afraid it's not something that I want to tell you."

His expression became sympathetic. "Oh, baby girl. I know already. I know I'm dying. I've known for a while now, I just wanted to wait until the doctors knew as well." His voice was almost a whisper as he confessed.

For the first time in my life, I saw my father as human. He wasn't a superhero anymore, impervious to pain, or illness or death. He was just another person, a body that would someday stop working. My reality altered in that moment and I was transferred to a place where my comfortable blanket, my bubble of safety that had always existed around the man before me, was cruelly ripped away and I had to see him for what he was – another man who would one day be nothing more than a memory. I felt exposed and lost, angry and confused.

And then it was lost. The numbness. Somehow, hearing my father admit he knew what was going to happen made it real. It. Was. Real. There wasn't anywhere I could hide and deny that it was going to happen. And that's when the dam broke behind my eyes.

My father motioned me to his bed and I sat down beside him. "I'm so sorry, Daddy. I'm so sorry." His arms wrapped around me and even though he was the one who was dying, he still put his own problem aside to comfort his child.

There's no feeling more helpless than having to tell someone you love that they are going to go away, that their life is going to end, that they are going to have to walk a journey to some unknown place without you — and that there wasn't a damn thing you could do about it.

Chapter Sixteen

Hunter

I wasn't able to sleep again that night. When Ellison and her dad hadn't returned home by six, I'd figured they were out having a good time. When they hadn't returned home by 10, I became nervous. But when they hadn't returned by midnight, I went into full on panic mode.

Around two in the morning, the headlights of Henry's truck bounced off my bedroom walls. It was so quiet, I was able to hear both truck doors swing open and swing closed, and the same sounds as the front door of their house opened and closed. I could hear Sasha and Bear barking welcome to Ellison and her dad. I jumped up from my bed when the dogs quieted and I quickly threw on some clothes and ran outside. I could see the windows in their kitchen light up as Ellison fed the dogs. I knew when she'd crossed the distance of her house to go into her room because the light turned on there. I knew when she laid down in her bed because the light in her room turned off.

I never felt more like a stalker than I did at that moment, but I couldn't look away. I walked around to see if the light in Henry's room was on and my heart jumped to find that he was in bed as well.

I had a decision to make at that moment. I wanted ... no ... I needed to talk to Ellison. I knew that Lily had warned me to stay away, but I also knew that I wouldn't be able to sleep again until I talked to her. But, it had nothing to do with me this time. I knew something was wrong with her. I could feel it. So I made the decision to talk to her. And at the time I'd made that decision, I knew that it was a stupid decision to make. Ironically, however, later on in life, when I remembered that decision, I would realize that it was probably one of the smartest decisions I'd ever made in my life.

My knuckles tapped on her window. Once ... twice ... three times. The light never turned on, I didn't hear her footsteps as she walked across the floor of her room. But I did hear the lock on the window click and I opened it without giving her the opportunity to change her mind.

Crawling in, I knocked over a stack of books she had piled up on a small table. I froze halfway in and halfway out just in case the sound had woken Henry. The last thing I needed was to be staring down the barrel of his gun. Ellison sniffled and when I turned my head to look in her direction, I found nothing but shadow. Damn, her room was dark.

A small voice broke the silence. "Don't worry. That noise won't wake up daddy. He's had a rough day." Another sniffle.

I crawled the rest of the way in. Stumbling over the scattered books, I moved in the direction of her voice. "Ellison? What's wrong?" My hands found the edge of her bed and I sat down, grateful to have found her.

"He's going to die, Hunter." It was a whisper. Her voice cracked as she said those words and my heart tore apart in my chest.

"My daddy is going to die and I'll be alone. I'll be on my own. I'll have to figure things out myself."

I reached toward the noise and my palm found the warm and wet skin of her cheek. Absently, my thumb wiped away the tears. "Tell me what happened, El. Just talk and I'll listen."

"And dump it all on you? That wouldn't be fair. It's my problem, not yours." She was quiet for a moment and I kept my palm to her cheek desperately waiting to feel her jaw move as she spoke again. "You've got enough of your own problems. You sure as hell don't need mine."

I inched closer to her and I noticed the bed dip as she moved to sit beside me. "El ... right now, you're obviously hurting and I'm not going to let you hurt alone. You say what you need to say. Pretend I'm not here. Pretend there's nothing to hear you. I'll take whatever load you can't bear and I'll carry it out of this room when I leave. But dammit, I'm not going to leave you here alone to bear it by yourself. So cry or scream or hit me. You do whatever you need to do. We'll keep the lights off. You won't see me, but I'm here for you to use me. Just talk El — don't think of me as poor pathetic Hunter who needs to straighten out his shit. Just think of me as a way to let go of everything that's hurting you." I paused but quietly added, "You've been taking care of me since I've been here, El; please — just let me take care of you."

I couldn't see her face. It was so dark; it felt like I was speaking into a void. Somehow, though, the darkness made it easier. There were no distractions. It was just me and El — our thoughts, our feelings — and the truth of what made us who we are.

She grabbed my hand and pulled me down to lay behind her and it felt like it took forever for her to speak again. The breeze from the fan in her room knocked her scent against me. Her fingertips traced along my hand that was resting on her stomach from where my arm wrapped around her. My body was buzzing to be in her presence — but it wasn't sexual, it wasn't anything she could do for me. It was about her — about making her better — about, for once, being there for someone other than myself, no matter how it tore my heart out to do so. It was about love.

I was finally learning what that word meant.

"You know what I need? I need to stop feeling what I'm feeling right now." I could feel her body turn around and my breath was stolen to know that her face was inches from mine. "I need to feel something different — anything different than this. It's not the thoughts in my head that are hurting me, it's the feelings that are consuming me. I need you to help me feel something else."

Her lips brushed across mine and I should have pulled back — but I was a selfish bastard. She wasn't thinking straight, she was crushed, and I knew better than to take advantage of that. But I just. couldn't. pull. away.

Her tongue slid along the crease of my lips and I opened up allowing her to brush her tongue along mine. Our mouths molded to each other and when a small moan left her mouth to float into my mouth, I shivered. I couldn't see her, there was nothing but the sounds of our actions to hear, and it made touching her even more amazing. My hands explored her face and my fingers eventually buried themselves into her hair. Our hearts beat against our chests that were plastered against each other. My body was completely obliterated by an emotion I'd never known. It wasn't lust, it wasn't a desperate need for a release. It was more than that. So much more and it hurt to feel it. It caused tears to well in my eyes and my mind to shut down for short spurts of time. Her nails dragged along the shirt at my back and I pressed closer to her. When I felt her foot wrap around and her legs spread beneath me, I had to fight to do what I knew was the right thing to do.

Pulling back, I was breathless when I said, "We can't do this. I'd be an asshole to do this. You're not thinking clearly right now, Ellie, and I can't let this happen." They were the hardest words I'd ever spoken.

The room grew silent again — the only sound was the heavy breathing of our bodies. "You said you're not here. So, technically, you wouldn't be an asshole. You'd just be taking care of me in the way I need to be taken care of. Please don't say no. Just let me lose myself in you for however long I can. Just let me hide in you for a few hours. Please." If the words that she spoke weren't enough to destroy me, the sound of her voice was. It was a quiet but desperate plea that she made to me in that moment.

She didn't need to say another word. If she needed an escape, I would give it to her. And if things had to return to they way they were the next morning, I was going to have to accept it. It didn't matter if it destroyed me in the process.

My mouth crashed against hers and her hands pulled at the bottom hem of my shirt. I grudgingly broke away from the kiss to allow her to pull my shirt off. My mouth immediately returned once I'd been freed of the material and I growled when her nails dragged down the skin of my back. I didn't care about anything at the moment but giving her what she needed. I didn't care if Henry heard us and walked in to shove the muzzle of his gun up my ass like he'd threatened previously. If she wanted this, if this would fix her, this is what she was going to get.

My hands wrapped around the sides of her abdomen and I pushed up, taking her shirt with me. She broke free of me just long enough to raise her arms above her to free her. When I brought my hands back down, my palms met with the skin of her naked breasts and her breath blew out breezing along my cheek and ear. I almost lost it right fucking there.

Our legs were entangled, our hips ground against each other as we pressed closer, were desperate to become one with another. I allowed my mouth to trail along her jaw-line, along her neck until my mouth met with that sweet spot where her neck joined to her shoulder. I let my teeth nip softly at the skin and her body bucked against me. The heat between us was suffocating and intoxicating. Sweat beaded on our bodies and skin slid erotically against skin. My jeans had become agonizingly tight but I didn't want to remove my pants. Not yet. Not until she made the move. I'd let her have whatever she wanted of me, but I wouldn't be the one to force it on her. This was her moment — with me — and I was allowing her to drive it at any speed she wanted.

My tongue met the edge of her ear and she groaned, her head falling hard against the pillow beneath her. Her chest pressed up against me and I moved to wrap my mouth around the hard peak of her breast. I slid my tongue around the rim of that peak and she moved under me, moaned under me, drove herself even farther inside of me. We were a tangled mixture of heat, of sweat, of salt and I couldn't get enough of it. I tasted every inch of her chest and stomach. I nipped at the skin I knew would twist her up inside. Her body trembled and shivered and my breathing became eratic and painful as I slowed myself down — as I allowed her to build the pace.

Finally, she reached down to grab me over the material of my jeans. I moaned out her name, let the three syllables slide over my lips to her skin where my mouth was still kissing her, still tasting her — still worshipping her. She fumbled with my belt and I pushed myself up off of her so that I could reach down and help her. The cool air of her bedroom snuck in between our sweat soaked bodies and a shudder ran over my skin. I pushed my pants down off my legs and could feel her under me trying to push her pajama pants off of hers. Grabbing the material of her pants, I ripped them down while she kicked at the material, desperate to remove the barrier between us. The only bit left was my boxers and her panties and my hand moved up to softly rub along the tiny scrap of silken material that she wore. Her breath came out in gasps and I reached up with my other hand to find tears trailing down her face. I leaned down and kissed each tear away while I rubbed along the sensitive skin between her thighs.

My heart broke above her, but I wouldn't let her know it. I wanted to be her island, her rock, and her strength. I wanted to take on the world for her and battle against anything that threatened her. Ellison was soft hearted — she didn't need pain to make her hard. It wouldn't be right. There was too much beauty in her heart and soul for that to happen.

My fingers slipped beneath the material and met with the slickened and soft skin beneath. My cock was hard against her thigh and every movement of her leg almost set me off. I grit my teeth against the inferno she was building within my body. Ellison wasn't just a girl I was with — she was an experience I would never forget. When I pushed my fingers up inside her, she bit down on my shoulder and a low growl built and vibrated from my chest over her body.

"Now ... I need you inside me now."

She didn't have to make the demand twice.

I pushed my boxers down and stripped her of that small triangle of silk. Her legs fell to either side of my body and I positioned myself at her opening.

"I don't have anything. Shit. I don't have a condom."

"Shut up, Hunter." And then her hands grasped the cheeks of my ass and she pushed me forward, slowly, inside her.

My mouth fell open. She wasn't thinking straight, but she wasn't taking no for an answer. Her muscles grasped around me and I began to move inside her — agonizingly slow so that I could keep this going for as long as she needed. Her body arched against mine and my mouth fell against hers. I explored every inch of her, my hands couldn't stop moving over her. I was being consumed by her.

Her hands came to my chest and she pushed up to roll me to my back. Climbing on top of me, she slid down over me again, burying me deeply inside her. She rocked over me, her body moving up and down, her hips rotating in seductive little circles. My head was glued back against the bed, but my hands found her breasts and I pinched and massaged their weight. She was exquisite, a fucking goddess that held me captive — that had stolen my ability to think or breath or speak.

When I felt her muscles start to ripple and roll along my length, I knew she was close. My hands gripped at her waist and I pulled her even tighter against me. Her hands came down on my chest and my fingers dug into the sensitive skin of her hips. She leaned forward suddenly, her mouth found mine and when I opened to allow her entrance, she screamed my name into my mouth, she released and let me swallow the sound of what I'd done for her. And that was all it took.

I lost myself and I swelled inside her before letting go and filling her.

My body quaked beneath hers as she fell limply against me — she was sated and obviously, exhausted. There was no telling how long we lay there. I'd grown soft inside her and her head was laid down on my chest. Her breathing evened out eventually and I wrapped my arms around her realizing she'd fallen asleep. My mouth curved into a smile to hear her breathe comfortably, to know that her tears had finally stopped falling. I didn't sleep at all that night. I just held Ellison on top of me as she slept. I allowed our bodies to breath in unison and only when the sun started peaking up over the horizon did I roll her to her side and get up from her bed. I didn't want her family walking in to wake her and find her naked, so I found her pajamas and dressed her before I tucked her in. Placing on single kiss on her cheek, I snuck quietly back out of her window.

Chapter Seventeen

Life returned to normal the following day as I knew it would. I was working on the porch separating the junk from the parts that could still be used. Most of the chemicals were unlabeled and I grew nervous just working around them. Placing them in a spot far out on the lawn, I walked back to the porch to see Ellison walking out with Sasha and Bear towards the trail. My heart fractured a bit. She'd not made a move to talk to me; she didn't even turn to look at me as she passed.

I didn't hold it against her. I knew the night before had been about that moment alone and that it wouldn't change the tension between us. I'd failed her by failing myself. I'd disappointed her by falling so easily back into the numbness of drugs when Tiffany had come down. It would take time to fix that problem between us, but I was more determined than ever to make sure it would be fixed.

Day after day went by and each day it was the same story. I worked tirelessly on the porch and Ellison pretended like I didn't exist. But, after a week's worth of mornings where Ellison walked by without acknowledging me or even looking at me, I couldn't take it any longer. Lily had warned me to give Ellison time, but I knew other stuff was going on in that head of hers and I knew she was trapping it inside without reaching out for the help she needed. She was distancing herself from everybody but her father — and her father was dying.

So, on the eighth morning that Ellison tried to walk past me, I allowed her to do so, just like every morning before that. Except, this time, when she entered the trail and disappeared into the overgrowth of the path she'd cut, I stepped in behind her and silently followed her along to the bigger trails beyond.

She noticed me almost instantly and turned to scowl at me before ignoring me and keeping up her pace. I smiled because I couldn't help but smile. Even her scowl was adorable and I was completely captivated by the girl who walked in front of me. I wasn't there to annoy her and I wasn't there to try and force her to finally talk to me about everything that had happened between us. I was there to lend her strength and I was there to let her know that she didn't walk her path alone.

It went on like that for seven days. There was absolute silence between us except for the heavy fall of our feet against the packed earth of the trail. The first few days she tried to teach me a lesson. She didn't stop at her normal places to rest and she didn't slow down when I tripped on a rock, fucked up my ankle and hobbled along behind her. I wasn't mad at her for it. She hadn't invited me and, essentially, I was hiking alone. But I refused to stop being there for her — whether she wanted me to be or not. Following Ellison for those days taught me many things about her. I already knew that she was strong, but I'd had absolutely no idea just how stubborn she could be.

Lily had said Ellison should come to me, and I hoped that by hiking out here everyday, following behind her with Bear and Sasha, she would eventually turn around and talk to me. No such luck. Everyday when we returned to the houses from our silent march, we went our separate ways. I would walk inside and the calendar would be stuck to the kitchen wall, front and center, letting me know I was running out of time to fix things with her. I had exactly a month left before I returned home and, at the rate it was going, I might get her to a point where she would wave goodbye as I climbed into my uncle's truck to head back to the plane. I couldn't allow that. I needed to get her to talk to me, but I needed to find a way to make her approach me.

Sitting at the kitchen table, I rested my head on my hand and stared up at that calendar like a little bitch. I had no idea what I could do to make Ellison approach me. I tried leaving her alone and I tried being there for her. And if there wasn't a stop watch ticking down the hours I had left with her, I would have kept being there for her, silently walking behind, acting like the stalker she knew I was.

Lily walked in and as soon as she caught sight of my face, she frowned and sat down at the table beside me. "I take it today was another quiet day?"

"Yeah." I huffed out a sigh and sat up straight in my seat before stretching my arms above my head. "I have to give it to you, Lil. You know your friend well. I've been following behind her like another one of her dogs for days now and the most I've gotten out of her is a scowl cast over her shoulder and a snicker when an errant tree branch slapped me in the face when we passed through an overgrown part of the path. She hasn't said one word to me and she barely even looks at me.

Lily nodded her head. "Yeah. That's the difficult thing about Ellison. Once she's made a decision in her head, getting her to change her mind is damn near next to impossible. In fact, in the entire time I've known her, I've only seen it happen once or twice."

"Well, that makes me feel better, Lily. Thanks for that."

She shrugged her tiny little shoulders and sat back in her chair.

It was obvious that I had a problem that needed to be resolved. Unfortunately, I had no experience in this area because, before I'd come down here, I'd never cared if someone was not talking to, or upset, with me. Typically, I would brush them off and be thankful that I had an excuse for not dealing with them. Plus, when it came to people like Tiffany, I never had to make much of an effort to get her to talk to me. The girl never shut up and the endless voicemails, text messages and emails made it next to impossible for me to ignore her. Most of the time, I read them out of curiosity and would eventually fold and contact her. And maybe that's what it takes with a stubborn person. You can't get in their face to force their hand, but if you can put enough bait out there, and if there's even a bit of interest in them, eventually they'll break down and take it.

It occurred to me that what I needed with Ellison was bait. Unfortunately, I had no electronic means of putting messages out there; and, even if I had the means, Ellison wouldn't see them anyway. I'd never seen her get near a computer and, although she had a cell phone, she never took it anywhere with her. It seemed that, lately, all the girl did was stay home except for her daily hike. I'd attempted putting myself out there on those, and it was getting me nowhere.

And that's when it hit me.

"Hey, Lil? Do Ryan and you have plans for tonight?

She shook her head 'no' and an eyebrow cocked over her eye. "Why?"

A smile crept across my face when I thought about just what kind of bait I would need to get a message out to El. It would cost some money and I knew exactly to whom I could go for that, but I needed help in the execution.

"I need you to take some pictures for me. And I need to borrow your phone again."

She scowled. "You're not calling Tiffany, are you?" The scorn in her voice was amusing and you'd think Tiffany was her arch nemesis by the way Lily said her name.

I laughed; half because of what Lily had said, and half because I suddenly had a good feeling about fixing things with Ellison.

"No. I'm calling my mom."

. . .

The next week was busy. I'd called my mom like I told Lily I would and, after three hours of soul spilling and begging, my mom finally relented to wiring me the funds for my project. It didn't hurt that she'd already talked to Bill after Tiffany had returned home to report about me, and Bill had assured her I was doing a great job on the house and seemed to have straightened up. With the money she sent, I refilled Lily's minutes after using them up, I bought some screening for Bill's porch, and I'd purchased the supplies I'd needed to bait Ellison.

Seven days into the baiting project and I was finally finished. During that time, I'd stopped following Ellison out on our hikes. The first day didn't seem to faze her because she left at her usual time and returned at her usual time without bothering to glance in my direction. On the second day, I noticed her head turn to look at me as she entered the narrow path, but that was the only acknowledgement I received. Days three, four, five and six were the same. But, on day seven, she passed me while I was repairing the last broken board on Bill's porch and she stopped for a moment to watch me. I forced myself not to look up at her from what I was doing. She didn't approach me and she didn't say anything, and, eventually, she made her way out to the trail. But it was the fact she'd stopped that made me grin. It meant she was still interested and it meant that it was time to put out the bait.

On day eight, I was outside scraping off the remaining bits of paint on the porch in order to prime and paint it. I'd replaced all the rotting wood and I'd removed the torn and tattered screening that looked like it might have been original to the house. I heard Ellison's front door open and close and the usual barking of the dogs as they were introduced to the first bits of sunlight in the day. I was tired as fuck because I'd been up until almost before those bits of sunlight appeared over the horizon; but, I'd spent the night executing my plan and now I would get to watch it unfold and discover if it would work.

She passed me by without a glance, probably because I was staring right at her. But I smiled anyway, grabbed the hiking pack that I'd also purchased with the money my mom had sent, and I followed behind her. When we entered the path, she turned to look at me. She sighed when she saw me, but I swear there was the tiniest smile peeking out at the corners of her lips. I smiled brightly — flashing the dimples, of course — and took my place with the dogs following her onto the trail.

We passed a low hanging branch just as the path broke out into the trail and hanging from that branch was a little plastic bag tied to a string. Inside that bag was a note. It was like an archaic text message and I knew the plastic bag would piss Ellison off because I didn't belong in nature. She ran up to it almost immediately and ripped it off the branch. Looking down at it she must have noticed it had her name on it. She glanced back at me and her brows furrowed between her eyes. I just smiled and shrugged my shoulders at her. I'd hoped she would take the note out and read it, but instead she just shoved it in her pocket, plastic bag and all, and kept hoofing it up the trail.

I wasn't worried though, because I knew that it was just the beginning. We approached the second mile mark of the hike and a person was standing up ahead. He stood on the sideline of the trail with his hand waving out at us. The only thing about it was, he wasn't moving and he looked just like me. Ellison stopped in her tracks and the dogs ran ahead to investigate. When they approached the man, they jumped up and knocked him over. It didn't take much for them to do so considering he was a cardboard cutout of yours truly. I'd had Lily take pictures of me is different positions until I was satisfied with a few I could have blown up and made into life-sized images.

Ellison slowly approached and I silently followed behind her. When she reached the cut-out she noticed the note it held in its hand, also wrapped within a plastic bag. She looked back at me confused at first, but eventually, she rolled her eyes and grabbed the note off the cutout and shoved it in her pocket.

We continued walking and I tripped over my feet when she spoke.

"You do realize you can't leave that cardboard out here, right? It's not good for the environment."

I smiled. "I've already got that covered, El." The guy at the print shop had assured me that the cutout was biodegradable, but I still had plans to walk the trail again with garbage bags in an effort to clean up the remnants of the bait.

She didn't respond.

Mile three came and went but when we reached the four-mile mark, another note hung in a plastic bag from another cardboard cutout. I was in a begging position for this one, which helped, because it hid the box tucked into the brush behind it. Ellison sighed up ahead of me, but still approached "Begging Hunter" and tried to pull off the note.

The note was secured to the cutout with a large staple so Ellison had to pull hard to free it. But, there was also a string attached to that note and when she gave it a good tug, the string was pulled and it opened the top of the box that was hidden in the brush behind the cutout. As soon as that box was opened, a hundred butterflies escaped that box and flew all around Ellison. It was a magical moment. The different colors of their wings surrounded her almost instantly and she spun slowly within the cloud of butterflies, her lips finally breaking out into the smile I'd missed seeing on her face over the past two weeks. The butterflies landed in her hair and on her hands and she stood still until the cloud finally dispersed and took off in separate directions.

She turned to look back at me with a questioning expression on her face. I shrugged my shoulders and explained, "The guy at the garden shop assured me they are an indigenous species to Florida to they won't be messing up the environment or anything. I just thought the little guys needed to be freed."

"Uh huh." She shoved the note in her pocket, but I didn't miss the smirk on her lips when she turned back to continue along the trail.

By the time we reached mile seven, the sun was higher in the sky and luckily; it was beating down on our backs something brutal. I could see the sweat sliding along Ellison's skin and I knew she was just as miserable as I was in the heat. At the opening of the path that led to the spring, there was another Hunter cutout. This one held a sign in his hands that read, "Hot? Tired? Need a dip perhaps? You should check the grass and pay your buddies a visit." Underneath those words was an arrow pointing towards the water.

Ellison stopped again. She glanced over her shoulder at me, but then turned to walk the path to the spring. When she approached the grass patch where'd we almost had sex the first time she found a blanket, and on top of that blanket was a large box.

Opening the box, she discovered two masks and two snorkels. Inside the masks were notes that read, "The fish miss you and so do I." She smiled but turned her head in an attempt from letting me see it. I noticed anyway despite her attempt.

She picked up the smaller of the masks and moved to walk out to the edge of the spring. After placing her pack on the rocks to the side, she stripped off her shirt and shorts and jumped into the water before placing the mask on her face and swimming out into deeper water. Hunter junior stood at attention to see her strip down to her bra and underwear, so I took a moment for him to calm down before following behind her.

In the distance I could see the small piece of Styrofoam that floated on the surface of the water. I placed the mask on my face and looked under the water to watch as Ellison approached it and found the smaller, waterproof case that hung from it and was weighted down to keep it from floating to the surface. Ellison grabbed the case and pulled it free of the float. After she'd accomplished that, I swam out to her side and we spent a good half hour just watching the fish move in multi-colored waves beneath us. Every once in a while, Ellison would swim down and move within the center of the school and it was a beautiful sight to watch. She looked peaceful — happy — and even if was only for a brief moment, I was ecstatic for having given her that small bit of peace.

When it was time to return to shore, I grabbed the Styrofoam float and pulled it to shore behind me. I took the masks and snorkels and stowed them away in the box, along with the float. By the time I returned to the trail, I noticed that Ellison had been watching me. She had a strange look on her face, but she smiled when I caught her before turning to complete the trail, shoving the case in her pocket as we walked. That was the last of my surprises, but I was happy to know that I'd gotten my messages out to her.

~   ~   ~

The hike back was quiet as usual. Except, this time, it was a comfortable quiet. Not the kind of quiet where I could tell that Ellison was mad that I was following her and she was calling me a stalker in her head. No. That had been the old kind of quiet — the new kind felt like acceptance.

We reached the houses and we both were beat down and tired. Even though I was drenched in sweat and my feet were killing me, I smiled brightly. The first part of my plan had worked.

Lily, Bill and Henry were standing by Ellison's porch when we rounded the corner from the trail and their six eyes locked on us almost immediately. Lily looked worried, Bill looked distraught, and Henry looked like he was going to follow through with his previous threats against me. He might have been sick, but he still looked like he'd find a way to kill me and feed my body to the gators.

"Hey, everyone. Daddy? Why are you home so early?"

Henry reluctantly peeled his eyes off of me to look over at Ellison. "I had an incident at work. It wasn't anything you need to worry about, I'm just going to go inside and go to bed."

Ellison nodded her head and Henry shot me one more eye dagger before turning to walk inside. Once he was out of earshot, Ellison looked to Lily. "What happened?"

Bill cleared his throat and answered. "He passed out at work today. Said he's just tired and that he hasn't been sleeping well. Besides the receptionist at his job who had a little bit of medical training, he wouldn't let anyone else take a look at him. They called me to go pick him up and he demanded I bring him home and not ask questions. Is everything alright with him, Ellie?"

Ellison's face fell and I groaned to realize that this news would destroy all the good feelings I'd just worked hard to build up inside of her.

"No. He's just been tired like he said. I'll go inside and see what I can do for him."

I didn't know why Ellison and her father continued to lie about his health, but it wasn't my place to say anything, so I kept my mouth shut. Ellison waved at us and made her way back to the house before opening the door and disappearing inside.

Bill and Lily walked over to their house and I walked over to the porch to finish up the scraping despite how tired I was from the trail. Ellison needed time, I would give her that time, and I'd done what I could to get my messages out to her.

The only thing I could do at that point was to wait patiently and see if the messages were enough to get her to approach me.

Chapter Eighteen

Ellison

By the time I got inside, daddy had already gone to his room to lie down. I sighed a heavy breath and showered before going into my room to take a nap. When I threw my shorts on top of my hamper, the case in the pocket of the shorts fell out and rolled across the carpet to land at my feet. I ignored it, not really in the mood to worry myself with my problems with Hunter. My father's illness was draining me emotionally and I didn't have any room left in me for more problems. By my calculations, he was leaving in three weeks and he'd return to the life he'd known before. There was no point in muddying up both our lives with a relationship that could never happen.

I wasn't able to fall asleep no matter how hard I tried. I was physically exhausted from the hike, but I couldn't get the notes out of my head. It also didn't help that I couldn't get the night I'd had sex with Hunter out of my head either. I don't know what I'd been thinking that night, but he was exactly what I'd needed at that moment. I needed the release, the feeling of something besides pain and heartache. And I hated to admit it, but he delivered. In fact, I couldn't get it out of my head for the next week about how he'd delivered. I could still feel his lips traveling over my skin and the perfect strength to his hands as they'd explored every part of me. My hands remembered the feel of his body, the way his muscles moved beneath his skin, and my mouth watered to remember the salt taste to his skin and lips.

And I won't even get started on what he felt like inside me. Let's just say a volcano erupted within me and I was pushed over an edge so high, my fall back to the ground almost felt as good as the trip it took to get to that edge. He was amazing in bed ... that was for certain.

My eyes peeked open when I finally gave up on sleep and they slowly traveled over to look at the case that sat on my floor and the hiking shorts on the top of the hamper. Huffing out a breath, I pushed my weary body up from the bed and walked the short distance to retrieve the notes. Carrying them back to my bed, I laughed to think about what he'd done to get them to me and I had to give him points for originality. The butterflies were a good touch ... I could admit that. I wondered if he'd known I wouldn't read the notes when I found them because I noticed that he'd numbered them to help me remember the order. He was a sneaky bastard, but I smiled thinking about how much time he must have spent putting the whole thing together. The least I could do was read what he wanted to tell me.

Opening note number one, I carefully unfolded the page and saw that it wasn't very long.

Hey, Ellie. I know you don't want to talk to me much and I know that I've been annoying you lately by following you on the trails, but I want to explain. I was hoping my presence would get you to talk to me, but it wasn't only about that. I want you to know that you're not alone in what you're going through. Just like the days on the trail, I'm always behind you, I'm always available to listen and I'm willing to walk through whatever you need me to walk through to prove that to you. I don't want you alone and I don't want you carrying the weight of everything that's happening right now by yourself.

That was it, I turned it over in my hand to see if there was anything else, and when I found nothing, I moved on to note number two.

I know you well enough to know you haven't read the first note by the time you're grabbing this one. And I'm okay with that. I actually prefer you read these when you have time to really think about what I'm saying. So consider this note my thank you. For everything, El. When I came down here I was nothing more than a punk kid looking for his next fix. I still don't agree with the 'addict' word, but I will say I was inching close. I needed an escape from life and a way to numb the feeling that I was wasting my time and throwing my life away. You opened my eyes. You made me realize that there was more to this world than the little bit of it I'd allowed myself to explore. Most importantly, you made me realize that there was more to me. I've been taking your advice and I've been working in silence. I've been thinking and I've been desperately trying to find something special in my life to work towards. While writing this, I have to be honest and say I haven't found it yet, but at least I'm trying. I know you didn't do much more than wake me up, but you were the only person who found the way to do that, or who took the time to care. And for that, I'll never forget you. When I return home in three weeks, I won't be returning to the drugs and parties. I'll go to school and I'll make something of myself like you said. I don't ever want to lose touch with you and I hope that we can fix things before I leave and remain friends. That's important to me. You're important to me.

I smiled at the end of the note. Not because of what Hunter claimed he felt about me, but because of what Hunter claimed he felt about himself. He was a better person than the one he'd been when I met him, and I was happy to know that he would act in a way that would better his life, instead of destroying himself with one drugged fueled party after another. However, I remembered these were just words on paper, I couldn't really believe him until his actions showed me he was serious in what he'd written, and that would take time. I couldn't let myself get too excited because the words were probably nothing more than a load of shit he was trying to feed me. Moving on to the next note, I removed it from the plastic bag and unfolded the page.

By now, you're probably thinking I'm full of shit ...

I couldn't help it. I laughed out loud when I read it.

But I promise you Ellison: I'm not. I'm begging you to please give me another chance to show you just how serious I am. I know we can't be more than friends and I know that we only have a few weeks left to spend time together. But I'm begging you to please spend that time with me. I've missed you and I need you in my life. I'll accept whatever you are willing to give me, just as long as I know you'll talk to me. I've been miserable these past couple of weeks. Absolutely. Fucking. Miserable.

And those words broke my heart. I felt bad for acting the way I had. Part of my reason for staying away from Hunter was my feelings for him. I didn't want to get too close only to have to let him go at the end of the summer, but it was unfair for me to deny him friendship. He'd done nothing to me on purpose and he couldn't be blamed for the boneheaded mistake he made about Tiffany. He had tried to break up with her, he'd just gone about it in a really stupid way. After thinking it over, I realized I'd been a bitch to him for something that was an honest mistake — and I felt really bad for having acted that way.

Moving on to the case, I spun the top over the bottom to open it up. Inside was a small, rolled up note, together with a silver ring. I recognized the symbol on the ring as the Irish Claddagh, and the two hands holding a crowned heart were extremely detailed where they'd been carved into the silver. My brows furrowed in confusion, so I quickly unrolled the note.

No! Don't throw the ring out! It isn't what you think!

Dammit. I laughed again. It was apparent he knew me well and that he'd been paying more attention than I'd realized.

The ring is a promise, El. It's a promise that I won't go back on what I've been telling you. I bought one for myself as well and I'm wearing it to remind myself of the friendship between us. I realize I'm weak and it's going to be hard for me not to get home and immediately fall back into old habits. So, I hope that by looking at the ring, and knowing who holds its match, it'll help me make the right decisions. You don't have to wear yours and I understand if you don't. Just knowing you have it is enough for me. I love you Ellison. I can say that knowing what it means to love someone this time and you were the one who taught me exactly what that meant. I'm not going to get into the details of 'love' and 'in love', because you don't need that right now. But I do love you and I'll never stop.

I gasped and tears welled at the back of my eyes. I fell back on the mattress of the bed and held the ring and notes to my chest. I couldn't believe he'd gone through so much effort to get them to me and I realized how big of a bitch I'd been to him over the past two weeks. I couldn't deny that Hunter had been there when I needed him. But then I thought about whether I had been there for him. When that girl had visited and when I saw how quickly he'd gone back to the drugs, I'd been angry. Really angry. However a good friend would have helped him get through it, would have stood by his side to push him through the mistake — and all I'd done was desert him. I was ashamed of myself. And I knew that I needed to talk to him. I pushed myself up from the bed and slipped the ring over a finger on my right hand.

With a smile on my face, I walked out of my room in search for Hunter, but stopped short when I found my dad sitting in the living room. He was relaxed back on the sofa and music played from the radio in the corner of the room. A beer was held in my father's hand, surprising me to see it.

"Daddy?" I moved to sit next to him. "Everything alright?"

"Ellison, baby, I need to talk to you about some things and I want you to listen without arguing. I've made some decisions and I'm firm in them and I want to make sure you understand my wishes.

"Okay." It was all I could say. When he had that tone of voice, I knew there was no budging him.

Putting his arm around me, he pulled me into his side. "When your mother died years ago, El, my life stopped. Well, I can't say that entirely because I had you kids and I loved every minute I had with you. But my heart stopped beating the same way it had before I lost her. I've thought about her every day that she's been gone and I've looked forward to finding her again when it's my time to go. So, when that happens, Ellison, I don't want you feeling sad for me. You're going to be upset, honey, and I know that, but I don't want you worrying about what happened to me. I want you to know that I'm happy to be able to finally find her again. In fact, the thought has made my heart beat for her again."

More tears threatened my vision and I was really getting pissed off at the amount of them I'd spilled over the summer. Between Hunter and my father, I had to drink craploads of water just to keep from dehydrating from all of the damn tears.

"I'm not going to accept treatment, Ellison. They said it wouldn't cure me, so I don't see any use in spending every dime I've saved up to buy myself a few more months. That money can go to far better things, such as your education."

He grew quiet and *Fire and Rain* by James Taylor started playing. Daddy smiled and softly sang along to the song. I'd always loved to hear daddy sing — it meant that he was happy, that he was relaxed ... that was rare for him. I listened to him sing and I laid my head against his chest and enjoyed listening to the beat of his heart against his ribs. I didn't know it then, but that would be the last song I heard my father sing, and the significance of the song's words never escaped me.

"So what's going on with that boy?"

The change in topic surprised me, but I answered, "He's been following me on my hikes."

"Do I need to be worried? I noticed how upset you got over finding out he had a girl back home. You didn't need to say it for me to see it. He hasn't messed you up, has he? If so, I have to carry out some promises I made to him."

I laughed. I knew daddy wasn't joking about those threats. Henry James was not a man who went back on his word and he never said a thing he didn't mean.

"No, he hasn't messed me up. We're friends, daddy. He's just been hiking with me. Said he didn't want me to be alone right now."

"He knows?"

"Yeah." I knew it upset him, but I couldn't be blamed for not being able to keep it all inside. "He caught me crying, and ... "

He put his hand up to silence me. "No, baby, that's fine. It doesn't look like he's told anyone. So it's fine. I can't expect you to go through it by yourself and I know your brother isn't around enough to help you with it."

I sniffled and wiped a tear from my cheek. Laughing, I said, "He's been following me like a puppy on those trails too. He knows I'm mad at him for what happened with Tiffany, so he's just followed behind without saying anything. He was just trying to be there for me when I was ready to talk to him again."

Dad chuckled. "The boy's got it bad apparently. But that doesn't mean you can trust him, Ellie. He's got a ways to go before he's worth a shit and you don't need to carry his problems while at the same time carrying yours."

"I know."

His arm tightened around me. "Well, okay, El. I trust you to make the right decision. You always have. Now go ahead and get wherever it is you were going. I'm going to sit around here and relax for a little while then I'll put on a pot of stew for dinner."

I nodded my head and stood up. "I'll see you in a bit."

When I walked towards the door, Sasha and Bear followed behind me. I opened the door and stepped out to find Lily coming up the steps of the porch.

"Ellison James. I've allowed you to be a stubborn bitch for far too long. I wouldn't be a good friend to ya if I didn't kick your ass for being stupid, so I'm here to kick your ass — 'cause you're being stupid."

I stopped dead in my tracks , but made sure to close the door so my dad couldn't hear us.

"That boy spent a week — A FULL WEEK — preparing all those cutouts and surprises for you and if you haven't seen that he's trying, you're fucking blind. You don't need to go and run off to have sex with Hunter, but you could at least be his friend. He's trying to be yours and you're too damn caught up in your anger to see it. It's about time you take the blinders off for once and see that's he trying to change."

I held my hand up to show her the ring. "I know, Lil. I was actually on my way to find him."

Her eyes widened and she stepped back. "Well, I'll be damned. Ellison James has finally learned to pull her head out of her ass. I never thought I'd see the day."

I lifted my middle finger while smiling sweetly.

"Fuck you, Lily. Really. I mean it."

She was a bitch. But I loved her anyway.

Chapter Nineteen

Hunter

I walked those seven fucking miles to pick up the remnants of my plan to talk to Ellison. And for those seven fucking miles, I chastised myself for not having placed all the little surprises within the first fucking mile so it would be easier to clean up. Of course, that wouldn't have worked because the spring was seven fucking miles away and I was pissed off at the spring for not being closer.

Fucking stupid spring ...

My legs stopped working at mile six. For the rest of the hike to the spring, I had to pick up my legs with my hands just to put one foot in front of the other. By the time I finally reached the spring, I collapsed on top of the table.

I'm not sure how long I lay on that table. I'm sure my back would protest when I got up, but at that moment, it was the most comfortable place I'd ever been. My entire body felt like it weighed a ton and I needed to catch my breath before dragging all the shit back the seven fucking miles it would take to get home.

And I hoped the forty-eight miles of walking it'd taken me to execute this plan were worth it. Ellison may have thrown the notes away when she returned home. I had no way of knowing one-way or the other. I realized that Ellison was teaching me more than to care about other people and myself, she was teaching me patience. Sure — her way of teaching me patience was really fucking annoying — but she was teaching it to me nonetheless.

I fell asleep on the table and I was surprised to wake up to water falling on my face. Great. The last seven fucking miles would end up being seven fucking WET miles. It couldn't get any better than this. I pushed myself up into a seated position and looked out over the water. I imagined Ellison's fish swimming beneath the surface and I remember the look of her swimming among them. I smiled to think about it and realized that, whether she talked to me again or not, those forty-eight miles had been worth it. I'd made her smile and that was more important than anything else.

"I've created an addict."

My body spun around at the sound of El's voice. She stood at the end of the path leading to the spring. "I'da figured the twenty miles you've already walked today would have been enough. But, look at you. Out here walking twenty more. Whatever are you going to do when you go back home?"

I laughed. "Guess I'll be spending a lot of time walking around Central Park."

Her laugh was melodic and my heartbeat sped up from hearing it. She walked to me slowly and I couldn't help but search for her hands. She had them folded behind her back. That little bitch. She knew I'd look for the ring as soon as I saw her. She crawled up on top of the table with me and we sat facing each other in the rain, neither of us caring. She brought her hand from behind her back and grabbed my hand and put her ring next to mine.

"You read them."

"I did."

"And?"

She breathed out a resigned sigh. "And — I realize that I've been unfair. I should have been there for you rather than getting pissed off and ignoring you. I was disappointed, but that didn't mean it was okay for me to turn my back on you ... "

"El — just stop." I put a finger against her mouth. And I may have held it there for a few seconds too long because I really loved her mouth. "This isn't about anything you've done to me. I completely understand. I just want things to go back to the way they were, okay? You know, to before Tiffany, to before next time, to before everything that went wrong between us."

"Next time?"

My cheeks may have reddened. "Never mind." Her eyebrow arched over her eye, but I chose not to explain. "I want to be friends, El. I want to go back home and be able to feel like I can call you, or text you, or whatever the hell it is I need to do to get in touch with you. I want to know you. That's really all it comes down to. I just want you to let me know you."

She got a funny look on her face. It was a mixture of happiness, and sadness — and something that I didn't recognize.

"Can we talk about what happened that night in my room?"

My spine straightened to a point of being painful and every muscle tensed when I waited for her to continue. I was afraid she was mad — and I knew that I had this coming. I'd hoped she would tell me it was the best sex of her life and that she couldn't live without more of it, but more likely, she thought I'd taken advantage of her.

"Because I have to admit ... I .... "

It was obvious she couldn't say whatever it was she was thinking, and the blush on the skin of her cheeks was all I needed to see. I leaned over the table and I kissed her. It wasn't a soft kiss and it wasn't a small kiss. It was a real kiss — the kind of kiss that love stories are built around. It was a kiss that said hello and it said goodbye. It was the beginning and the end of a summer that made me want to grow up.

Pulling back, I looked in her glistening blue eyes. "I'm sorry. I had to do that."

"I'm not entirely upset that you did."

We sat there; our hands tangled together and stared at each other for the longest time. The sun started to set behind her and I groaned to realize it was time to head back.

I stood up from the table first and reached up to help her crawl down. We were standing toe to toe and I lifted her chin up to look down into her eyes. "So, is this fixed?"

Smiling brightly, she answered, "It is."

"Good." I grabbed the box and blanket from the grassy path and then reached over to grab the trash bag that carried the crumpled cardboard Hunters. "Is there any way I can convince you to help me carry this stuff back?"

She laughed as she walked ahead of me and shook her head. "Not a chance."

~   ~   ~

The next three weeks were a blur. Ellison and I still hiked daily and I finally finished the porch. Bill was on his way home and I was slapping on a big red bow after slaving my ass off fixing the screens as a surprise.

"Damn, Hunter. It looks good. Maybe you should skip Harvard and work with a handy man until you can start your own business or something." Lily stood with Ellison behind me surveying the finished job.

"Don't think so, Lil. But if one of you could help me with this stupid fucking bow, I'd appreciate it."

Ellison laughed and stepped up to hold the ends of the bow so I could secure them. I was leaving that night and the tension between us for the day had been tough to deal with. It wasn't an angry tension, but one filled with sadness and loss. My insides were breaking apart, but I tried to keep anyone from noticing how hard I was taking my impending return home.

"It's perfect. Dad is going to be so damn surprised. He's been trying to fix this place up for years."

We stood staring up at the porch for a few minutes. Nobody spoke and the significance of that porch meant more to me than just being a simple porch. It was something that had been forgotten, something that had been neglected and misused and I'd fixed it. Hours of labor had gone into the porch and, to me at least, it sparkled. It was brand new once again and would have many years ahead of it as long as it didn't get weighted down in trash and debris — as long as it was loved and cared for, it could last forever.

"I'm going to go inside and start dinner. We should celebrate your last day here, Hunter, and if I start cooking now, there'll be just enough time to eat before El and I have to drive you to the plane." Lily bounced her way up the porch steps and the screen door slammed behind her when she disappeared inside the house.

I sat down on the steps and stared up at a girl I didn't want to let go. "I can't believe the summer's already over."

Sitting down beside me, Ellison reached out to put her arm around my waist. "Me neither. Seems like the days just flew past. Makes me sad to think I won't have my hiking partner. I'll have no one to laugh at anymore for tripping over a root or a rock, or even getting slapped in the face by a branch." She winked at me and I laughed.

"I fucking hate nature."

Chuckling, she commented, "Yeah, well, you and nature seemed to hug and make up over the past couple of weeks. Maybe when you get back home, you can spend some more time with it and get to know it better." She reached over and took my hand before quietly adding, "Might keep you away from all those parties you couldn't avoid before you came down here."

I squeezed her hand and let out a loud sigh. "No worries, El. I won't be attending any of those parties. I'll be at my parents' house long enough to pack up and then I'll be moving to Massachusetts for school. I plan to actually attend class this time, so I'm sure I'll be busy." I nudged her with my shoulder to get her to look over at me. "You need to be getting ready for school yourself. It starts up soon and you'll be out there doing your thing and showing those other students how awesome you are in your element."

"I'll be in a classroom for the first semester, at least. It's not exactly 'my element'."

"You'll be perfect, El. Just like you always are. Seriously, I feel bad for Finn. Competing against you would suck."

She smiled a sad smile. "Yeah, well, if I start school. I'm thinking about holding off until next year — especially with everything going on with my dad."

My shoulders dropped and a little painful lightning bolt shot through my body. I wanted to demand she start school on time, but I also knew her dad was more important and couldn't be put off until some other time. "If you need anything, El. All you have to do is call me. As soon as I get back home, I'm setting you up some social networking accounts and texting you the user names and passwords. We'll be connected in a hundred different ways. You'll never be able to get rid of me."

Her brilliant blue eyes sparkled up at me. "I could just refuse to turn on the computer."

"Then I'll send smoke signals and carrier pigeons will be pecking at your window. I live in New York. There's an endless supply of pigeons. They'll be pecking day in and day out."

"But you'll be in Massachusetts"

"I'm sure there's pigeons there as well."

She laughed but things got quiet and it felt like a blanket of misery had settled on top of us. "I'll miss you, Ellison. You know, if things had been different — if we didn't live a thousand miles away from each other and if we'd had more time — I wouldn't have let you just make me a friend."

She looked up at me and opened that lovely little mouth of hers to argue. Placing my hand over her mouth, I silenced her. "Nope. I'm not letting you argue.

I know you can't help it, so I'm not holding it against you. But you need to accept that, if circumstances had been different ... " I motioned between us. " ... This would have happened. It would have happened on those trails, it would have happened in these houses and it would have happened at the bonfires. I don't care if Mr. Sensitive-Guitar-Guy was watching. I would have called you 'my girl' and there would have been nothing you could say or do to stop me."

"You're full of yourself, Hunter. In fact, I think you're so full of shit, your eyes are turning brown as we speak."

"You think so?"

"Yeah, I think so."

Well, damn, if I didn't have to show her how much she was wrong. Leaning over, I said "You should take another look. My eyes couldn't get any bluer." When I was close enough to her, my mouth latched to hers. She jumped in surprise, but I wrapped my arms around her to keep her from making a break for it. Her hands came up to my face and I flinched in anticipation of her pulling my hair out or smacking me upside the back of the head, but when her fingers curled into my hair, pulling me against her, and as she opened her mouth to deepen the kiss, my heart beat faster and blood rushed through my head making it close to impossible to hear anything else. With every movement of her lips against mine, my heart broke a little more. I loved this moment; I loved the girl that I was holding. I wanted nothing more than to lay her out right there and show her how much I loved her, but I knew I couldn't — I knew it wouldn't be fair to either of us in the long run. Breaking apart from that kiss was like stabbing myself in the gut — but I did it and I smiled when I looked into her beautiful face and noticed how her eyes were still closed and how her lips were swollen from the intensity of the kiss.

Slowly, she opened her crystal blues and a smile peeked out on the corner of those swollen lips.

But then she pinched my nipple.

Hard.

"Ow, Sonofabitch!"

She laughed. "I told you what would happen if you tried that again."

When she let go, I put my arm around her shoulder and pulled her against me. "Yeah, well, at least this time you didn't bite me. That makes me think we're making progress."

"Nah — I'm just leading you on."

I chuckled. "You're a cruel woman, Ellison James. Very cruel, indeed."

Chapter Twenty

We arrived to the plane with about a half hour to spare until the time I was scheduled to leave. Mr. Klimpt opened the gates to the private airstrip, but rather than driving me back in his golf cart, he allowed Ellison and Lily to escort me back to the plane in Ellison's Jeep. I still hung on for dear life as she drove, but it broke my heart to realize it would be the last time I rode in the death trap she referred to as a 'car.'

Reaching the plane, Ellison skidded to a stop and Lily jumped out to immediately cross the tarmac and up the stairs into the plane. The entire ride over, all she had asked was if there would be time for her to tour the interior before I left. I was happy to give her as much time as she wanted. The last thing I wanted to do was board that plane.

I stumbled out of the back seat and resisted the urge to fall to the ground. My equilibrium took a second to stabilize and once I could walk again, I turned back to grab my bags.

"Now that is some fancy transportation, Hunter. I know I'll never see the inside of one of those in my lifetime. It's hard to imagine your parents own it." Ellison laughed nervously to my side. Placing the bags on the ground, I turned to her and pulled her against my chest.

I looked up at the plane. Sunlight reflected off of the silver exterior, almost blinding in its intensity. "Yeah, mom and dad are what you would call the ultimate consumers. If it's new and it's something the neighbors haven't already acquired, they have to have it — to set the trend, I guess. You should see my dad's garage. He's an avid collector of cars."

"Well, he is Bill's brother. Why do you think Bill has a shop? He just can't afford the collection, so he tinkers on other people's vehicles. Guess both of them worked around cars a lot growing up. It's hard not to love something that spent your life around."

It was a new perspective into my father that I hadn't considered before and I was somewhat stunned by what Ellison had said. "And here I thought he was just trying to show off." I squeezed her body to mine when she laughed. That was one of the things I was going to miss about her the most. She always had a different way of looking at things. It wasn't that Ellison could see the good or bad in people, it was that she saw the *real* in people. She didn't excuse and she didn't place blame on people either, she simply pointed out the most rational explanation for their actions.

I didn't know what to say to her and the tension was killing me. We both were trying hard not to be upset, or at least not to admit that we were upset about my leaving. Even though I'd told myself all summer that this moment would come, that I would have to say goodbye to her, I could never have prepared for the absolute desolation I felt. It was like a void expanding in the center of my body, slowly growing and hallowing out the places that it reached.

I knew I had important things waiting for me back home. I knew that college was something I needed to take seriously. But even knowing that, I wasn't able to shake the feeling that I was making the biggest mistake of my life by climbing on that plane. I'd never felt for anything in my life that way I did for Ellison and regardless of how much waited for me at home, none of it compared to her.

213

The silence between us was too much, but it gave me time to think of some way not to have to leave. And then it hit me ...

"Do you remember when you told me that I need to be a pirate?"

Ellison pulled away to look up at me. Her lips twisted up in confusion. "Yeah. Why?"

"I don't know. I was just thinking that you were right. I should live life like that — well not exactly like that, but at least how I want. I don't want to go home, El. I don't want to leave you, I don't want to leave Lily and Bill. I feel like I'm leaving my family — my actual family. I'm going to back to live an apartment off campus, by myself, and I have no desire to be there."

"You have to go to college, Hunter ... "

I put a finger over her mouth to silence her. "I know I have to go to college. But I don't have to go to Harvard. I don't have to follow in my father's footsteps and become everything they want.. I can go anywhere in this world and become what I want. I can go to school here just as easily as I can go to school there. You're the one who told me that. I don't see any difference about where I choose to go to school."

It was slight, but I could see her head shake in disagreement with what I was saying. So I pushed harder. "El, you need people by your side right now. With everything that's going on with your dad ... "

"Exactly, Hunter! With everything that's going on with my dad. It's going to get ugly. I don't know if you realize how bad it's going to get, but you don't need to be worrying yourself with my situation or Lily's or Bill's while you're in school. That's why I'm not starting right away. I know better than to attempt it."

214

"I know, El and that's why I should be around. Not only will you need help, but so will Lily and Bill when they find out. Henry is family to them as well."

"So you'd be dropping class and homework and everything else every time you thought I needed something. No, Hunter. I can't do that to you. Your focus needs to be on school; not on what's going on here." Tears welled in her eyes and she pulled apart from me entirely. Her arms immediately wrapped around her mid-section. When she'd stepped farther away, she continued. "You have a full scholarship to a top university. You have a brain that can do amazing things with the information you'll learn there. You need to be there. You need to become something incredible, in whatever the hell field you choose, and you need to make a difference because you're the type of person who can."

"I'll start late … "

"Hunter, please. Please don't make me feel any worse about this than I already do." She looked down at her feet and spoke quietly when she admitted, "I'm mad at everything right now. I'm mad at cancer itself, if that makes any sense. I'm mad that it's taking my dad's life, I'm mad that it's taking my dad from me and that it's affecting my brother and everyone else. I'm mad because I feel helpless to do anything but prepare as best I can for it. It's like a damn tornado and the minute you hear sirens, the only thing you can do his hide and wait as it mows you down. So, I can't stop that shit. But I can stop this. I can keep it from altering your life in any way. You need to go. Don't worry about me. We'll talk over whatever social site you want, but we'll do it while you're in Massachusetts being brilliant like you are supposed to be."

I slowly walked up to her. Arguments to what she said slammed against my thoughts, but I knew better than to voice them. Ellison had made up her mind and it was like punching your way through a brick wall to try and get her to change it. We would end up fighting, and that was the last thing I wanted to happen between us before I left.

Reaching her, I noticed the tears that streamed lightly down her cheeks. My hand moved to brush them away and my thumb ran over her lips. Her sad blue eyes locked with mine almost instantly after I'd touched her.

"Why can't I just stay here and love you?" A single tear broke free of my eye. I felt it make its path down my cheek. It grew cold against the heat of my skin and my body trembled from the strength it took for me to keep the rest of the tears to follow in its path. I was pleading with her with that one sentence. I knew something was wrong with what I was doing. My heart felt like it had been placed in a vice and I struggled to breath around the pain that was constricting my chest.

When she saw me cry, her tears fell harder and her face contorted from the sobs she was attempting to choke back. She tried to look away, but I grabbed her chin and pulled her face back to me. Leaning down slowly, I placed a kiss on the tears staining her cheeks. She continued staring up at me. Her body was completely still. When my mouth fell on hers she didn't step away like I swore she would. She stepped forward, hesitantly wrapping her hands around my neck while I took her into my arms. My tongue brushed across her mouth and when she deepened the kiss, my heart fell into my feet. This was her way of saying goodbye. It was her way of taking the last chance she had to love me and actually doing something with it. I couldn't hold it back any longer and we both cried during that kiss, our combined tears sliding along our mouths, adding salt to the taste of our lips.

The engine for the plane started behind us and I forced myself to break away from the kiss knowing that Lily would come bouncing back at any second. My entire body tensed to look down at Ellison knowing it would be the last time I'd see her in person for a long time.

"I'll be in touch with you as soon as I get home. Keep your phone on and try and check the computer every once in a while, okay."

She smiled. "Sure thing."

My eyebrow arched in disbelief that she would actually do as I'd asked. When Lily finally returned, I turned to her and said, "Hey, Lil, make sure Ellison checks her computer and phone every day. She says she will but I'm not sure I trust her."

Lily smiled brightly and put her arm around Ellison who then rolled her eyes. "Are you serious? You're siking Lily on me? That's unfair."

My shit eating grin took up the majority of my face at that moment. "I figured it would be a reliable method to ensure my interests were met."

They both laughed just before Lily lost the smile on her face when she realized it was time to say goodbye. She walked up and hugged me tightly. Looking up, she lightly patted me on the cheek. "You be good up there. Don't do anything stupid, and please, for the love of all things holy, please do not go anywhere near 'Crack Whore Barbie'. That woman is nothing but aggravating and I'm really upset you stopped me from whipping her ass."

My smile was genuine as I looked down at my tiny, yet surprisingly intimidating cousin. "I'll keep my distance. I can guarantee that. She's going to school in New York so I won't even be in the same state as her."

"Well, thank God for small miracles. Alright, Cuz, I'll talk to you soon." She hugged me once more and walked away to wait in Ellison's Jeep.

I stared at Ellison while she looked everywhere but me. It crushed me to see her fighting so hard against what she was feeling.

"So, I guess it's time."

She looked at me finally after I'd spoken to her. "Yeah." She stepped toward me and reached down to take my hand. Absently, her finger spun the silver ring around mine. "You take care of yourself up there, Hunter. Have fun, live life, but do it in a way where you're not hurting yourself. Just be smart about what you do from now on."

"I will. You'll get to hear all about it every day when I'm constantly texting and emailing." Smiling sadly, I leaned down to place a kiss on her forehead. She nodded, sniffled, and then stepped away from me.

"Aright, I'm going to make the first move and get the hell out of here. Have a safe flight. I'll talk to you when you get home." She spun on her heel and didn't give me time to respond. I could tell it took all her strength to keep taking each step away from me and as the distance was put between us, my heart beat a little bit slower and a little bit longer to watch her walk away.

Grabbing the bags from the ground, I made my way to the plane. The pilot stood at the top of the stairs and smiled down at me as I approached. "Good to see you again, Mr. McCormick. Did you enjoy your time in Florida?"

I put one foot in front of the other as I forced myself up those steps. I looked back over my shoulder and saw Ellison climb up in her Jeep. The brake lights quickly flashed and flickered away as she sped toward the exit runway. As she made her way out, her tires squealed while they ripped through the sand, and howled when they found purchase on the underlying asphalt. I heard the pilot above me gasp into his open palm at the sight of it.

He chuckled after a second and commented, "It's a good thing that girl is not your pilot; you'd never see New York!" He turned to enter the plane. Blowing out a deep breath, I lifted my feet up another three steps and boarded a plane that would take me over a thousand miles from where I wanted to be.

~ ~ ~

The flight back sucked because I couldn't sleep the entire way. I wasn't sure what I was going to do when I got home from the airport because I'd never been at the house and awake when the sun was shining. After exiting the flight, I waited patiently for my father to pick me up. Fifteen minutes passed and finally I saw the cherry apple red Porsche come pulling up to the curb. I folded myself into the small car and my father hit the gas faster than I could pull on my seat belt.

"Welcome back, Hunter. How did it go down there?"

His tone of voice told me that even though he was asking how I liked my trip, he didn't really care about my answer either way. He was going through the formalities of conversation typically expected of a normal, well-adjusted family.

"I know you've been talking to Bill, so I'm surprised you even have to ask that question."

He scoffed at my response but didn't attempt to speak to me again the rest of the ride home. Pulling into his garage, I rolled my eyes to see that he'd added to his collection since I'd been gone. El's words replayed in my head and I tried to remember that maybe my father's fascination with the cars was a reminder of his youth rather than merely an outward reflection of his success and wealth.

When I walked through the living room of the main house, my mother stood up from the couch and crossed the room to hug me. She pulled away to look up at me and ask, "How'd it go down there?" She seemed genuinely interested to know.

"It was good. I'd like to spend more time with them now that I've gotten to know them better. Maybe we could fly them up for Thanksgiving in three months. They could stay the entire four days."

Yes. I was attempting to corner my mother, but it really irritated me to think about how they'd all but rejected Bill and Lily and how they'd done nothing to help, even when Lily's mom was killed.

My mom fidgeted in front of me. Her hands nervously wrung over each other and she looked to my father across the room for support. "Hunter, I don't think now is a good time to talk about the holidays. I mean, they are so far away, who knows what will come up between now and then." She patted me on the shoulder and walked me towards the French doors at the back of the house. "What I do need to talk to you about is what you will be taking with you to Massachusetts. The movers will be here in three days. We'll need to have everything sorted and ready to be packed when they arrive."

I was feeling hostile at that moment and I continued pushing the issue with Bill. "I'll be taking everything. That way you can turn it back into a guest house which will be perfect for when Bill and Lily come visit, right? They'd have their own place to stay outside of the main house."

Huffing out a breath, my mother's hand fell forcefully against the door handle before she threw the door open in front of me. "Hunter, I told you, I don't want to talk about it. If you plan on taking everything, that's fine, but the furniture will need to stay. We rented you a fully furnished apartment near the school. You'll have no need for anything. Your father and I wanted to show you how proud we are of you going to school, so we spared no expense in the home you'll be staying in while you are there."

Smiling, she looked up at me like I should be jumping up and down clapping at her generosity. However, the only thing I was thinking was that, once again, my parents were throwing out money to appease me, as a distraction to avoid having anything to do with me as a person. Not once had my father said he was proud of me. I wouldn't have cared before the summer, but now it felt like a slap in the face.

Tightening my grip on my bags, I stepped outside.

"Oh, Hunter. Your father also purchased another car for you to use. It's parked by the guesthouse. Try not to destroy it this time." She smiled again and closed the door.

I looked up at the guesthouse and dreaded the climb to get to it. However, when I'd halfway tackled the horrid climb, I noticed that it wasn't as hard as it used to be. El's damn hikes had not only straightened out my thought process, they'd built up my physical stamina. For the first time in my fucking life, I felt like I could run a marathon without keeling over dead at mile two.

I pulled my key from my pocket and let myself into the house, immediately heading back to my bedroom to throw down my bags. When I walked in the room, all my electronics and credit cards had been returned to me. They were layed out neatly on my bed and in the center sat a set of keys to the new BMW sitting outside in the driveway.

I picked up my phone almost immediately and plugged it in. Flicking it on, I quickly typed out a text to Ellison.

Me: Made it home safely. Miss you guys already.

It was a quick message that was intended to see if she'd turned her phone on like I'd asked her to do. I hoped for a response, but deep down, I didn't expect one.

Looking over my room, I groaned at the amount of work it would take to pack everything up. I pulled open my junk drawers to find piles of drug paraphenila, loose change, concert ticket stubs, photographs and other momentos of a life lived on the wild side. Picking up the differents odd and ends, I tossed most of it in the trash bin to the side of the bureau. What I'd once considered trophies of a life lived well, were actually reminders of a lot of time wasted.

Chapter Twenty-One

Ellison

Me: Yes, I got your messages, all 20 of them. You're seriously driving me crazy with it Hunter. I've been out hiking and I come back to you freaking out and accusing me of ignoring you. Calm the hell down or I'll turn the phone off.

He wasn't really freaking out, but it was fun to accuse him of it anyway. But he was driving me absolutely crazy with his constant barrage of communication. I'll admit, my cheeks reddened every time he sent something, but 20 messages? That's just insane.

Hunter: You know, your phone is portable, it can be carried with you on your hikes and then you won't miss anything while you're gone. Plus, it's a safety factor. What if you fall down and break your ankle?

Me: I hike to get away from technology. Why would I bring it with me? You're wasting my minutes.

Hunter: I just added more to your phone ... Lily's too ...

As soon as I read that, a knock sounded from my bedroom window. Rolling my eyes, I tossed the phone on my bed and opened the window to find Lily standing with a grimace on her face.

"Would you please text Hunter back so he'll leave me the hell alone?!" She tapped her foot on the ground and held her phone on to show me the litany of messages she'd received.

I chuckled. "Oh, that boy has gone overboard, now."

Placing her hands on her hips, she asked, "What in the hell did you do to him, El? I know you two had a thing for one another and all, but this is a little ridiculous!"

A little over a month had passed since Hunter left for school. Normally, we only spoke at night and on the weekends when he wasn't in class, but he had the day off for some school event, and just like the week before he actually started school, he had nothing better to do but sit around and message me. He was doing really well about avoiding the wild parties and friends that would tempt him back to alcohol and drugs. To fill some of his time, he joined a non-profit organization that focused on sick children and I was proud of him for having done so.

"Why don't you come inside, Lil. Walk around front. The door's open."

Lily smiled and bounced her way around the house. I picked up the phone from my bed.

Me: Did you really feel it was necessary to send Lily over here?

Before Hunter could respond, I heard the front door open, followed by a loud crash and the dogs barking.

"Ellison! Get in here! NOW!"

I ran from my room and when I rounded the corner of the hall, I saw my father sprawled out on the floor near the coffee table. The phone dropped from my hand to the floor when I ran to his side.

"Daddy?! Oh god, Daddy are you okay?"

My father groaned and his head rolled around on the floor. His eyes were closed and he didn't seem capable of responding.

"Lily! Call an ambulance!"

I carefully ran my hands over my dad's skull. When I reached the back, it felt sticky and wet and I pulled my hand back to find blood smeared into his hair. "Shit! Dad, I need you to talk to me right fucking now! Do you understand?!"

He moved his hand up to touch his head. "El?" His voice was weak and his face contorted from pain.

"You must have fell and hit your head on the coffee table. What hurts?" Tears distorted my vision as I looked over the rest of his body to try and find any other injuries. Nothing looked out of place.

"My leg feels like someone slammed into it with a sledgehammer, and my head. I was walking in here and my damn leg gave out from underneath me."

I had to stop the bleeding on his head until help could arrive. "Don't move. I'm going to go get a towel for your head. Help is on the way."

Pushing up from my crouched position, I faintly heard my dad bitching about help having been called, but I didn't care. I was in full panic mode and I would call in an entire army if it would help. Running back, I placed the towel under his head and breathed out a sigh of relief to see that it didn't immediately soak up a lot of blood. I prayed that meant the injury was superficial. Lilly ran back inside.

"They're on their way." Taking a position next to me, she looked like she wanted to reach out and help but she was too afraid to move. She didn't ask any questions, but just sat quietly beside me until we heard the sirens from the approaching ambulance.

~   ~   ~

"It appears Mr. James' leg broke from a tumor that had developed in the femur and weakened the bone. It's a painful break, but it can be managed with pain killers." The doctor paused and looked at me.

"So, are they going to take him into surgery tonight to fix it?" It was simple. A broken bone. I'm sure there were millions of them that occurred every year, and it was something that could be repaired easily. I wasn't concerned.

"Ms. James." His voice sounded sympathetic. "They're not going to set the bone. There's no point. We can put him in a protective cast to keep it from becoming worse, but that cast would have to come off within a few weeks."

"Well, then how in the hell is he going to walk again?! What do you mean they aren't going to fix it? I'll come up with the money to pay for the surgery, just tell them to get in there and do it!" I was mad and scared and shaking where I stood. I couldn't understand why the hospital was refusing to fix my dad's leg and would just leave him like that. He needed to be able to walk.

The doctor breathed out a resigned sigh. "Ms. James — I'm sorry. I believe its time for your family to consider your options from this point forward. Your father is refusing treatment for the cancer and his care from now on will only be palliative — to keep him from feeling pain. We don't typically render that type of care long term in the hospital, however there are programs that can assist you. They have their own facility where your father can be transported or he can receive care at home as long as there is someone who can provide 24-hour care." He paused again and breathed a slow breath. "The disease is progressing quickly, Ms. James. It may be time for you to make arrangements. As for now, I can give your father a prescription for oxycodone to help with the pain and I can provide you with a phone number for the local Hospice. It's an excellent program and they can walk you through the process."

"The process? What process? And I don't know about the oxycodone. Isn't it addicting? How will we get him off of it?"

His expression didn't flinch. I briefly wondered if doctors were taught to remain so serious and impassive in medical school. "Your father is dying, Ms. James. I can't tell you how much time he has left but any addiction he develops will not be a problem. There are steps that you are going to need to take to prepare for his death. That is where Hospice can assist you. I recommend you give them a call today if possible. We'll keep your father here until transfer arrangements can be made."

~   ~   ~

After quickly thumbing through the paperwork, I looked up at the Hospice representative who'd come out to my house. She quickly assessed the space and we agreed to set up a hospital bed in the living room for my father. She told me that they would provide the bed, a system for me to use to lift my father and that they would work directly with the doctors to obtain prescriptions and other medical care that my father would require.

"Ms. James, the first couple days or weeks will be the easiest part of this process. Since you will be your father's caregiver, you will be in direct contact with our nursing staff 24-hours a day if need be. If there is ever a time where the task becomes too much, or if you need to leave the house for an hour or two, a nurse can sit with your father during that time."

Her face fell and she reached over to take my hands into hers. "I'm sorry this is happening to your family. We'll be with you every step of the way and if you need anything, you let us know. I also want you to remember to take of yourself during this time as well. Caregivers tend to forget that they have needs. The last thing you need is to make yourself sick during the coming weeks. The paperwork will explain everything."

We went over the arrangements and she explained how to use the equipment and how to administer my father's medications. When she left, I closed the door and fell against it. My entire body hurt, my heart, my bones, my skin — everything. It was quiet in the house except for a soft vibration. I looked towards the hallway and saw the screen of my phone light up on the floor. Stepping away from the door, I approached the phone to pick it up. Hunter had texted me more than 15 times. I scrolled through the texts, but didn't really read them. He was upset that I hadn't responded, but not in an angry way. He was simply concerned. My thumb moved to hit the button to respond back to him, but I couldn't push it down. I had nothing to say. My world had just been hit by the beginning of the storm and I'd become almost catatonic to see it coming. It was as if my reality had shifted and even though I was still part of my life, I was only watching it rather than participating. My body wouldn't let me do anything more than feed the dogs and crawl in bed. I didn't even have the strength to shower. I held the phone to my chest, felt every time that it vibrated with a new message. I didn't look at them and I didn't respond back. I couldn't.

My father would be arriving from the hospital the next morning and all I could do was curl up under my blanket and lay there while I waited.

Chapter Twenty-Two

Hunter

Me: Well have you tried going over there?

I'd broken down and texted Lily again around midnight when I didn't hear back from Ellison. Lily'd responded that Ellison's dad had fallen and was taken to the hospital, but she didn't have much information beyond that. When she told me she let Ellison drive to the hospital by herself after the ambulance left, I almost reached through the phone and strangled her.

Lily: I walked over there a little bit ago and knocked on her door and window. The lights are out and I think she's asleep. I'm sure she's just tired. I talked to Jake and he's heading home now to see what's going on.

"Fuck!" I threw my phone across the room, but then immediately ran over to make sure I hadn't broken it. The screen was cracked, but thankfully it was still operational. It was the only somewhat reliable source of contact I had with Ellison. It was on rare occasions that she turned on her computer and she didn't really like social networking — most likely because she wasn't interested in taking the time to learn it.

Every muscle in my body tensed and clenched. I paced helplessly through my apartment not sure what I could do. I wanted to jump in my car and race to the airport to catch the next flight to Florida. I didn't give a shit that I had to be in class the next day. Ellison was more important. But I knew that if I pulled that maneuver and it wasn't a serious issue, Ellison would be pissed. She'd warned me when I left that the stuff going on with her would distract me from school. As usual, she'd been right. Even over a thousand miles away it was affecting me. But my heart wasn't here, it wasn't in the walls of that fucking school or in the walls of this apartment. It was in a small wooden house in the middle of nowhere fucking Florida and THAT was where I should have been.

Flicking my phone on, I typed out another text to Ellison.

Me: I'm flying down. I'm worried and you're not responding, so I'm flying down.

It was a cheap trick, but I knew Ellison would respond if for nothing more than to yell at me for even threatening to leave school. I waited for what felt like an hour, but eventually my phone chirped. Snatching it from the table beside me, I pulled up the message.

Ellison: It's nothing, Hunter. My dad broke his leg. Everything's fine. See - this is why you don't need to be involved in this. You're too damn willing to drop everything. Now stop. It's three in the morning, I know you have class tomorrow and you need sleep. I'll talk to you tomorrow.

I knew she was lying but I also knew that was all I was going to get from her. I tossed the phone back on the table and leaned forward to hold my head in my hands. Blood rushed through my veins and my headache pounded in time with it. I'd been fucking miserable since I left Florida. The week before school was a joke and I'd spent most of my time at the guesthouse avoiding my parents. Ethan had come by a couple times, but when I told him I wasn't interested in partying, he eventually gave up. He'd informed me that he and Tiffany had hooked up when she returned from Florida and I wished him luck. For some fucking reason, he thought I'd be upset, so you can imagine his reaction when I laughed so hard, I'd started clapping. I was that happy about it because I knew it meant I wouldn't have to deal with her before I left for Massachusetts.

After I arrived here, I kept to myself. I made acquaintances obviously, but I I was quick to side step any romantic advances and I kept my friendships to the people who were more serious about school work than their social lives. Ellison had yelled at me for becoming a recluse, but I couldn't help it. I wanted to impress her — to make her proud. I'd never wanted that before and the desire was too much to ignore. I finally joined a non-profit group to appease her and keep her from worrying that I'd become some creepy guy holed up in an apartment who only saw the light of day when he had class.

Luckily, there were only two more weeks of school before we got a break and I intended on returning home and using my parents plane to fly down to see Ellison. I would only be able to stay for a day or two, but I had this overwhelming urge to hold her, to talk to her in person, to take care of her in any way that I could.

~ ~ ~

The morning after that night, Ellison had laid into me over email. If I'd printed the email, I was sure it would have been several pages long. She let me have it for my threat to fly down and she let me have it for my constant messages. I had no idea where her anger had come from because, even for Ellison, the length of the email was a bit much. I didn't text her for the rest of that day trying to give her time to calm down. However, when I texted her the following day, she would only respond with one word phrases or curt explanations. It's been like that for the past two weeks,

232

which only made me more determined to fly down and find out what was going on with her.

I'd left school as soon as break started and I was pulling up to my parents' house in New York. As usual, my mother had the place decked out for the holidays and everything looked perfect and cold. I sat in the car looking up at the perfectly placed lights and the festive ornaments and bows she had placed throughout the large yard. But, despite the obvious attention that had been paid to the detail of the display, there was no warmth to it — no love.

Climbing from the car, I grabbed the bags I'd packed for the trip and walked inside the house, tossing my bags down in the foyer. My mother must have heard something messing up the perfection of her décor and came flying down the hallway.

"Hunter! Honey, why are you home so early and why aren't you putting your stuff in the guesthouse? You'd be more comfortable there. I refurnished it." A fake smile appeared on her face and I groaned.

"I need to use the plane. I'm going to Florida for a few days."

Mom never lost her fake smile when she said, "Well that's not going to be possible. There is a little less than a week left before Thanksgiving and you need to be here. It wouldn't look right if my son didn't come home for the holidays."

I scoffed. "Mom, I'm going to Florida, one way or the other. If I have to drive, I'll drive, but I'm going. If you let me take the plane, I can make sure I'm back in time to play the perfect child for your friends."

Her jaw dropped. "How dare you? I want you around for the holidays because that's what families do and not because I'm just trying to make a good impression."

Brushing past her, I walked to the kitchen and yelled back over my shoulder. "I'm going, mom. You can decide how I get there, but nothing is going to stop me."

I sat down at one of the barstools and grabbed a pile of my mail that my mom had been saving while I'd been gone. Flipping through the assortment of envelopes, I tossed most to the side and chuckled at the amount of junk mail I'd received over the few weeks I'd been gone. I also tossed out the phone bills and credit card statements because my parents' accountant took care of those electronically. However, on the bottom of the stack, I found a plain white envelope, addressed to me, but without a return address. The writing was nothing more than chicken scratch and I immediately ripped open the top and extracted a two page, handwritten letter.

Hunter:

I'm not good at writing out long-winded shit, but I'm going to attempt to clarify some things with you that I've been considering.

Before reading the rest of the letter, I flipped to the second page and scrolled my eyes down to the signature. It read 'Henry James.' I almost dropped the paper from my hands. Why the fuck was Henry writing to me? Flipping back to the first page, I continued.

You know I'm not your biggest fan, and I'm not writing to retract my earlier threats. I meant every single last one of them and even if you fuck up after I've passed away, I'll still find a way to pay you a visit. I can promise you that. I just wanted to get that promise out of the way before moving on to why I'm writing this.

I've noticed something over the past couple of days and I can't sit around and ignore it. I don't have time for that. I know that before you left you were hiking daily with El and I know the reason she allowed that was because you followed her around until she had no choice but the talk to you. I'll admit, that was pretty slick and I'd used that maneuver on Ms. James plenty of times during our marriage, so I won't hold it against you. I'm not proud to admit this but I found some notes in Ellison's room one day after she'd returned from one of those hikes. My curiousity got the best of me and I read them. I'm sure you know what was in those letters because you wrote them.

When I first met you, I thought you were looking out for yourself over the needs of my daughter. I know what it's like to be a man your age and the last thing I wanted was for my daughter to fall for the crap I assumed you'd been feeding her. But then I read the letters, and you surprised me. I'm not saying I trust you any further than I did before I read them, but it made me consider the fact that you might care for El more than I realized.

So, before I leave this life, I wanted to correct some things that could become mistakes later on. Since you left, my daughter has been in a funk. It wouldn't be obvious to the outside observer, because, let's face it, my daughter is good at concealing her thoughts. But I'm her father and I can tell. Even after her break up with Finn, she never acted sad or lost. It pains me to see her act that way now.

What I'm attempting to say is this: I know Ellison cares about you and I suspect that you care for her more than I originally believed. I see no reason for you two to go your separate ways if there's a chance that you can make her happy, and THAT is all I want for my daughter. I still think you're a punk kid and I still think you have tons of growing up to do, but you have potential and I think that if you straighten up your shit, you can be the person that makes her happy. So, consider this a challenge. Before I die, I want to give you my blessing for pursuing my daughter, but I only do so with the condition that you become a man and not a boy. A man will look out for her over hisself and a man will take care of her no matter what it takes — I think you can be that man.

Don't go showing this letter to my daughter in an attempt to win her either. That's a punk maneuver and once Ellison reads this she'll be pissed you went against my wishes. But I will tell you this: if you want to be with Ellison, if you really love her as I suspect you do (considering her damn phone goes off about every five seconds), then grow the fuck up. Do something with your life and do it for yourself and for her. Be something she can be proud of, be something she will accept into her life. I've raised her not to put up with bullshit and I'm sure by now, you've learned that. Don't expect anything less with her. Most importantly, be her equal. She's an amazing person and it'll be difficult for any man to be worthy of her time. So make yourself worthy.

That's the only advice I can offer you, son. What you do with it is up to you.

Henry James

I read the letter three times to make sure that I understood it correctly. Henry James — the man who'd explained to me numerous times how my life would end badly if I messed with his daughter — was asking me to go after her, to not give up in my pursuit, and to become the person worthy of her. My jaw must have hit the countertop because my mother's curiosity was peaked to see the expression on my face.

"What is that, Hunter? Who is that letter from?" She attempted to take it from my hand, but I pulled it to my chest. Henry had intended this message for me, man to man, and I was going to honor that.

Standing up suddenly, I looked at my mom while folding the letter back into its envelope and shoving it in my pocket. "I have to go. Am I allowed to take the plane, or ... "

"You're not going anywhere, Hunter."

My entire body tensed and rage began to bloom within my head and chest. "Excuse me?"

My mom's expression was stern. Her brows furrowed between her eyes and her lips were pulled into a thin line. "Your dad is on his way home now. You're not going to screw up the holiday season for us by, once again, making a stupid decision. We sent you to Florida to learn about what it's like to live in poverty, not for you to join those people."

The way she said 'those people' made my stomach turn. It was obvious she viewed Bill and Lily as nothing of value, as something less than her and disposable. That little bit of rage within me grew in intensity until it was an inferno of loathsome contempt towards the woman who'd raised me.

"You can't stop me." I stalked in her direction and noticed how she backed up a few steps when I approached. "*Those people* have more strength, honor, determination and intelligence than you can ever hope to have. What's more important is that they have a heart, something which appears to have turned cold within you. Bill raised Lily as best he could as a single father. He gave her everything and he raised a beautiful person in the process, however you and dad turned your backs on him when he needed you. You could have done something, but you chose to turn your noses up at him because he didn't fit the mold of your perfect

237

fucking family! Bill McCormick and Henry James raised two amazing children and they did it in the best way they could, meanwhile you and dad raised a fuck up — but you were too fucking busy to even notice. Luckily for you, *those people* stepped in and did something about it. They accomplished something in three months that you and dad couldn't bother to complete over a 19-year period. So, no mom, I'm not going to sit around and prance for your friends to make you look better — because it's not your achievement."

I pushed past her and walked quickly to the foyer.

"How do you expect to get there, Hunter? You don't own your car and we're not giving you permission to drive it to Florida."

I turned around to find her with her arms crossed over her chest. Her gloating expression showed me that she thought she had me cornered. I intended to show her that two could play that game.

"Then have me arrested, mom. Be sure to raise enough of a stink about it that it's all over the news. I'm sure it'll be much easier for you to explain that I couldn't join dinner because I was sitting in jail than it would to simply explain that I was visiting relatives."

Her eyes narrowed and her skin took on a red tone. I'd cornered her right back and she was too focused on her precious image to continue with her threat. I turned back around, grabbed my bags and stepped out of the house determined to fix a mistake and find the only person that mattered.

Chapter Twenty-Three

Ellison

It was like he'd given up as soon as he was put in that hospital bed in the living room.

When they'd first transported dad to the house, he looked the same, spoke the same - acted the same. But over the past two weeks, I've watched him age 30 years. It's like nothing I could have imagined. It was almost as if I'd taken photos of him every day for those 30 years and created a fast moving flip book. The only difference was I couldn't flip it back to the way he was before he got sick.

Before they brought him home, I'd been up all night, barely able to fall asleep while I wallowed in self-pity. The only thing that broke up the 'pity party for one' was the aggravating text I received from Hunter when he'd threatened to leave school. The one fucking thing I didn't want for him and he threatened me with it immediately when the shit hit the fan. I'd pushed myself out of bed that morning and typed out a lengthy email about it. He was the one good thing in my life that my father's cancer wasn't destroying, and I couldn't allow him to mess that up. I'd tucked him away in Massachusetts, far enough that he wouldn't be dragged into the desperate helplessness of my life. I wanted him to stay there, to become something. It was the only victory I felt like I had over this nightmare situation — letting him go was the hardest thing to do, but he was a star that I launched into the sky so that his light would be protected from the shadow that was slowly creeping into my life. If nothing else, I could look at that light and think that at least one thing hadn't been tainted by my father's disease.

And Hunter threatened to fuck it up by coming back.

I haven't been responding to his texts very much, in fact, I've kept my phone tucked away in a drawer most of the time. I have nothing to say to him, nothing to tell him that wouldn't make him want to rush down even more. I've dropped 10 pounds already over the last two weeks. I've been a constant caregiver to my father and I've only had breaks when Jake or the nurses were here to let me sleep. I could sleep forever and it wouldn't be enough. I'm exhausted, I'm beat down and my heart is torn from my chest every day and every hour — it feels like it never ends. But I keep getting up, keep brushing off the pain of watching my father die to cook for him, clean for him, and administer his medications. I can't tell Hunter those things. I couldn't lie to him either. So I just said nothing.

The paperwork said his disease could progress rapidly and they hadn't been lying. It's not even something that I could explain because any words I used wouldn't accurately describe what it was like. Each day was a new problem — a new hurdle to be jumped and an avalanche of pain to be avoided. My father was in so much pain and even the morphine barely touched it. I couldn't stand to see him so weak, so confused. It wasn't him. And that's the thing about cancer. You don't lose the person on the day they die, you lose them when they become so weak that they are no longer the person you used to know. I was caring for a shell of a man that used to be my father, and only on rare occasions did he seem to come out of the fog. The brief glimpses I had of who he'd been meant more to me than anything, and even though they only lasted for a few seconds, I cherished every single second that he had them.

It started slowly. He slept a lot, the pain medications at least did that for him. I could handle when he slept because I could pretend that everything was okay — like he'd fallen asleep watching movies on the couch. But over the weeks, when the meds weren't working as well anymore, they'd switched him to a different type and what was once a nightmare became a living Hell.

He had a break with reality that lasted two full days. For forty-eight hours I didn't sleep, didn't eat, didn't bathe, could barely find time to run to the bathroom. Most of the time, my father thought he was five years old again. He kept asking for his mom or his dad — he would cry for them like a child who'd been separated from his family. He didn't recognize me and he was afraid of me. I cried while attempting to remain strong for him — to take care of him. Watching him break was leaving me broken right there beside him. There was nothing I could do to calm him down and it was like some twisted dream from which I couldn't wake. Here I was taking care of the one person who I used to be able to go to for advice, but he couldn't give me any and I was lost as to what I had to do. Eventually, I was able to calm him down. I read him old books I found on my shelves from when I was young. There's nothing like reading a children's book to a grown man who reacted like any normal five year old would to hear it. He smiled, he clapped, and I'd read the story to him enough times that he'd memorized and could repeat it back to me.

I thought the worst was over when he remembered he was an adult. I was wrong — so.fucking.wrong.

At first he was obstinant. He kept trying to get out of bed when I knew that he'd fall and I wouldn't be able to pick him back up. His bones were so weak they would break from the pressure of my grip. I had to remain constantly by his side to keep him in bed and he was so angry. He was suddenly my father again, calling me by my full name while demanding I let him go to work. It was bad enough when he was angry at me, but when he became terrified, I almost lost myself to his madness. Every time I tried to give him his medication, he cried. He accused me of trying to kill him, he kept asking me why I would do that to him when I was supposed to love him. He didn't understand that he was sick, he thought I was making him sick. He blamed me for everything that was happening to him.

I was angry with him and that anger only made me feel guilty for having felt it. He was losing his life, he didn't know what he was doing, yet I was selfishly taking his comments personally and feeling resentment. What about me? What about my exhaustion and terror and pain?! I worried that I wasn't giving him enough love, that I was thinking about myself too much when I took a minute break. I became worried that I wasn't strong enough to keep going.

He fell asleep finally. Forty-eight long hours and he graciously closed his eyes and let dreams take him. I couldn't sleep. I was too afraid that if I fell asleep he'd wake up and hurt himself. I needed help, but there was nowhere I could go — nobody who could help me. Even though Lily and Bill were aware now that daddy was dying, they couldn't come here. He wouldn't want to be seen in this condition. Calling the nurse would have only resulted in him being forced into the hospital and I couldn't do that to him either. So, I sucked it up and stayed awake.

I was in the kitchen drinking coffee when he woke up again. He sat up as much as he could and looked straight ahead of him. His eyes moved up and down as if something was standing in front of him.

"Anna?"

I looked over to where he stared. There was nothing. But that was mom's name he'd just said.

"Oh, Anna. You look so beautiful."

My shoulders straightened and I pushed off the counter to walk into the living room but stopped — I just stood there and listened. Tears welled at the back of my dry and tired eyes and I listened as he argued with my mom. From what I could understand by the things he was saying she wanted him to go with her, and he refused because he had to stay here for the kids. It wasn't an angry argument, just a normal disagreement that sounded like ones I heard between them many times before mom had died. It was oddly comforting and I laughed softly to myself. I was desperate for anything to be hopeful about and hearing him talk to her had given me the smallest bit of light. The paperwork had said that when people died they talked to people who passed before them. It was supposed to be normal and expected. They advised to just go with it, not to argue and say that the other person wasn't there. Now, to hear it and see it, to know that it happened often enough to have to be acknowledged, it touched me — made me wonder if we truly did go on after we ceased breathing.

My arms came up to wrap around my abdomen and I leaned back against the counter. I gained a bit of strength when I listened to him talk to her. I pretended that I could hear her voice as she responded to him. It's crazy, I know, but when you're in a situation as futile as mine, you become desperate for any bit of happiness or hope you can find. It hurt to think it might simply be another symptom of the illness, but it also calmed me. It gave me a reason to believe that when he finally passed, he wouldn't be alone and he wouldn't just be gone — as if he'd never existed in the first place.

Eventually, after talking to my mom for what felt like an hour, my father fell back to sleep, but he did so with a smile on his face. I didn't move, just stood at the counter with the dogs sitting sympathetically at my feet and I knew that they were grieving too. From around the curtains over the windows I saw headlights pull up to Bill's house. I looked at the clock and noticed it was late. Chuckling to myself, I thought Lily must have missed curfew again.

I startled when someone knocked at my door.

Chapter Twenty-Four

Hunter

It was a 17-hour drive back to Florida. I got lost about 15 times and had to pull over and sleep for a few hours at a shady as hell rest stop in Georgia. I was afraid that I'd wake up to my car being on blocks because I was in a bad area, but my eyelids felt like 50-pound weights over my eyes and I pulled over anyway. Thankfully, I lived and my car wasn't stripped before I'd made it to her house. I stood outside debating whether to knock or wait until a decent hour.

Walking around the house, I noticed that the bedrooms lights were off, but I swore I saw a dim light on in the living room. I knew Henry would kill me for showing up at three in the morning, but I had to see her, to talk to her, to know that she was still in one piece — that she was okay.

Walking up the steps to the door, I prayed that Ellison answered the door and not Henry. I didn't want to piss the man off within the first five minutes that I was back, but I was willing to take that chance to see her.

After she threw the door open and after I saw the shock turn to a murderous look in her eyes, I kind of wished it had been Henry who answered after all.

"What in the hell are you doing here?!" Her voice was whisper quiet at first, but her tone told me she was a hundred percent pissed off. She quietly shut the door behind her. "Explain to me right now why I'm standing on my porch looking at you when you are supposed to be a thousand miles away."

She looked like shit and it was a punch to the stomach to see her initially. Her clothes were stained and wrinkled and I would have placed a bet on the fact that she'd worn them for several days. Her hair was up in a messy bun. Bits and pieces of it were pulled out at the sides, sticking out in every direction. I could see the bones of her shoulders through the thin cotton shirt she wore. Her cheeks were sunken in and her eyes would have been as well if they weren't so swollen from crying. The blue of her eyes looked neon compared to the dark red rims that surrounded them.

"El, don't be pissed at me." I stepped toward her and she stepped back nearly pressing her back against the door. She held up her hands to stop me from getting closer. My hands fisted at my sides to notice that no emotion was clear on her normally expressive face. She looked raw, hollow — as if every bit of life and vitality had been drained from her, leaving a weak shell in its place.

"Ellison, what's going on?" My voice broke when I whispered out that question. I don't know why I kept my voice so low, but looking at her, I worried that anything louder could break her. She'd been fighting, that much I could tell. I could barely shake the driving need I had to wrap my arms around her and not let go.

She looked at me; just stood there staring out of empty and passionless eyes. "You need to go home, Hunter. There is no reason you, of all fucking people, need to be standing in front of me right now."

Her voice shook as she spoke and I could see her eyes glisten with unshed tears. I swallowed down the frustration that was drowning me in that moment. My throat hurt, my stomach cramped and the blood rushing to my head pushed along the headache slowly creeping up the back and sides of my skull.

"I'm here for Thanksgiving. I don't have school for a week, so I had time to get down here. I wanted to see you." It was like talking to a mental patient. The person standing in front of me looked like Ellison, but her words, the way she spoke and the way she was holding herself, she wasn't the girl I'd left behind a little over a month ago. I spoke slowly, clearly, in an attempt to calm down the rage I saw simmering behind her eyes and beneath her skin. "Will you tell me what is going on? You look ... "

"I know how I look. I didn't need you driving down here to tell me how I look. I have a mirror."

Fuck, there was no emotion to her voice at all. Normally, I could pick up something; anger, frustration, teasing humor — but this, this was mechanical and cold.

"My dad is dying, you know that. His condition worsened, but that's all you need to know. Enjoy your Thanksgiving with Lily and Bill, and then go back to school. I'll text you when I'm not so busy later on."

The cracked quality of her words carved splinters from my heart. I'd known she was avoiding me when I texted her, but I didn't know why. My answer was the haggard and spent shell of a woman that stood before me.

She leaned back against the door and folded her arms over her chest. "I won't be accepting visitors for a while. I wish I could say I'm glad to see you, and if you really are just here for the holiday, that's fine, then I'm glad. But come Saturday, you better have your butt headed back up north." A single tear finally escaped her eye and I reached up to wipe it away. She flinched when I did so and I pulled my hand back to my body to see her react in such a way. She was fighting and she was fighting hard — but against what, I had no idea.

Her resolve broke in front of my eyes and she doubled over as if she was in pain. Her back shook with her fitful breath. I reached out and placed my hands on her shoulders, pulling her body against mine. She crumbled when I finally had my arms around her. I leaned back against the railing of the stairs to take her weight and I silently held her as she shattered completely within my grasp. My shirt stuck to my skin where her tears had soaked through the material and, even though I fought hard not to join her, I couldn't fight back my own in reaction to her pain. I wanted to question her, talk to her, make her think of anything but whatever was going on behind the front door, but I knew she wouldn't answer. I was afraid to speak at all, for fear that she'd remember that she didn't want me here and would make me let her go.

I don't know how long we stood like that, but eventually her sobbing stopped, her breathing shallowed and her body relaxed. I gently nudged her. "El?"

She'd fallen asleep standing up. What had made her so fucking tired? When her legs started to collapse beneath her, I caught her and picked her up to carry her inside. There was nothing that could have prepared me for what I saw when I entered her house.

Medical supplies were scattered over every available surface of the house. In the middle of the living room was a hospital bed, and in that bed laid a man who at one time would have been Henry James. I was shocked to see how much he'd changed over a few weeks. His hair had greyed and his skin sagged over his bones. He was motionless as he slept and his jaw hung open from how deeply he breathed.

Rather than tearing across the room as they normally would, Sasha and Bear slowly approached me. When they reached me, they rubbed their heads softly against my legs and sat down at my feet while I stood in shock taking in the details of the house. It was chaos. Dishes stacked in the sink, towels and blankets in piles on the floor. Amongst the boxes of supplies and bottle after bottle of medications that lined the counters and tables were wrappers tossed aside, most likely when Ellison had been moving quickly to do something for her dad.

I placed Ellison on the couch and grabbed the blanket at one end to pull it over her. She immediately curled in on herself and grimaced in her sleep. Even when unconscious, she couldn't find peace. I stood in the middle of that living room not knowing what to do. I couldn't leave her in these conditions. Anger boiled inside of me to wonder if anyone had been helping her. Grabbing my phone from my back pocket, I typed out a rapid text to Lily.

Me: Where is Ellison's brother? Who has been helping her with her dad?

Yes, it was three in the morning and no, Lily hadn't been expecting me. I was going to give her a couple minutes to respond and then march over there and bang on her window to wake her up if she didn't. Luckily, she did.

Lily: What the fuck? Do you know what time it is? Why do you want to know about Jake and how the hell am I supposed to know?

Me: Because I'm at Ellison's fucking house and it looks like a hospital fucking threw up all over the place. Who's been helping her?!

Lily: You're here?! Oh shit, Hunter, she's gonna be pissed that you're in there. This is Ellison we're talking about. She won't let anybody help her, she doesn't want anyone seeing her daddy like that.

I didn't give a shit if Ellison never wanted to speak to me again. I was going to get her help. There was nothing that could make me leave her in this condition. If she woke up and got pissed, fine ... I'd just devise a way to make her get over it eventually. I was willing to take the hit.

Me: I'm going to clean up her house. Text Jake and tell him to get his ass home, now.

I didn't wait for Lily to respond before shoving the phone in my pocket and going to work on the house. I found trash bags in the kitchen and pulled one out to pick up and throw away all the emptied medical wrappers and other miscellaneous trash I found littered around the room. After I had that cleared, I gathered together the scattered supplies and medications and placed them on the coffee table so that they were easily accessible to her. After picking up the towels and blankets and placing them in the wash, I got to work on the kitchen, washing and drying dishes before placing them in the cupboards.

Every so often Ellison would stir where she slept, but she never woke up. She groaned in her sleep and cried and it took everything I had not to lay down beside her to comfort her. Mr. James never woke up and I was thankful for that. Eventually Jake came lumbering through the front door looking like he'd just rolled out of bed.

"Hey, man; Lily texted me. What the hell is going on?" He closed the door quietly behind him and took a seat in one of the overstuffed chairs by the couch.

Looking between El and her father, I motioned for Jake to follow me to the back bedrooms. I was afraid we'd wake her up by talking and I wanted her to get as much sleep as possible. I wouldn't be surprised to learn that she'd not slept over the past few days given her appearance when she'd answered the door.

After I'd closed us into Jake's room, I turned to him and he jumped to see the expression on my face. Normally I would have laughed to see a guy his size move like that, but I was too pissed to find it funny. "Where the fuck have you been? Ellison looked like she hadn't slept in DAYS and the house was a fucking mess when I got here!"

He blinked and then shrugged his oversized shoulders. "I've been working. I come home and try to help her, but dad feels weird having another guy take care of him. You know how he can be. The nurses come around as well, but Ellison lies to them and tells them she's fine."

"So, why haven't you told them what's really going on?"

He looked at me like I was an idiot. "Have you met my sister? She'd remove my balls if I did that. She's afraid with the issues dad's been having, they'd want to put him in the hospital — strap him down and shit. I've been coming and going — but mostly going. I just feel like I'm in her way."

That wasn't why he was staying out of it and I could tell by the pained expression on his face. He looked tired and ashamed. It was apparent to me that Jake wasn't handling the situation well and rather than charging at it head on like Ellison, he was avoiding it to pretend that it wasn't really occurring.

I sighed in resignation. "Can you at least be around for the next day or so and let her get some sleep? She's going to make herself sick, Jake, and, no offense, but I don't think you can handle losing both of them."

Jake nodded his head that he would and I turned to leave the room. "I'm going to leave before Ellison or your dad wake up and find me here. Do me a favor and keep in touch with me if any of you need anything. I don't give a shit if it's early or late, let me know what's going on with her, okay?"

He nodded again and when I started to open the door, he quietly asked, "Did you get his letter?"

I stopped suddenly and remembered that the letter he was asking about was currently folded up in my pocket. Turning back to him , I responded, "Yeah, I got it yesterday. Why?"

"I'm not asking what was in it or anything, but he was really adamant that I mail it to you and not let Ellison know about it. Seemed like it was important or some shit, so I just wanted to make sure you got it."

I could tell he wanted to know, but I wouldn't break Henry's confidence by talking about it — not now anyway. "No worries, Jake. I received it."

He nodded again and I left the room and slowed down as I passed through the living room. Glancing at the couch, I noticed that Ellison was still asleep. It was restless, but it was better than nothing. I wanted to go touch her, kiss her on the forehead to let her know I was there, but it could wake her up and that was the last thing she needed.

Letting myself out of the house, I was met with a cool breeze. I slowly walked down her steps and over to Bill's house. They didn't bother locking their doors out here so I was able to get in with no problem. I made my way to the spare bedroom and lay down on the bed, completely exhausted, but unable to sleep. Ellison's situation was worse than I'd imagined it could be. Thanksgiving was four days away and I had to leave to go back to school in six, but I wasn't sure I was going to make it back.

Considering my options, I felt torn between knowing she'd kill me for staying and leaving her alone with people who were too afraid to force her to let them help. I didn't care what Ellison wanted and I had to care about what she needed, and she didn't need to be left alone. School could wait, it would be there the next semester, just like it had been there all the semesters before. Dropping out now would hurt my GPA, but that stupid fucking number wasn't as important as the girl who was sleeping in the house next to me. Rolling to my back, I reached up and squeezed my temples between my fingers.

I hated what she was going through. I hated that she was battling something she had no hope of winning against. I hated the helplessness that she lived with and I suddenly understood the futility of hating a disease that had no cure.

But then — something occurred to me.

That night was the beginning. A moment where thoughts clarified in my head and a passion and drive bloomed within my heart. My hatred and anger enraged me to a point where a disease - a concept - a thing that held no true form or mass had became a dragon that needed to be slayed, a problem that needed to be eradicated. It didn't matter that my focus was solely revenge for what it had done to Ellison; I made a decision that night and everything seemed to snap into place.

I hated cancer. I hated what it did to Henry and I hated what it did to her. Ellison wanted me to make a difference and I decided to do just that.

Chapter Twenty-Five

I emailed my professors the following day. I had to drop my classes and I begged in each email that they withdrew me from the classes in such a way that it didn't screw up my GPA when I started back again. I knew it would be a week before I heard back from them, and, to be honest, I didn't give a shit if they all refused to withdraw me. I was staying there for Ellison and I had no fucking intentions to return to Harvard.

I walked out to the living room and Bill choked on his coffee to see me appear from the hallway.

"Holy shit, boy. What are you doing here?"

Lowering my weight into the chair beside of him, I leaned forward and laid my head on the table. "I came back last night to spend Thanksgiving with you guys ... and to see Ellison."

Bill's expression softened. "Hunter, I'm afraid you drove a long way for nothing, son. She's dealing with her daddy and we haven't seen much of her in the past few weeks. I've tried to go over there a few times, but Henry didn't want anybody visiting him." His expression darkened when he remembered the condition of his friend.

Pushing up from the table, I settled into my chair and closed my eyes against the sunlight coming in through the windows. "I know. I saw her last night." Pausing for a second, I breathed in a deep breath and asked, "Would you mind if I stayed here a little longer than this week?"

Bill looked at me. "How much longer?"

"Don't know. I'm thinking about transferring to school down here. I just wanted to know if I'd need to find a place for myself or if I'd be able to stay here with you and Lil." It didn't matter if he told me no. It just meant that I'd have to add finding an apartment to the list of things I had to do.

Laughing softly, he replied, "She'll beat down you for it, you know. She wanted you up there — not because she wanted you gone, but because she didn't want to drag you into this with her."

I tensed to hear what he was saying.

"After you left, I overhead her and Lily talking in the living room. I don't like to eavesdrop, but when it comes to your children, it's one of those things you do. Sometimes it's the only way you have to find out what's going on in their lives." He looked down into his coffee. "From what was said between them, I have no doubt that Ellison James loves you, Hunter — and I know that's no easy accomplishment." He smiled slightly. "I was a little surprised that you boarded that plane, thought for sure you'd refuse and challenge that girl the way you did on those hikes."

I chuckled. "You heard about that?"

He nodded. "Yeah, Lily told me about and so did Henry. We were amused to say the least. At 19, you'd already figured out the passive aggression needed when you're dealing with stubborn women. It took Henry and I at least three years of marriage to our wives to figure out that trick." Looking up again, he smiled. "But, then again, you're the smart one in this family, so I'm not surprised."

"I won't get dragged down by what's happening, Bill. But she will if I don't do something about it. I'm

256

transferring to school here. She won't like it and she'll probably stop speaking to me because of it, but I don't care. I'll be here whether she likes it or not because she needs someone regardless of her adamance that she doesn't."

Bill reached up to pat me on the shoulder. "Spoken like a real man. Good to see that you're finally growing up. Honestly, I didn't think much of you when you first came down here all those months ago, but you've changed, kid. You can be proud of that. I'm not impressed with much anymore, but I'm impressed with you. Guess they were right when they said that behind every great man is a woman ... because all it took to straighten your ass out was Ellison James. You should consider yourself lucky that she took the time." He paused in an effort to give me a minute to absorb what he'd just said. "Of course, you can stay here, but I wouldn't expect open arms from Ellie."

"I don't."

He sighed. "Regardless of how she treats you for the coming months, just remember that girl loves you. I'm happy to see you back, and it's about damn time you realize that just because Ellison packed you up, it doesn't mean that she's done with you. She tried to do what she thought was right for you and by coming back, you're doing what is right for both of you. She's not thinking straight right now, Hunter, and you need to love her think for her. Not about the stuff with her dad, but about the stuff that comes after his death ... about the rest of her life."

I felt two arms wrap around me from behind and I looked up into the teary eyes of my cousin. "You're staying?"

Her blue eyes blinked and I smiled. "Yeah. I'm staying."

"Oh thank god because I thought you were a dumbass for climbing on that plane and I didn't want to believe it!" Her little arms squeezed around my neck and I coughed from the lack of air. "Oh! Sorry." She let me go and sat down in the chair beside me. "So what are you going to do to get her to talk to you again? 'Cause as soon as she finds out you're not going anywhere, she's gonna kick your ass and forget you exist."

I laughed. I'd missed listening to Lily talk like she was stuck in fast forward.

"Don't know, Lily, but I won't give up until she does."

~   ~   ~

I'd spent the morning catching up with Bill and Lily. They'd been concerned about how I'd left things with my parents, but I didn't care. I'd left out the details of the contempt my mother had shown toward them because they didn't need to know that they were thought of so poorly by family. It made me want to strangle my mother even more just to think about it while I was around them.

Two things were made clear though in my talk with Bill: Ellison loved me enough to send me away and I loved her enough to refuse to stay where she sent me. It was an impossible situation, but one I'd endure until she was thinking straight again.

I started that afternoon being there for her. Knocking on her door, I was immediately greeted by Jake whose large body blocked my view of the interior of the house from the doorway. "Hey, man." He stepped outside and closed the door behind him. "El's in the shower. She slept in some this morning and gave

258

dad some medication so he's back to sleep. I'm staying long enough to give her time to get cleaned up."

"How is she?"

"As good as she can be, I guess. She was pissed to find out that you'd cleaned the house last night, so she's still got some spirit left in her. I guess that's a good sign."

I smiled. "Yeah, it is."

The front door opened behind Jake and Ellison peeked her head out. Her eyes narrowed as soon as she saw me. Stepping out, she looked better now that she had on clean clothes and her hair was washed. Her eyes were no longer empty and she appeared more human than zombie as a result.

"Jake, go inside with daddy. I want to talk to Hunter alone for a bit if you don't mind."

Jake looked sorry for me when he turned to walk inside. "Good luck to you, man. I'd hate to be in your shoes right now."

Ellison looked back to scowl at her brother before turning that scowl in my direction. "Let's walk down to the driveway so we don't wake up my dad by talking."

Oh shit.

"How loud are we going to get?"

She pointed to the driveway and I sensed the imminent shit storm. I didn't care though. She wanted to play stubborn, I was ready to play stubborn.

She brushed past me and led me to the other side of Bill's house before she stopped. Spinning on her heel, her finger was immediately in my face when she asked, "What the fuck do you think you're doing coming into my house and cleaning up? I would have taken care of that — I have that fucking house under control."

I scoffed. "Yeah, El. It really looked like that. You fell asleep standing up for fuck's sake, how exactly do you think you have it under control?!" That was going to piss her off, but I said it anyway. Someone needed to point out the problem.

"So then you should have just woken me up and sent me back inside! You had no right coming in there. Dad would have been pissed to know that you'd seen him like that!"

Grabbing her by the shoulders, I held her in place when I responded, "You know what, Ellison? I understand your desire to protect your father's pride, but I think if he were conscious enough to talk to you about it, he'd choose your health over how other people looked at him! You can't keep refusing help because you fear upsetting your dad!"

She tried to pull away, so I just wrapped my arms around her and held her still. Her knee came up into my leg and I winced but kept holding on. She could beat on me with both of her fists if she wanted to, but I was going to hold on to her and make her understand what I was telling her.

"Don't you tell me what I will and will not do! This is my life, Hunter, not yours! I'll make whatever fucking decision I want and you'll go back up north where you belong!"

I laughed. It wasn't a funny 'ha ha' laugh, either. Nope, it was a laugh that meant there was no way in hell I was going to listen to what she was saying to me.

"No, Ellison, no I'm not. This might be your life, but I'm making it mine as well — because YOU are my life! I don't give a shit what you say or do. You can ignore me, you can hate me — hell — you can put my picture on a wall and throw darts at it if that's what makes you feel better, but I'm not going anywhere. While you're taking care of your dad, El, I'll be taking care of you and there's not a damn thing you can do about it. You might be worrying about the coming weeks, but I'll be worrying about the rest of your fucking life and I'll be damned to let you force me out of it."

Those must have been fighting words, because the next thing she did was slam her hands against me with such force it almost knocked the air out of my chest. I tried to hold on, but when she took both my nipples between her fingers and twisted, I released her in response to the pain.

"Fuck! Ellison, that shit hurt!"

"I know it did, that's why I did it. And you can expect that reaction from me every time you think you're going to overpower and force me to stay still when I don't want to!"

"Well, then fine!" I shoved my chest out at her and held my arms out to my sides. "Go ahead and rip them off then, El, because you can expect that I'm going to hold you every fucking day until you stop breathing!"

She looked at me like I was nuts. Her voice was a whisper when she asked, "Why can't you just go home?"

We stood staring at each other for a few seconds. It was eerily quiet where we stood, almost as if the birds and bugs had stopped to watch, curious to find out what would happen between us.

We locked eyes and I walked up to her. Grabbing her by her chin, I tilted her angry face up in my direction and held on when she tried to pull away.

"I am home. Why can't you just accept it?"

My lips fell on hers and I kissed her with everything that I had. I told her I loved her with that kiss, I told her that I would protect her, that I would care for her and that I would fight for her every fucking day if that's what it took for me to be with her. My knees almost buckled to taste her again and I didn't want to take pleasure in forcing my mouth on hers, but I couldn't help it, I was estatic. I realized in that moment that my life couldn't be lived unless she was in it and I would take on the whole fucking world for her if it would get her to stand by my side.

Slowly, she wriggled out of my grasp and her eyes burned holes into me. Without looking away, she reached up and wiped my kiss from her mouth. If it had been raining, steam would have risen from her head because the woman was as heated as a damn oven, she was so pissed.

"Do us both a favor and go back to school, Hunter. Go do great things and live a great life. If there's anything left of me by the time you graduate, then fine, come back and find me, but for now, you need to be someplace else."

I couldn't tell if her tears were from pain or frustration, but the fact that they fell told me she needed me more than she realized.

"Not a chance in hell, Ellison James." Walking towards her again, I noticed the small steps she took to keep distance between us, so I just walked faster. I gripped her by her arms and pulled her shaking body against me.

"Tell me you don't love me. You want me away from here? You want me to believe that we're not meant to be together? Then fine! Just tell me you don't love me - that you can live the rest of your fucking life without seeing me and you'd be perfectly content with it! Because you need to know that I wouldn't be content. I've been miserable since I left here. All I can think about is what it feels like to talk to you, to laugh with you, to hold you and kiss you and argue with you! Even when you're annoying the living shit out of me by being as stubborn as you are, I still can't get enough of you. I love you, Ellison. I've found something that I feel passionate about in my life just like you asked — I found you! You are what I'm passionate about, you are the person for whom I want to live and breathe and I'm determined to do whatever it fucking takes to get you through this! For once in your fucking life, let somebody help you!"

She pulled away from me again and stepped back quickly towards her house. I followed her. When she'd almost reached her door, she turned around. "I don't love you, Hunter." It was a gut punch and shot to the chest all at the same time to hear her say it, but her tears told me she was lying. "Now, go home."

She turned back and I yelled after her. What I had to say was harsh, but she needed to hear it. "Your dad is the one who's dying, Ellison, not you! So, when you can get it through your thick skull that you need help and that your life will continue on after his ends, I'll be outside waiting for you to tell me. I'll be right fucking here waiting for you to realize you're pushing away your future because you're too damn stubborn to realize you can't take on the world and all of its problems by yourself!"

I planted my ass on the hood of my car and stared at her back as she walked away. My heart slammed against my chest and my lungs dragged in air, desperate to replace the oxygen I'd lost by screaming. My hands hurt from fisting as tight as I held them and my body trembled from the flood of emotions that coursed its way through my veins.

She paused for a second before she opened the door and I thought she was going to say something. She didn't. When she went inside, I settled against the car determined to stay there day and night until she admitted that she needed me in her life.

An hour passed and I shifted in my seat on the hood. I heard the door open and close at Bill's house, but my creepy stalker eyes remained trained to Ellison's front door. Bill walked up beside me and silently handed me a bag of frozen peas. I looked at him in question.

"It's for the nipples. That looked like it hurt."

I laughed and couldn't blame him for watching. Ellison and I were screaming right outside of his living room window. I placed the bag to my chest and, oddly, it helped. I'd been too mad to realize the skin where she'd pinched me was swollen and inflamed. When I breathed out a sigh, Bill chuckled.

"I learned to use frozen peas instead of ice after Emily hit me in the jaw for the third time after I'd pissed her off. The woman had one hell of a right hook and I found that the peas were less messy."

I laughed softly. "She must have been a strong woman."

"She was."

He unfolded a lawn chair and sat it down in front of my car. "Think this might be more comfortable than where you're at now."

I smiled while sliding down the hood to sit in the chair. "Thanks for worrying about me, Bill."

He laughed. "It's not you I'm worried about. This is a really nice fucking car and I'll be damned to let your big ass dent it." He clapped me on the shoulder and looked over to Ellison's house.

A small sliver of rage wound its way through my body when he mentioned damaging the car because it made me think of its owner. "It's not mine, so I don't give much of a fuck."

Bill huffed out a breath. "Don't matter whose name is on the title, it's still an impressive ride and I won't put up with you abusing it in my driveway."

I didn't respond. My mind kept mulling over the looks of disgust on my parents' faces when I'd mentioned inviting Bill and Lily up for the holidays. Eventually, I gave in to my curiousity.

My eyes were trained on Ellison's door when I asked, "What happened with you and my dad?"

He took a deep breath and let it out slowly before answering, "Ellison's mama happened."

My eyes immediately shot to look at him. "What?"

Bill sighed again and grabbed another lawn chair that he'd brought with him. Unfolding it, he took a seat beside me like he had a story to tell. "Well, Anna, Emily, your dad and I all grew up together. Anna and Emily were best friends. They were the same age as your dad, but I was only a year and a half older so I ended up hanging around with them most of the time. Eventually, as we grew older, your daddy fell for Anna and I fell for Emily. Your daddy dated Anna for few years in high school and he was about as smitten as a man could be

265

with a woman. Henry moved into town during my senior year and we became friends. After a few days, he became one of the group. Anna and Henry had something special almost instantly and after a few months, she decided that she wanted to be with him. It broke your dad's heart to lose her. He reacted badly and got angry with me for not cutting Anna out of my life. But, she was Emily's friend, and there was no way in hell I was leaving Emily. I thought he'd gotten over it by the time he went off to college, but after he left I didn't hear from him very often. He lived down here for a few more years after he finished school and we got you kids together every once in a while, but then his business took off and he moved up north."

"Holy shit. Did my mom know about Anna?"

Shrugging his shoulders, Bill looked at me. "Don't know how she would unless he told your mom about her."

I returned my gaze to El's house and sat back in my chair. I noticed how every once in a while she would look out the window, but fling the curtain back in place every time she saw me. I tried to imagine what she was doing inside.

Jake came outside after a few minutes and shot us a strange look before crossing over to us. He turned to look back at his house and back at us. "Do I want to know why you two are parked in lawn chairs staring at my house?"

Bill and I looked up at him in unison. Finally, Bill laughed and answered, "Hunter is sitting outside the house waiting for when your sister will admit she needs him."

Jake joined in Bill's laughter. "Wow, you'll be parked out here for a while. Hope you have a tent or

266

some shit in case it rains." After the two had quieted down, Jake waved and walked off. "Later. I'm off to work." He turned back to me. "I'll be home around nine. I think she can handle things fine until then. Dad's been sleeping a lot."

I nodded my understanding as he climbed in his truck and took off. After Jake's truck pulled away onto the street, Bill stood up. "Guess I should grab you the rest of the supplies you'll need." He disappeared into the house a few seconds later and I settled into my chair even more. It was going to be a long couple of days.

Chapter Twenty-Six

Ellison

Hunter had been camping outside my house for close to two weeks. On Thanksgiving Day, I'd watched as Bill and Lily brought him out dinner and sat with him while he ate it. I could have sworn he would at least go inside for the holiday, but no. He maintained his silent vigil in the driveaway day and night like he said he would. I was pissed off because I knew he was missing class, but he'd already told me he had no intention of going back.

I hated to admit it, but Hunter coming down here had changed something in my brother. Whereas, he used to avoid the house, opting to crash at Finn's place or some girl's house, Jake was now coming home when he wasn't working and it felt good to finally have some help with my dad - even if was just stuff like cleaning up and watching him so I could shower, it was still something.

The nights were getting colder and on this particular night, the temperature dropped suddenly to 35 degrees. The wind was blowing something fierce against the windows and it howled as it tore through the canopies of the trees. I looked outside and noticed Hunter wrapped up in his jacket, sitting in the chair outside of the tent he'd set up his first night there. He looked miserable and I shook my head at his persistence.

They'd found a medication that worked to control my dad's anxiety and pain and he slept most of the time for the past week. When he did wake up, he was more like himself for the short period of time he remained conscious. Jake was watching an old Christmas movie on television and dad woke up. Sitting up, he looked around for me and I rushed over to him to hand him some water. He could barely drink because his swallow reflex was weakening, but he was able to get small sips down. After he taken what he needed of the water, I sat beside him as he watched the movie with Jake. After a while, he finally spoke.

"Why don't we have a Christmas tree, El?"

It was an odd question and I turned to him with a confused look on my face. I didn't have an answer for him beyond how odd it felt buying a tree when he was dying. "I don't know. I haven't been able to go get one, I guess."

He nodded and after a few more minutes he said, "El, I want you to go get Bill and Lily and see if they want to come over here and talk to me. I know I've been difficult, but I can't exclude them from saying goodbye."

My eyes widened to realize what he was saying, but I got up to do as he'd asked. When I stepped out the front door, he added, "Baby girl, I'm sorry for everything I've put you through. You've done a good job taking care of me — don't ever think you didn't. I love you Ellison."

I swallowed the lump in my throat. "I love you, too."

Weakly nodding he added, "And get a tree will you? It's the holidays. We should have a tree." I could barely understand him because his voice was so frail.

Closing the door behind me, I stepped down the stairs and walked in Hunter's direction. He didn't move at first and I couldn't tell if it was because he was in shock or because he was frozen.

"I need you to do me a favor."

That got his attention and he stood up immediately. That's why my teeth went "tsk" when I saw that his lips were blue from how cold it was outside.

"I need you to get me a Christmas tree."

His jaw dropped, but he seemed to bounce back from his shock pretty quick when he nodded and grabbed his keys. "It's midnight, El, so I'm not sure what I can do, but I'll try." He surprised me when he got in the car and took off to get the tree without asking questions. I'd expected a little bit of drama after I'd gone so long without talking to him, but the minute I needed him, he did what I asked without being upset with me for it. I'll admit: it impressed me.

After Hunter left, I retrieved Bill and Lily and was surprised to see that daddy was still awake by the time we'd gotten back to the house. Bill's face fell as soon as he saw Daddy and Lily did a poor job of attempting to hide her gasp. I couldn't blame them though. My dad looked like he was over 100 years old and he'd looked nothing like that the last time they'd seen him.

Jake and left the room to let Bill and Lily speak to dad and eventually Lily came back to the bedroom where we were to allow Bill some time alone with him. I could tell she'd been crying and I put my arm around her to comfort her as much as a could. After another hour had come by, I saw headlights pull up outside and I ran to the front to open the door. Hunter dragged the tree inside and I smiled to see it.

Placing it on the ground, he looked up at my dad and nodded in his direction. The room grew quiet and I looked over to see how my dad would react to Hunter's presence. It felt like an hour before my dad finally nodded back at Hunter and said, "Come here, boy."

Hunter approached him and my dad held out his hand. Hunter gently took it and they shook. Daddy looked up at Hunter after that and asked, "You remember what I said?"

Hunter smiled. "Yes, sir."

Daddy nodded and lay back on his pillow. "Good."

What was that about?

I shook off my question and all five of us got to work decorating the tree. Daddy was in and out as we did so. He seemed to enjoy finding us in the room when he woke up and, by the time the tree was done, he had a front and center view of it. He smiled and fell back to sleep. When he didn't wake again after a long period of time, Bill and Lily excused themselves home and Jake went to bed. Hunter and I were left sitting on the floor near the tree.

Reaching up to rub at the back of his neck, he yawned. "Guess I need to get to bed myself." I looked over to him and smiled. He squeezed my shoulder before standing up and moved to grab his jacket.

"Hunter?"

"Yeah?" Turning back to me, he looked exhausted as he continued to pull the jacket over his body.

It was too damn cold for him to sleep outside and I knew he'd get sick if he attempted it. "Why don't you sleep in my room? I tend to fall asleep out here for dad. It'd be easier for me to ask for help from you if you were inside the house, you know?" I was lying, but if it got him to stay inside, it was worth the lie.

He looked surprised to hear me suggest it. "Are you sure?"

"Yep. It's cold as shit outside and I don't feel like walking out into that if I need something. So, just stay in my room until the weather warms up, okay? Then you can go back to your makeshift campsite." Another lie — and I think he knew it, although he wasn't calling me out on it.

He smiled just before he stepped forward and kissed me softly on the cheek. The contact sent shivers down my spine, but I didn't let it affect me more than that.

"Thank you."

"You're welcome."

We stood a little too close to each other for a very long time. The heat of his body rolled down the side of mine and I could hear every breath he took beside me. I started leaning into him, but I felt so fucking guilty that he was here. Initially, when he'd told me he wasn't leaving, I'd been crushed. I felt like the one thing I was trying to protect from all of this had been exposed and I'd lost every fucking battle I fought. He was the one exception, but all that was ruined when he'd not returned to school.

"Did you drop out? Is that why you're still here?" I had to know. I hoped that he'd just taken an emergency leave of some sort.

He looked distraught to hear me ask that question. "Yes. It's not going to affect my GPA because the professors understood I had a serious problem, but I won't be going to back to Harvard, El. I've already told you that I'm staying here."

My stomach hurt and I felt sick to hear him say it. I wasn't sure how I was able to cry after all the crying I'd been doing over the past weeks, but somehow, my body found a way to produce tears and I could feel them slowly trailing down my cheeks.

"You were the one thing, Hunter — the one thing that my dad's illness didn't destroy. The one thing that I was able to protect and the one victory I had over all of this. You ruined that for me by coming back." My voice cracked as I spoke, but I wanted him to understand how I felt.

He looked at me for a long time. His eyes searched my face and my body — and they briefly flicked to look at my father before locking back to mine. His voice was quiet but deep, the timbre carrying perfectly as he slowly responded. "Have you ever stopped to think about that for a second, El? You are bound and determined to have at least the one victory by protecting me — but to accomplish that task, you're pushing me completely away in the process. So, while you may be winning one small thing, you're losing something much bigger than you realized."

My breath caught and my heart constricted at what he was saying.

"School will be there when I get back to it, wherever I end up going, it'll be there. You need me now and I need to be here for you now. We need each other. I know you were lying out there when you said you didn't love me. You're a horrible liar."

I chuckled. He was right - I was a horrible liar.

His finger came to tilt my chin up to face him. Whispering, he said, "I'm not going to kiss you in front of your father, but know that if we were anywhere else, that is exactly what I would be doing to you right now. So, I'm going to bed to keep myself from doing what I want to do at this moment. Please — I'm begging you - get some sleep as well."

I sniffled and tried to blink back an errant tear. "I will."

He smiled as he released my chin and turned to walk into the hall that led to my bedroom. I watched him as he moved and when he was out of sight, I went around the room to turn off all the lights but the ones on the tree. I sat down in a recliner next to my father's bed and reached out to hold his hand in mine. My eyelids were heavy and my vision was fuzzy from exhaustion but I couldn't help and stare at the tree for a little while before falling asleep. Decorating it was the last thing I would ever do for my father.

~   ~   ~

The first thing I noticed was how cold his hand was in mine. Standing up, I saw that a red glow emanated from behind the curtains. The sun had just crested over the horizon, providing just enough light that I could see around the room. Pushing up from my chair, I moved to my father's bedside and looked down at his face. His eyes didn't move from sleep beneath his lids and I placed my hand on his chest to find that he wasn't breathing. Quickly I moved my hand to his neck and I couldn't find a pulse. I almost collapsed right there on the bed when I realized he was gone.

The numbness returned almost instantly. I felt shattered, broken and out of touch with everything. I felt disconnected and reality had altered and shifted, leaving me behind in a world that no longer existed. It was a moment when the adrenaline left the body because the battle had been fought and all the emotions you'd been holding back came rushing through in a painful and suffocating wave, draining you of every drop of energy you had left. And even though I knew those emotions existed, I couldn't connect enough to feel them. It was clinical and cold and it felt like a protective bubble of sorts. A soft place where I could float and my mind or heart could be protected from the full brunt of the impact. I'd just lost a friend, a parent and the only person I could rely on for advice and support. He wouldn't be there to walk me down the aisle, he wouldn't be there to know my children. But even through the numbness, one emotion did force its way through me. I was suddenly terrified of everything.

I don't know how long I sat there staring at him, but when I'd sat there long enough, I pushed up from the bed and slowly walked in the direction of my bedroom. The door squeaked when it opened and I padded through the dark room and crawled up onto the bed. I lay my body over Hunter's and my cheek rested against his chest so I could listen to his heartbeat. The movement from his breathing soothed me. I cherished the feel of his body beneath me in that moment and I buried my face against him so that all I could smell was him. My hands came up to grasp the sides of his shirt when I curled into a tight ball beside him. I was hiding in him — again.

"Ellison?" He sounded out of it when he first woke up, but within seconds he was more alert. "El, what's wrong?"

I didn't answer at first — couldn't say it out loud because, to do so, would make it real.

"Ellison?" He shook me and then pushed up on his elbow to try and look at my face. "What happened?"

I sounded like a fucking robot when I finally answered, "My dad ... he died."

Chapter Twenty-Seven

Hunter

Sitting up, I tried to process what she'd just said to me. I wanted to ask her to repeat it, but, at the same time, I didn't want to make her say it again. Not something like that. I pulled her body against mine and I noticed how still she was in my arms, every muscle in her body was tense.

"What do you need me to do, El? Whatever you need, please, just tell me what to do."

"I need you to wake up Jake ...."

I jumped to hear her voice. I was expecting her to fight against me helping, to pull her usual obstinate bullshit, but she didn't even attempt.

"There's a phone number to the nurse and the funeral home written down on a piece of paper. He needs to call them." She sounded distant and lost.

Reluctantly, I rolled her to lay her on the mattress and I stood up. I moved to exit the room and she said, "When you get done with that, will you come back ... please."

I nodded 'yes' and she curled up into a ball, hugging a pillow to her chest.

Walking down the hall to get her brother, I couldn't help but peek into the living room to look at Henry's bed. I couldn't imagine what El was going through and I hated to admit that I was glad she'd asked me to go back to her room — the last thing I wanted to do was walk in that living room and see Henry up close. I didn't know if I could handle it.

Jake was obviously upset when I woke him up, so I tried to calm him down enough to get him to make the calls. Once he was able to go take care of it, I returned to El's room. I crawled behind her on the bed and pulled her to me. She didn't say anything and I could tell she wasn't sleeping either. I stayed quiet as I held her. Within an hour, the nurse had arrived and needed to speak with Ellison. I woke her up and stayed with her as she dealt with all the details. Once the funeral home had arrived, Ellison was filling out paperwork for them and I took the opportunity to speak to the nurse privately.

She smiled when I approached her and I introduced myself. "Hey, I'm Hunter, El's friend. I was hoping you could tell me what I need to do for her over the next few days. I'm worried about how she's acting and I'm not sure if there's something I should be doing."

The nurse looked sympathetic when she answered, "Everyone grieves differently, Hunter. From what I can tell with Ellison, she's in shock right now and that's to be expected. The best thing you can do is let her deal with this as she sees fit, as long as it's not in a way that can harm her. Be there for her, but don't force yourself on her. I've gotten to know her over these past few weeks. She holds things in, I can see that, but for the next week or so, let her handle this in a way she feels comfortable — give her time before trying to push her through it, okay?"

I nodded and waited for everyone to leave. The medical equipment was left behind and that made the scene more depressing. Ellison sat on the couch staring off into nothing. Crossing the room, I picked her up and cradled her to me as I carried her back to her room. We slept for the rest of the day.

~   ~   ~

The next two weeks were busy. I didn't see Ellison much because she was dealing with funeral arrangements and financial and estate matters. While she was busy with those things, I went to the local college and went through the application process. I hoped that they could offer me a scholarship much like Harvard. It wasn't that my family couldn't afford school, it was just that I didn't want to ask my parents for another fucking dime. At the time I applied, it was too late to start school again during the spring semester, so I applied to start the following fall. It would give me eight months without much to do, but it was the best I could do with the choices I'd made. I'd been accepted almost immediately, but a decision was yet to be made regarding the financial arrangements for my education. At some point, I needed to return up north to collect my stuff from the apartment my parents had rented for me, but, luckily, I had time to get those arrangements handled before starting school in Florida.

Ellison and I saw each other in passing and she would politely stop and talk to me, but she was distant again — almost as if she operated on autopilot. The energy that normally exuded from her was absent. The nurse's words kept replaying in my head and I tried to give Ellison time to handle her father's death in a way that was comfortable for her. I couldn't understand what she was going through and I searched online trying to find information that would help me talk to her or interact with her in a way that was healthy for her.

When I saw her, I wanted to say the normal things: *'He's in a better place, his pain is over, life goes on'*, but it wasn't what she needed to hear. Maybe it comforts some, but it wouldn't comfort Ellison, she was too unusual to be satisfied with the standard phrases that accompanied the deaths of the people we love.

I'd cleaned up the campsite I'd erected in the driveway. I vacillated between keeping up my vigil until she was ready to talk and worrying that the site would be a reminder of what she'd just gone through. I was angry, I was frustrated and I had a desire to beat the shit out of something — anything — just to work out the negativity and powerlessness I'd felt in the weeks since Henry James died.

Over the course of those weeks, Jake had been coming and going for work and whatever the hell else it was he did on a daily basis an I noticed that Finn was showing up with him again, now that Henry was gone. It pissed me off and I stared his ass down every time I watched him climb out of Jake's truck and walk to Ellison's house. Where the hell was he when she was taking care of her father? If he really cared about her as much as everybody said that he did, why hadn't he been there to help her when I'd been in Massachusetts? I felt sick to see him coming around again and I wanted nothing more but to tear into him and call him out for the asshole that he was — but that wouldn't help Ellison, so I didn't.

It was Christmas and Ellison hadn't stepped foot outside of her house. Jake and Finn were nowhere to be found and I stood outside Bill's house looking over in the direction of Ellison's window — once again assuming my typical stalker persona. I'd bought her a small present but I never wrapped it because I didn't know if I should give it to her. It was an impossible situation — I didn't want her to miss the holiday and, at the same time, I didn't want to remind her that the holiday had come and gone and her father hadn't been there to spend it with her. I didn't want her spending the day alone.

Standing outside, I noticed rain clouds gathering in the sky. The sun was beginning to set in the distance and I gathered my jacket around my shoulders to try and keep out the chill that was quickly settling around me.

Ellison's front door opened and I watched as she stepped outside. She was wearing a thin t-shirt and shorts and I wanted to scream at her for dressing like that when it was no more that forty degrees outside. She turned to walk between the houses in the direction of the path she'd cut that led to the hiking trails behind her house.

"Ellison?" I called after her, but she didn't acknowledge me or respond. She just kept walking.

So, we're back to this, are we?

As we'd done so many times over the summer, Ellison disappeared within the brush of the path and I jogged to catch up and follow along behind her. I didn't like that she was heading out when it was getting dark outside and I was pissed that she wasn't wearing any clothes to protect her against the cold in the air. It wasn't my place to say anything, however, so I diligently followed behind.

Ellison seemed to be in the worst place of all and after we'd walked for an hour and when there were now thick black clouds rolling along the darkening skies, she took a turn she'd never made before.

The path she took wasn't intended for humans. That much was certain. It was narrow and littered with roots and other obstacles that slapped me in the shins and face as I passed. Ellison didn't seem to mind, so neither did I.

Thunder rolled above our heads and I saw lightning flash between several of the clouds in the sky. I wanted to call out to Ellison and demand she return to the house. The storm above us was angry. It was one of those storms that could take lives where it passed and I didn't want us to be caught in the middle of it when we had no shelter from its strength. Ellison reacted to the cracks of lightning by speeding her pace out towards wherever it was she was going.

"Ellison, I think we need to turn around. The storm is really bad. It would be dangerous for us to be caught out here."

There had been many days and nights during the past summer where I'd been introduced to the Florida storm. They came in fast and hard, they ravaged and they destroyed. And, sometimes, they killed. Lightning created fires where it touched and winds knocked over large trees. Two storms had destroyed the progress I'd made on the porch and I'd spent the hours after they passed trying to repair the damage they'd done. It was an exercise in patience on those days where I killed myself working only to have the sudden storm come and fuck up everything I'd worked to accomplish. If that had happened at the beginning of the summer, I would have lost my shit and given up. But, during the months I'd been in Florida, I'd learned that obstacles would happen and that roadblocks were a normal part of life. Character was built in jumping those obstacles and crashing through those roadblocks and I learned to appreciate them for the person they were creating within me.

"Go home if you're scared, Hunter. You have no obligation to stay."

The bitter tone of her voice shocked me and I didn't respond. It was obvious she was determined to go wherever it was that she was going and I had no other choice but to follow her blindly. My weary eyes looked up into the black depths of the clouds above us and I swore that if Ellison wanted me to walk with her into the middle of that storm, I'd do it.

Twenty minutes passed as we walked the narrow path and raindrops started to fall on my shoulders. Light at first, I was able to keep pace with her, but when those drops became heavy, when they landed in my eyes and distorted my vision, I became worried. In the distance, I saw lightning touch the earth and I worried that a fire would ignite from how dry it had been over the past few weeks. Despite the inclement weather, Ellison never slowed her pace. She was going somewhere and nothing was going to stop her from reaching her destination.

Eventually the path she followed broke apart, splitting open into a massive field with a single and small patch of trees in the middle. Ellison hoofed it out onto that field, the lightning illuminating her skin as she went. The thunder was ceaseless and the winds tried to tear the clothes from my body. However, I wouldn't give up. I pulled my shoulders back and I marched behind Ellison onto that field. The ice cold rain stung against the skin of my face and visibility was getting to the point where I couldn't see 10 feet in front of me. But I didn't care. Wherever she was going, it had to be important.

When we reached the edge of the small bundle of trees in the center of the field, I thought she was going to seek shelter. But when her body went down, when she dropped to her knees and when she raised her face into the sky and screamed as loud as she could at that storm, I shattered. My heart, my soul, my mind … all of it broke open and my entire body tensed to see her in so much pain.

I ran to her and dropped to my knees behind her. I didn't touch her or try to stop her, I just sat there and made sure she knew she wasn't alone. That was all that mattered. I was letting the same storm that threatened her threaten me because I refused to let her endure it without someone standing beside her.

Lightning flashed around us and I saw it strike the ground not a hundred feet from where we knelt. I pushed up on my knees and attempted to lean over her. I was afraid we'd be struck and I hoped that if it occurred, it would only hurt me. It was a stupid idea and I knew I could never protect her from lightning, but that knowledge wasn't enough to stop me from trying.

After a few minutes, she stopped. Her entire body went still, and she curled over on herself in the middle of the field where we sat. Her back shook from her sobs and I couldn't keep from touching her. When I placed my hands on her shoulders, her skin was cold to the touch. She was fucking freezing. I quickly stripped off my jacket and wrapped it around her.

"Ellison, we need to get under the trees. I'm going to pick you up. I'm going to carry you to a place where we can get out of this storm as much as possible."

She didn't respond, she just kept crying and whimpering, releasing all the pain she had stored up inside her into the chaos of the storm that surrounded us. I lifted her into my arms and cradled her to my chest. She fell against me like a broken doll and her hand came up to grasp me on the sleeve of my shirt. I moved quickly to seek shelter. I knew it wasn't wise to hide under trees in a storm, but, given no other choice, it was the only means I had to get her out of the direct wind and rain.

Sitting down against one of the middle trees, I silently held Ellison to my chest. I wrapped my body around her, attempting to warm her. I was almost completely folded over and it was an uncomfortable position to hold — but I held it anyway. I cried with her under that tree and I waited for her to release everything that she needed to let go so that the wind could carry it off somewhere far where it wouldn't hurt her anymore.

After a while, the storm's intensity lessened: the lightning stopped striking the ground around us, the clouds shifted away, and when the rainwaters subsided, Ellison's storm had also calmed. Her breathing slowed and she eventually moved to push the wet hair from her face. She didn't speak to me about it at first and I was perfectly fine with her silence.

I watched through the thin canopies of the trees as the moon came into view, accompanied by the appearance of what looked to be millions of stars. I'd never seen the night sky so clearly before and I was in absolute awe of how vast and beautiful the world was when you took a moment to notice it.

Ellison stirred in my arms and I looked down to find her staring at my face. She reached up and placed her palm over the cold and chapped skin of my cheek. The tears that had cascaded down her face only moments before finally eased and only a few still rolled along her skin, reflecting the light of the moon as they traveled.

"Why do you keep chasing after me, Hunter?" I could tell how raw her throat must have been by the scratch in her voice. I was thrown off by her question and it took me a minute to formulate a response.

I didn't answer her immediately because I felt like everything, all the times we'd spent together, all the smiles we'd shared and the tears that had fallen, and all the years I wanted to share those types of moments with her in the future hinged on my response. Why did I keep chasing after her? To most, she was just another girl in small town who was struggling like the rest of us in an attempt to find a place where she belonged in this world. Most of those people weren't lucky enough to know her like I'd known her — they hadn't talked to her, hadn't been shown the depths that existed within her. Much like the moon and stars that hung above us tonight, Ellison was a light that wasn't easily contained. She burned bright enough to break through the dense fog I'd walked in my entire life. Because of her, I'd opened my eyes when I hadn't even been aware they'd been closed — and for that, I'd chase her forever.

Clearing my throat, I reached up and pulled her hand from my cheek when I turned to look her in the eyes.

Speaking quietly, I confessed, "Because you are a dream and someone once told me that if I had a dream, I should chase it." It was a simple explanation, but somehow I knew Ellison would understand the honest weight of what I'd said.

Her eyes blinked slowly as she studied my face and as usual, she did something unexpected. She laughed. The corners of my lips turned up when I tried to suppress my grin. Her laughter sounded fragile, as if something so tiny could come along and break it apart - but it was there and my heart raced against my chest to hear it.

"That is probably the strangest thing I've heard you say yet." She sighed and pushed herself up so that she could sit beside me rather than in my lap. The cold wind stung the parts of my body that were exposed when she moved away and it made the loss of contact more painful to bear. "You're crazy for following me out here. You can get sick in weather like this."

I nodded. "Same goes for you."

Chuckling again, she quietly responded, "Yeah, but I have an excuse for being crazy. What's yours?"

My hands grabbed the side of her face so I could hold her stare when I answered. "I fell in love with a crazy girl."

Her responsive laugh was a short burst, but then she pulled away and her eyes drifted to look out into the distance. "I think we should get going home. We'll both develop pneumonia from being wet and cold."

"Oh, fucking thank you, because I didn't know how much longer I was going to be able to sit out here before I froze."

She laughed again and I smiled to hear it.

It felt like, finally, the storm had passed.

Chapter Twenty-Eight

The Florida winter came and went and spring was emerging in late March. In the time that had passed since Christmas, things had returned to a comfortable calmness within both houses. I still hadn't spoken to my parents, and when I returned to my apartment up north for a week to vacate my apartment, I sent them an email, letting them know.

Standing out in the driveway at the asscrack of dawn, my hiking packs were weighing me down while I waited for Ellison to get her ass outside. Her door opened and I was met with the familiar barks of the dogs as they charged down the stairs in my direction. Reaching into my pocket, I pulled out two small pieces of bacon that Lily had given me before I left the house. Ellison noticed me handing it to the dogs and laughed.

"I knew it. I knew there was no reason for those dogs to like you as much as they do. You've probably been giving them bacon since the first day you met them."

"Nope. It's like I said," I wrapped my arms around her as she approached me. "That was my sparkling personality ... plus I think Sasha kind of has a crush on me."

Ellison slapped at me playfully before pushing up on her toes to kiss me. Softly, at first, her lips brushed across mine and my tongue flicked out to taste the strawberry lip gloss she wore. Her mouth opened slightly and I took the opportunity to deepen the kiss while pulling her tight against me. She let out a small squeal and her hands came up to grip my hair. I couldn't help but smile when I kissed her. We'd slowly come back together after that night in the field. Although we spent almost every minute together, and fell asleep almost every night holding each other, I hadn't rushed having sex with her again. I didn't want to take advantage of a girl whose world had been ripped out from beneath her. That's not to say that it wasn't the hardest thing I'd done, but somehow I'd found the strength to abstain and keep my physical needs in check while I was with her despite the raging hormones that took hold of my body when I was around her. Even with something as simple as this kiss, I had to arch my hips away so she didn't feel my pants tightening against her hip.

She slowly pulled away from me after a few minutes. The small rays of light that broke through the tree limbs above us caused her blue eyes to shine when she looked at me. "Let me put the dogs up and we'll get going," she said.

I was surprised. "They're not coming with us?"

"Not today." She smiled.

"Why not?"

Her hands came to my chest and she pushed away from me to walk to her house. Looking back over her shoulder, she answered, "No reason." When I saw her wink after saying that I didn't know if I should applaud to have her back or run like hell because those words meant trouble. I groaned at the sight of the way her body moved as she walked away from me and decided that I'd be brave and tag along to see what she had planned.

After the night in the field, Ellison and I had fallen back into a pattern of hiking much like we'd maintained during the summer. It was as cold as a bitch most of the time, but something about those walks was therapeutic for us both. I assumed that during the quiet parts of those walks Ellison was working through the loss of her dad, while I was devising a plan on how to finish school and afford graduate school. Becoming a doctor wasn't cheap and I refused to ask my parents for help; I had cut up the credit cards once I'd used them to get my stuff. I'd taken a job bartending at The Tavern and worked two nights a week to help chip in on food and other bills at the house. The job wasn't that hard actually. I only worked Tuesdays and Thursdays and the place was always dead when I was there.

"Think it'll get hot enough for us to go swimming today?"

I looked at the back of her head like she was insane. "There's no way in hell I'm jumping in that water, El. I'm sure it'll be fucking freezing."

She stopped and turned to look at me. "Oh, come on." A mischievous smile touched her lips. "Stop being such a baby. I'm sure the fish miss us."

Laughing, I walked up to her and put my arm around her shoulder. Continuing up the path with her by my side, I answered, "Well they can keep missing us at least for another few weeks."

Ellison reached down and grabbed my hand and pulled me onto a small path that I barely recognized — most likely because it had been dark the last time I'd followed her down it. To see it during the day, I wouldn't have recognized it as anything more than an area that was thinner than the rest of the brush that surrounded us. After a few more scraps and slaps to my leg from the overgrowth, we walked out onto the field where Ellison had broken down.

I stopped in my tracks and was stunned silent to see the size of the field. I looked around at the amount of space that surrounded us. Above us was a boundless blue sky and beneath us was grass as far as I could see. There was nothing else and for some odd reason I felt unnerved to be standing in what felt like a sea of nothingness.

"It's scary isn't it?"

I wasn't surprised she knew what I was thinking — she always did. Walking up from behind, I wrapped my arms around her and pulled her against me. "Yes."

She nodded and said, "I found this place on accident. Bear had run off after a squirrel and by the time I caught him, I was at the edge of this field. It was frightening and awe-inspiring all at the same time. But I couldn't figure out why I was scared. I know a lot of people can't handle closed in spaces, but I think it's the wide-open ones that scare me the most. I feel exposed to the world and to myself, opened up so that I realized just how insignificant one person is in such a massive place. Despite how much this place scared me, I visited it often. It's a place for me to think."

She turned around so that she was facing me. "I don't want to be insignificant. I don't want to die and have that be it. I want to think that we go on, that there's a reason for all of this, and that by some grace we'll understand our purpose when we die."

She paused and rested her head against my chest. "But, it's different with you here. I noticed on Christmas night when you followed me out here. After the storm had cleared and we sat there freezing our asses off, I wasn't scared, I didn't feel small and I didn't feel alone — and I don't feel that way now.

She looked up at me again and when her eyes met mine a small spark ignited within me. I could never look into her eyes enough even if I did so for the rest of my life.

"You were right, Hunter. When you called me a liar ... you were right." Her voice grew quiet and she looked away quickly before her gaze locked back with mine. "I fell in love with you that first night in my room. You were the only person who could give me shelter, whose touch was enough to chase off all the pain I had inside me. I've never known anything like it. I feel it again now, out in the middle of this big ass field that normally scares the shit out of me. I feel grounded, like I'm not going to just float away when the Earth turns on its axis, you know?"

I laughed softly. I'd missed the weird shit that came out of her mouth and my heart was doing a happy dance to hear her talking like she had when I'd first met her. But even more than that, my heart danced to hear her tell me for the first time that she loved me.

Grabbing my hand, she walked us out onto the field in the direction of the small group of trees in the center. I was too busy watching her to notice that in the middle of those trees was a blanket spread out on the ground and a cooler set to the side. However, when I did notice, I did a double take before turning my confused expression to her and finding a beaming smile spread across her face.

"Surprise!"

I laughed out a broken and shocked chuckle while motioning to the blanket. "What's all this and how the hell did you get it out here?"

She pulled me down onto the blanket and crawled over to open the cooler. Pulling out sandwiches, fruit, drinks and chips, she placed them in front of us. "Lily and Ryan helped me haul it out last night. You'd fallen asleep, so I snuck out while you were snoring away."

I actually did wake up when she'd left the bed. I just thought she was going to the bathroom and I fell back asleep waiting for her to return. Grabbing a sandwich, I pulled it from the plastic bag and took a huge bite. It was absolutely perfect and we finished off the food pretty quickly. Lying back on the blanket, Ellison and I looked up into the tree canopy above us and noticed a small group of squirrels that were chasing each other, chirping their little hearts out in the game.

Ellison laughed. "Well, there's a sure sign of spring. Those little guys can't have sex with one another fast enough."

My lips twitched when I realized I knew exactly how the squirrels felt. Eventually they moved on and the trees were quiet above us. Rolling over, I pushed Ellison to the ground and crawled over her. She laughed when I kissed her all over her face and I pushed up to look down into her twinkling eyes. "What's so funny?"

She reached over and snagged the strap of her bag. "Got another surprise. It's not as fancy as butterflies, but I think you'll understand."

My brow arched over my eye curiously and I took the bag from her grasp.

She smiled. "Open it up."

Without taking my eyes from her face, I unzipped the bag and reached in to find a cardboard box. Pulling it out, my eyes settled on an unopened box of condoms with the words "next time" scribbled over the box in permanent marker. Choking on my own shock, my eyes flicked back to her face and she shrugged her shoulder.

"When I asked you what that meant before, I actually knew the answer. I just wanted to see if you would admit it."

My face hurt because my smile was a mile wide. The dimples were in full force and effect, the sudden blush to her cheeks giving away the fact that they still affected her. I pushed up so I was hovering over her and my eyes traveled down her body before slowly working their way back up. "Oh, you are asking for it now."

I couldn't help myself. My hands fisted in her hair and I was on that girl before she had a chance to change her mind. My mouth hungrily sought hers and when a small moan escaped her throat, I growled in response. Every nerve ending in my body was instantly alive. It felt like electricity sparked across my skin and I used my legs to force hers apart.

"Holy shit, Hunter! Aggressive aren't we?" Her words came out breathless and broken because I wouldn't stop kissing her as she talked. I responded with another feral growl and she laughed like I'd been kidding. When my hands released her hair to grip her shirt and pull it off her body, she realized how much I was NOT kidding.

I ran my mouth along the tops of her breasts and back up to her neck. When her body arched in my hands I became unglued. There was nothing stopping *next time* from happening and I wasn't taking any chances that something would come along and fuck it up. She writhed beneath me, seductively moaning and her breath caught with every new part of her skin that my mouth came in contact with. My fingers gripped roughly into the soft flesh of her body. Instinct and desire had cancelled out my ability to think and I was operating by pure need to dominate and conquer.

Within minutes I had Ellison naked beneath me. She reached down to remove my shirt, and I helped her by reaching up and ripping it over my head. My shorts were next. When I was stripped down to my underwear, I mentally surveyed her body again before touching, licking and kissing every inch of her skin. My hands got busy removing what little bit I had left on my body and when we were skin to skin, I groaned out of desperate want and frustration. Her taste was fucking fantastic and I could smell the traces of coconut from the sun lotion she'd put on for the hike. When I licked down her stomach and kissed her bellybutton, her hips bucked up in welcome. I moved farther down to bite along the insides of her thighs when she grabbed me by my hair and pulled me back to face her. "Inside me — now."

Her hand reached down and grabbed me and an almost painful jolt shot out from where she touched me. I grabbed the *next time* box, tearing the entire side off in my attempt to get a condom. Finally snagging one from the box, I ripped the package open with my teeth and Ellison laughed. I flashed her my dimpled grin and watched her melt beneath me.

Lifting her hips, I pulled her up while burying myself within her. Her head fell back and my mouth fell on the taut skin of her neck. The salt taste to her body drove every primal need I had into a frenzied state. Pushing myself up, I moved slowly inside her and watched as she wriggled beneath me. My mouth found hers again and we moved against each other in perfect unison igniting an inferno within me. Her fingernails trailed down my back and my hips bucked forward when she reached my lower back.

My mouth found her ear, "Fucking love you."

I felt her get off on those words, her muscles gripping at me hungrily and my name tearing from her swollen lips. I pumped into her, pulling her legs damn near up to her chest, and when I joined her in her release, my forehead rested on hers as my eyes locked with her gaze.

In a voice so soft and breathless I could barely understand, she responded, "I love you too." A tremor of ecstasy rippled along my spine at those words and my body floated in a void of everything good and pure and raw because she was the one who spoke them. Our hearts beat against each other, our chests collided from our labored breath.

Rolling to her side, I pulled her against me and we lay there together, our bodies calming, small bits of sunlight illuminating our skin where it broke through the cover of the trees above us. My face was buried in her hair and my hands couldn't stop traveling softly over her skin. She rolled over eventually, facing me, smiling at me and I grinned at her, my dimples standing proud. "Thank you ... " I tapped her nose with my finger. " ... for next time."

Her smile brightened but I covered it with my mouth and tasted her once again. Coming up for air, her eyes were opened wide and her beauty beamed out at me.

"Well, um, we should probably get dressed and head back ... we are naked in public currently and it would be bad if someone found us."

I groaned at having to let her go. Eventually we were dressed again and packing up the picnic to carry back home. Once everything was shoved into the basket, I grabbed my pack and starting walking out onto the field.

"What the hell? Aren't you going to help me carry this stuff back?"

I turned back to her and winked.

"Not a chance."

Chapter Twenty-Nine

Another few weeks flew past and I wouldn't have believed it was possible, but I fell for Ellison harder each day. She still had days where she broke down over her father and others where she wasn't actively upset, but quiet and reserved instead. I didn't push her on those days, but I paid attention to her triggers. Sometimes it was something as simple as what a person said, and others, she'd run across something that her father had used often. There was one day in particular where we were driving — thankfully with me behind the wheel — and a James Taylor song started playing over the radio. She doubled over in her seat and I pulled over worried that she was sick. She crawled over into my seat, curled up in my lap and cried. I tried to turn it off, but she grabbed my hand and shook her head, silently asking me to let it play. So I held her while it played, let her seek shelter in me like she'd told me in the field that day.

"This sucks, Hunter! Why are we doing this again?"

I looked over and laughed as Ellison's whole body shook from scraping at the old paint on her house. I'd noticed on the many days that I stood outside in the driveway waiting for Ellison to start our hike that the two houses didn't match. One stood proud — sanded and repainted, the porch rebuilt, the roof repaired and the landscaping trimmed and maintained. The other — well, that house still remained haggard, forgotten, damaged by the elements and time. I'd spent a summer fixing up one and I'd decided to spend the next summer fixing up the other.

"Because we need to make sure the surface is sanded down and clean before we apply the first coat of primer. A solid foundation ... "

She threw the scraper at me. "Oh, would you stop it with that solid foundation speech?!"

I laughed.

"I just want to know why we're sitting around fixing up this old house when we should be out there hiking or swimming or ... " A blush fell across her cheeks. " ... having picnics."

She walked over to me, seductively swaying her hips in her cute as hell attempt to deter my desire to fix up her house. I leaned against the stair railing and crossed my arms over my chest waiting for her to get close enough that I could grab her. When she reached me, I captured her in my arms and pulled her against me. She threw her arms up to push herself away while protesting.

"Damn it, Hunter, you're all sweaty."

Her laughter carried across the wind and I smiled. "So are you." I pulled her against me again and licked a line up her neck, nipping along the sensitive skin. My next words came out as a throaty growl. "I love the way you taste."

"Ew!" Her laughter howled out of her as she attempted to pretend she was disgusted with what I'd just done. But I didn't let go and I kept up my assault until her body went limp in my arms.

"You two should seriously get a room. I know daddy isn't going to be happy about the peep show outside if you keep this up."

Both our heads spun to see Ryan and Lily standing to our side. Lily smiled brightly and Ryan looked like he was trying to hold back a grin. I nodded in his direction and he nodded back.

Releasing Ellison, I bent over and picked up the scraper she'd thrown at me earlier. Holding it in front of her face, I said, "Think you'll be needing this."

She scowled at me before snatching the scraper from my hand. "You suck. You know that?"

"You'll thank me for it later."

I watched her walk back to the wall she'd been working on and I turned my attention to Lily. "Bill's finally come around, huh?"

After I'd starting working at the Tavern, Ryan and I became friends. We spent many nights sitting behind the bar talking. Ryan told me about the things he'd been through in high school and how difficult it had been for him to straighten up. He credited Lily for giving him a reason to want to make the effort. Over the months that I worked there I talked to Bill the following mornings, making a case for Ryan. It took a while, but eventually Bill seemed to come around. My best argument had been that Ryan wasn't any different than me, and all he needed was for people to believe in him to become a person worthy of Lily's time. Seeing Ryan standing on the property without fear of being shot was a good sign that my talks with Bill had been a success.

Lily's blush covered her whole face when she pecked Ryan on the cheek and answered, "Yep. Seems Daddy's going to give him a chance. So, to thank you, we've come over to help fix up the house. It'll get done a lot faster if we all work on it together rather than just you and Ellison."

I was surprised by her offer, and I responded by picking up some extra bottles and scrapers we had laying around and tossing the supplies in their direction. Once everyone was settled and working on his or her section, I smiled. Fixing Bill's house had been an exercise in patience, endurance, determination and desire. The act itself had given me time to reflect on my life, to think about my future, and to take pride in repairing something that had been neglected and forgotten over the years. And now it was time to fix Ellison's house, to repair something that had been damaged by the many seasons and storms throughout its life. Much like Bill's house, it would take time to strip away the fading paint, to prepare the house for the first coats of primer and to rip away and replace the rotten boards and shingles that no longer served their purpose. When it was fixed, when enough love and attention had been paid to the surface and to what existed beneath the layers of dust and decay, it would last a lifetime as long as it was given the same care and attention it had taken to repair it in the first place.

"So, did you find out whether you'd be given a scholarship yet, Hunter? It's been months. I'm surprised they haven't answered yet." Lily absently scraped at the chipped paint while asking me about the school's decision.

My arm came up to wipe the sweat from my forehead. "They answered a couple of weeks ago."

Ellison looked up from where she was working to pay attention to my response.

I let out a deep sigh, resigned to finally tell the truth, knowing it would disappoint El. "They declined. Unfortunately, because I dropped out mid-semester at

Harvard I was disqualified for an academic scholarship until such time as I can prove myself 'worthy'. So, basically, I have to pay for a year or two and prove I'm serious before they can offer me any type of financial assistance."

"But that's bullshit! You had an emergency!" Ellison's face was red with anger and she huffed out an adorable little breath that blew the loose hairs away from her face.

Shrugging, I went back to work scraping. "It is what it is. Just another roadblock that I have to work around until I can get to where I'm going in life."

"Where are you going?" Ryan piped up, keeping his eyes trained on the wall.

I sat back and my eyes flicked to Ellison. Her eyebrow arched and her lip twisted into a confused smiled. "Yeah, Hunter. Where are you going?"

I hadn't yet spoken to Ellison about the decision I'd made the night I returned to Florida and found Ellison completely buried by the cruel circumstances of her father's illness. Lily and Ryan stopped what they were doing and silently looked between Ellison and me.

The corner of my mouth crooked up at the side and I confessed, "I'm going to medical school."

Ellison's jaw dropped. "What?"

I shrugged. "I've always been good at science and math, so it wouldn't be unusual for me to pursue that path. Plus ... " I breathed out heavily to bring it up. Looking Ellison directly in the eye, I continued, "Do you remember what you told me outside of the plane when I went back home."

She nodded, but still appeared lost.

"When you said you hated cancer and asked if I knew what you meant? Well, I do know what you mean, I understand how it feels to hate it, and I decided I'd work to do something about it. I'm not sure how much I'll be able to change, but I can at least work towards finding a cure."

Ellison sat silently, her jaw hanging slightly open to hear what I'd told her. Ryan and Lily continued looking between us and Ellison eventually stood up and walked over to where I was sitting. When she was standing above me, I craned my neck to look up at her. A single tear ran down one sun kissed cheek and she lowered herself down so that she was straddling me on the ground. My eyes didn't leave hers and I heard Ryan and Lily silently excuse themselves and walk over to the other house. The sun shone behind Ellison making her hair glow around her face and I laughed to find ourselves in the same position we'd ended up in many times when we first met.

I started to say something, but she shook her head, placed her hands on the sides of my face and leaned down to kiss me. The strawberry flavor to her lips had become my favorite thing. When she swept her tongue across my lips I opened up to her and cherished the moment she deepened that kiss. It would never get old — the feeling of Ellison James kissing me. It was addicting, it was extraordinary, and it was something that would always, ALWAYS, keep me coming back for more.

When she stopped and pushed herself up to look at me again, she whispered, "You're amazing."

"I'd do anything for you, El."

Slowly, her lips pulled back into a toothy grin and I wrapped my arms around her waist, pulling her down so that her body covered me. We laid together on the ground for a few minutes, just holding each other before she asked, "How are you going to afford it, Hunter? Would your parents … "

"No. They haven't attempted to contact me and I have no intention of contacting them. I can do this own my own, El. I can work, take out loans, hopefully earn that scholarship back quickly. There are other options besides running back to my parents. It's the same reason I haven't driven the car since I returned home to get my stuff. I don't want anything from them if they can't accept you, Lily and Bill as family."

"I don't want to be the reason you stop talking to your folks." She got quiet and I saw a streak of pain flash across her face. "You don't get forever to fix things with them, Hunter. Trust me on that."

I sat up, but held her on my laps as I crossed my legs beneath. Her legs wrapped around my waist and I hugged her to me. "I know. But you are my family as much as they are. They are the ones who refuse to acknowledge you — not the other way around. I made my choice, El. I choose you."

She nodded and I grabbed her chin with my fingertips to get her to look at me. "And don't start thinking that if it wasn't for you things would be different between my parents and me. They wouldn't. The only thing that would be different than how things are now is I would be at college living my life the same way I had in high school. I'd still be lost if it wasn't for you. I'd have no drive, no focus, nothing to look forward to in my life. My parents didn't think enough of me to ever attempt to help me change. You did."

Blowing out a breath, she placed her hands on my chest. "If you say so." She broke her eye contact with me and looked around at the miscellaneous supplies that were littered around the perimeter of the house. "Are we allowed to give up on this today and go do something fun? It's Spring Break and they have a bonfire going out in the fields tonight."

I groaned. "Will Finn be there?"

She laughed in response. "You have nothing to worry about when it comes to Finn. He's accepted that I moved on and has finally moved on himself."

I knew I had nothing to worry about, but it was still fun teasing her every once in a while. Unwrapping my hands from her waist, I grabbed the cheeks of her butt and pulled her hips against me. Her legs tightened in response.

"Sounds good. But, I think I can come up with something we can do in the meantime."

She squealed and I sat up quickly to take her lips with mine. By the time I pulled away she looked stunned from the intensity of the kiss and I moved sideways to dump her off my lap. "Race you to the bedroom."

Her eyes flew open and she smiled while pushing up off the ground to race. We laughed as we wrestled each other up the stairs and we damn near hit the ground when we threw the front door open and attempted to squeeze past one another. Once we were in I slammed the door behind us and chased her through the living room towards her room. When I reached the hall, Sasha and Bear excitedly ran past my feet, tripping me in the process. Flying forward, I hit a wall before falling to the ground and hitting my head. I rolled on my back and held my head where it had hit the floor. Sasha and Bear took the opportunity to lick me all over my face.

"I win!" Ellison screamed out at me from the bedroom.

Opening my eyes, I looked up into the furry faces above me. They looked like they were smiling. "Traitors."

A grin came over my face and I laughed. If this was what the rest of my life was going to be like, I couldn't be happier.

Chapter Thirty

"There! The final touch has been finished and your house is perfect."

I stood back from where I'd installed a new doorbell on Ellison's house. She ran up the new wooden steps and paused with her hand hovering over it."

"Do I get to be the first one to ring it?"

I couldn't believe how excited she was over a doorbell, but I guess when you grew up without much, it was the little things that you learned to appreciate.

"Go for it."

She hit the button and chimes played in the house. Sasha and Bear barked in response. Jumping up and down, she threw her arms around me and kissed me on the cheek. "I love you and I love this house. Thank you."

Smiling, I kissed her back. "Don't thank me. You worked on it as well. So, since the house is done and it's still early, you wanna go for a swim and see your fish buddies?"

"That's seven miles away!"

"Well, okay, I mean, if you don't think you can handle it ... "

Her hand smacked me on the shoulder. "Oh, please, I can out-hike your ass any day. Let's go."

I opened the doors and grabbed our bags that I'd packed and set aside earlier in the morning. Stepping outside, her brow arched to notice that I'd planned on taking her hiking, and she grabbed her pack to toss it over her shoulder.

Normally, hiking the trail gave me an elevated heart rate due to the physical exertion; however, this particular hike had me damn near floored. I was giddy, I was nervous and I walked behind Ellison trying to keep my breathing even. When we reached the spring, she immediately threw her pack on the table and starting stripping off her clothes. I watched her undress and when she looked up again I smiled.

"Sorry, just enjoying the view."

Her lip curled. "It's hot as hell, Hunter. Take off your clothes and jump in the water with me." She didn't have to tell me twice.

When we reached the waterline, she looked out before jumping in and pulled me back when she noticed something floating on the surface out in the distance. Her head swiveled so she could look at me. "What's that?"

I shrugged my shoulder. "Don't know. Guess we need to swim out there to find out." I jumped in, pulling her with me, and it took a second for my heated skin to adjust to the cold-as-shit water. Eventually, I was able to move again and we swam out to the float. It was nothing more than a square piece of white Styrofoam, one that I'd used before. Recognizing what it was, Ellison dove under the water and grabbed the waterproof case I had tied underneath. When she resurfaced, she held the case up.

"Open it." My heart fell to my stomach and my skin tingled making it feel like every part of my body had fallen asleep. Nervous energy caused my chest to constrict. I could feel a lump form in my throat in anticipation of her reaction.

She twisted the case apart and pulled out a small, black velvet bag. Her eyes flicked up to mine and I couldn't speak while I waited for her to open it. Finally, she pulled at the little string on the side, opening the bag and she pulled out the ring from inside it.

Her eyes looked over the ruby heart shaped solitaire that was set into the platinum band.

I cleared my throat to settle the lump that had formed.

"Will you marry me, Ellison?"

Thank god the water in the spring was as crystal clear as it was because she dropped the ring almost instantly in shock. My eyes followed it as it floated to the bottom and I made a mental note of where it had landed.

"Oh my god!" Her hand flew to her mouth. "I'm sorry, Hunter, I didn't mean to drop it!"

"I don't care if you dropped the ring, El." I grabbed her chin to pull her face up from the water to look in my direction.

Her eyes met mine.

"Will you marry me?"

When I noticed a tremble to her bottom lip, I got nervous. Tears broke free of her eyes, and she nodded "yes." A flood of happiness and relief assaulted my body when she finally opened her mouth.

"Yes."

That was the best fucking "yes" I'd ever heard. Diving beneath the water, I retrieved the ring from the bottom. Resurfacing, I looked at her, placed the ring on her finger, and pulled her into me before kissing her like my life depended on the feel of her lips against mine. Pulling away, I pointed to the ring.

"I bought that for you for Christmas, but given everything that happened, I never had the chance to give it to you. I didn't intend for it to be an engagement ring when I bought it, but over the past seven months I've fallen for you more every day. I know I want to spend the rest of my life with you, and I know the ring isn't much, but I'll replace it with a diamond one day."

She held the ring to her chest and shook her head. "No. I don't want you to replace it. It's perfect. I never want to take it off my finger."

"But you deserve the best."

She smiled up at me, reaching out to pull me against her. "I have him." Throwing her arms around my neck, she kissed me until we could no longer breathe. The sun shone down on our skin and the rainbow wave of fish swam beneath our feet. It was a magical moment, one that would forever be a cherished possession in my heart and thoughts. And it was there, in the spot where we'd first learned about each other and where we'd first kissed, that we started living the rest of our lives together.

~   ~   ~

When we finally reached the houses in midafternoon, Ellison ran inside her house to get a shower and I went over to Bill's to grab some clean clothes. Even though I was spending every night with Ellison, I still tried to keep up the appearance that I lived at the other house. Walking in, I waved to Bill and turned to meander down the hallway to grab my clothes. I decided to jump in the shower while I was there, and when I got dressed and moved back into the living room, the front door was open and Bill was nowhere to be seen. My curiosity was piqued so I stepped out the front door and my eyes fell on the sleek black paint of a restored 1970 Mustang. I could tell that a lot of time and money had been put into the car and I knew whoever drove it here wasn't a local.

"Fuck."

Bill was talking to someone who was sitting in the vehicle and I groaned wondering who from my former life had just shown up. There was only one person I could think of that would be driving that particular car. Walking around the side, I stopped suddenly when I saw my father. As soon as I came into view, their conversation stopped and my father and I stared each other down.

"Why are you here?" My voice was an octave lower than normal and rattled against my chest from anger.

He blinked, but the bored expression on his face didn't change. He stepped out of the car and I noticed that he was dressed in a suit as usual. The sunlight streaming through the trees glinted off the solid gold watch on his wrist. "Good to see you too, Hunter."

When he stepped towards me I stepped back. "I didn't say it was good to see you, I asked why you're here."

"Now, Hunter. That's no way for you to speak to your father. He came all this way to see you. The least you can do is be cordial." Bill's low voice boomed out, but I didn't look away from my father's face to acknowledge what he'd said.

My father waved off Bill's warning. "Save your breath, Bill. Hunter has spent 19 years treating me like I'm not worth his respect."

"Why. Are. You. Here?" I didn't care to hear anything come out of his mouth other than the purpose for coming. I wanted to settle whatever score he had, deal with whatever bullshit he was about to start, and get him the fuck out.

"I came to talk to you. I think you've made a big mistake by dropping out of Harvard and coming here. I was hoping I might be able to convince you to fix that mistake before you throw your life away." He took a step towards me and I didn't step away this time. I was fucking livid and I wasn't backing down. I hoped he'd take a few more steps and be within my reach so I could toss his ass back in the car and make him leave.

"I don't care what *mistake* you think it is that I'm making. I haven't asked for shit from you since I've been down here and you need to get in your car and drive away. If you have something you need to discuss with me, you can text me."

"You mean, on the phone that I pay for?"

Shit. I hadn't thought of that.

"And how would you suggest I take the BMW away with me? Since you're not asking for anything from me."

"Fucking tow it for all I care. I haven't been driving it."

"Hunter?" Ellison's voice called out from the front of the car and my dad turned to look at her and

312

froze. His entire body seemed to tense for a second and his eyes were glued to her.

Bill went to say something to her, but she pushed past him and offered her hand out to my dad. "Hi. I'm Ellison James. You must be Hunter's dad. You two look just alike." Her smile was genuine and when my father didn't extend his hand to shake hers, I was glad that he hadn't touched her, but at the same time, pissed because I wondered if he'd instantly judged her unworthy.

I moved to stand next to El and looked up to see that my father's eyes were opened wide and he looked like he'd seen a ghost. Bill walked up and put his arm around my father.

"She looks just like her, don't she?"

My dad's response was so faint you could barely hear it. "Identical."

Ellison leaned into me and I could tell by the way she held herself that she was spooked out by my dad's reaction.

Eventually, he seemed to snap out of it. Clearing his throat, he offered her his hand. "My name is John McCormick. I'm sorry I reacted that way. It's just that you look exactly like your mother."

Shit! I'd forgotten all about what Bill had told me about my father and El's mom when they were younger.

"Well, thank you. I considered my mom to be very beautiful, so I'll take that as a compliment." Her smile could have melted glaciers it was so warm. "It's nice to meet you, I'm Ellison James. I'm Hunter's girlfriend."

"Fiancé." I corrected.

Dad's eyes shot to me almost instantly and I couldn't determine by his expression what he was thinking. I rolled my shoulders back and looked at him in a way that dared him to say anything. Bill interrupted before he had the chance.

"Fiancé? When exactly did that happen?!" Stepping closer, he grabbed Ellison's hand and looked at the ring. "Well, I be damned ... "

"Why don't we all just go inside and talk about this. There's a lot going on and I think we'd be more comfortable if we weren't standing out in the driveway."

I hated Ellison's suggestion. There was no way in hell I was letting my father in either of those houses.

"I don't think that's ... "

"Actually, son. I think Ellison's right. Let's go John, it seems like we all have something to talk about."

My dad grudgingly followed Bill inside his house and I was left out by the car with El. I narrowed my eyes at her and she scowled at me in response. When she didn't back down I rolled my eyes and reached out to pull her to me. "Why did you invite him in? I want nothing to do with him."

"Tsk. Whatever, Hunter, obviously, he's here for something and there's no point not hearing him out."

"I already know why he's here. He came to tell me that I'm a fuck up for having moved down. It doesn't matter what I do with my fucking life. To him, if I don't attend Harvard, I'm a failure. So, I don't see why I need to take the time to listen to him say it again."

Her expression remained impassive when she replied, "Because he's your dad. The fact that he came down at all tells me that he cares for you. And maybe he is a fuck up — but, so were you when you came down. I didn't hold it against you and eventually you turned things around. Why can't the same thing happen with him? You'll never get anywhere if you avoid people in a stubborn refusal to resolve your differences. All that gets you is a bunch of pissed off people sitting on opposite sides of the earth that are miserable. Give him a chance, Hunter."

Technically, I could have kept arguing, and if it had been anybody else, I would have. But looking down into her concerned blue eyes, I had nothing else to say. Well, except for one thing.

"If even one harsh word about you comes out of his mouth ... "

She placed a finger on my mouth to silence me. "Then I'll handle him. I'm willing to work out differences, Hunter, but I'm not somebody's doormat. You, of all people, should know that's true."

I allowed Ellison to lead me inside the house and we sat down at the kitchen table with my father and Bill. At first the discussion was strained. My father was still startled by Ellison's presence and I was on the edge of my seat, waiting for him to say one wrong word about her. Yes, I knew El could handle herself, but I still refused to let anybody speak badly of her. I made my case for living in Florida by explaining my intent to go to medical school. I didn't go into detail as to why. My reasons weren't as important as the fact that I was determined to do it. It was a long conversation, one in which I talked the majority of the time and, surprisingly, my father sat back and listened. By the time it was done, he didn't respond. His eyes flicked back and forth between Ellison and I and, after a few minutes, he nodded.

"If you're that determined to stay here, Hunter, I realize there's nothing more that needs to be said about it. So, I won't argue." Breathing out a long breath, he sat back in his chair and admitted, "To be honest, I'm surprised, and somewhat proud to see this side of you. I never thought you'd straighten up your act and I'm glad to hear that you've finally made a decision to do something with yourself, regardless of how I disagree with the manner in which you'll accomplish it."

I was stunned and Ellison hit my leg under the table when I'd failed to respond. It was the first time my father relented to anything I'd said and I didn't understand why. However, I wasn't going to press him about it so I nodded and thanked him for understanding.

Eventually, the conversation moved on to more casual topics and as the sun started to set, Bill and my father walked outside. Ellison and I remained at the table and she smiled over at me, tapping her foot against the side of my leg. "See? Told you that if you just talked it out, you could resolve it. You two still have stuff to work on, but at least you're communicating again. It's a start."

I playfully grabbed her hair at the back of her head and pulled her to me. My mouth brushed across hers and she immediately pressed herself against me, kissing me in a slow and seductive way. I heard the engine of my father's car start and she pulled away from me. I responded with a frustrated groan to the loss of contact.

"Would he just leave without saying goodbye?" Her eyebrow quirked in an adorable way and I laughed.

"Yep. That's pretty much how it works."

Her lips puckered and her face scrunched up. She was mad and I was inwardly laughing at her reaction. She stood up and moved to the window. Pulling the curtain back to look outside, she turned to me with a smirk on her face. "Maybe you should come take a look."

My brows furrowed in confusion, but I got up to stand beside her. When I finally turned my attention outside, my jaw dropped to see Bill and my father standing in front of the Mustang, toying around in the engine and laughing with each other. I'd never seen my father appear even the slightest bit carefree and it was unnerving to witness it.

"Looks like two other people had some making up to do as well."

All I could do was nod my head in response.

Ellison slipped her arm around my waist. "Well, come on. We need to fix dinner. It's rude not to offer him something before he has to make the drive back."

~   ~   ~

When dinner had finished, my dad stood up and apologized that he had to cut the night short. We said our goodbyes and Bill walked him to the front door. He was halfway through when he stopped and turned back to look at me. "Hunter, could I talk to you outside, please?"

Just fucking great …

I somehow knew his acceptance was too good to be true. Ellison nudged me to follow him and I sighed when I stepped outside. We approached the car and he turned to me, before briefly looking towards the house and back in my direction.

"I'm surprised to hear that you are engaged so young. I won't say it doesn't worry me, but … " A deep breath escaped him and his shoulders dropped in resignation. " … I understand. Ellison has a unique vibrance in her, much like her mother had. I know how infectious and life altering someone like that can be." He frowned while remembering back to a girl he'd once loved. "I didn't chase after her and I didn't put up much of a fight when I lost her. I'm not saying I don't love your mom and I married her as a consolation, but I will say that I know there aren't many people in this world as open and alive as Anna was and as Ellison appears to be. That's something that is difficult to find and have to let go."

I listened to what he said, shock settling along my spine to hear him admit something so … human. My entire life, the only things I'd heard him say to me were the mechanical words expected of a parent towards a child. Even his posture seemed different; it was soft rather than rigid.

"How are you paying for school?"

"I don't want … "

He held up his hand to silence me. "Hunter, I know you want to do this on your own. I get that. But school, especially graduate school is expensive; and you're about to have a wife to worry about. I'd rather you focus on your classwork than pay for rent and tuition. I have the means to put you through college, and I plan to do just that. I also offered the same to Lily."

The surprise must have been apparent on my face, because he laughed to see my expression.

"Bill has been on his own with her for too long. I held a grudge that I shouldn't have. I guess it's time that I make it up to him."

He clapped me on the shoulder and climbed into the car. Looking back out at me, he said, "Please have the school financial office call me. I want to take care of this for you."

I nodded and stepped back so he could shut the door. Starting up the engine, he waved before he pulled out of the driveway and disappeared down the road. I heard the door to the house open and close and Ellison's footsteps as she approached me from behind.

Wrapping her arms around my waist, she rested her head against my back and held me. My hands came up to hold hers and I absently toyed with the engagement ring on her finger.

"See? I told you to give him a chance. I don't think he's as bad as you thought — just misunderstood. Everybody has a story, Hunter, and that story will cause them to act in ways that other people won't be able to understand. But, you give a person enough time, eventually, they'll open up, and it will all make sense."

A smile crept over my face when I realized that once again, Ellison had improved my life. And maybe that's what I'd always needed. A tenacious blonde who wouldn't take shit from me and who called me out on my mistakes — and a woman who, by her very existence, brought something to life within me.

Epilogue

- 2064 -

The auditorium was silent. Not a single person spoke or made a sound while their eyes remained glued to Hunter at the podium. His head was bent down and his posture looked tired and frail. Finally looking up, the audience could see a tear rolling along the wrinkled skin of his cheek from the illumination of the stage lights. Clearing his voice, he straightened his spine and rolled his shoulders back in an effort to finish what he'd come to say.

"I started college with Ellison that year, but, the passion of being newlyweds overtook us and she became pregnant during the second semester. I argued with her for the first four months of her pregnancy about her decision to withdraw from school in order to raise our first son. I didn't think it was fair that she should have to give up her dreams in order for me to continue forward in mine." Chuckling to himself, his shoulders shook with mirth and a smile cracked his lips.

His voice boomed out louder, prouder, when he continued, "She put me in my place when I'd said that, and she told me that there were many ways in this world to make a difference. Sometimes, it's the things you do yourself, and other times, it's something as simple as raising a child to be remarkable. As soon as she knew she'd be a mother, she chose the latter path."

His eyes took in the audience, the faces were shadowed in comparison to the lights glaring down on his body, but he still tried to meet their eyes, tried to make them understand. With his eyes locked to the nameless faces before him, he confessed.

"I wasn't able to save her. Despite how tirelessly I worked, how many hours I devoted to finding a cure for the disease that killed not only her, but so many people that came before her, I didn't discover it in time." His hand hit against the podium, the sound of the strike echoing out across the large space. Tears welled in his eyes and his body sagged at the sudden drain in strength that accompanied remembering when she'd died.

Hunter gained his composure to finish his speech. "Ellison had once said that she feared being insignificant — she feared she was one small person who could only hope to bring small changes to the people and environment that she loved." He looked down at the wood of the podium and traced a vein of the wood with his finger.

Looking up, his voice bellowed out when he finally reached the end of the story he had to tell.

"Ellison is anything BUT insignificant. She is the reason for my success; she is the smile and the light that drove me along my path in life. She is the reason so many people can stop fearing a disease that carries the pain, the heartache and the tears of every person it has touched directly or indirectly. Whereas, I'll be accepting the credit for the cure, and whereas it will be my research and methods that will be used and applied to finally eradicate something as heinous and far reaching as cancer — the true credit belongs with a blonde-haired girl with blue eyes and a smile that would light up even the darkest corners of this Earth — the credit belongs with Ellison."

His vision was distorted by his tears, but even distorted, his eyes widened to see one person after another stand up, bring their hands together and applaud. It was a steady wave as they rose from their seats and the light applause rapidly became a booming ovation before him. But Hunter couldn't smile with them. Despite having succeeded in his quest for a cure, he still considered himself a failure, because he hadn't been able to save her.

Slowly, he stepped away from the podium and made his way down the stairs. Silently stalking back up the carpet through the center of the room, the audience continued to applaud, their faces following him as he passed. At the end of the row of people stood two men. They held out their hands to steady him as he reached the door and they walked him through and to the car waiting to take him home. Once packed in the car, the older of the two men turned to him.

"Do you want to go straight home?"

Hunter shook his head. "No. There's one place I want to visit first."

~   ~   ~

Placing the roses at the base of the granite slab, Hunter traced his finger over her name where it had been carved into the stone. He brushed away the dirt and errant leaves that littered her grave and he leaned forward to kiss the stone that marked where Ellison's body had been interred. The two men reached down and assisted Hunter back to his feet, and the three men stood staring down at the grave.

Hunter sniffled and wiped at his nose with the handkerchief he'd pulled from his pocket. "You know boys, your mother would have been proud today. If she could have been here, she would have stood at the podium with me and she would have argued with me about my crediting her with the accomplishment. But she would have smiled as well — because, despite her argument, she would know that what I said was true."

Jeremy, Hunter and Ellison's oldest son, spoke first. "I didn't know the entire story until tonight. I find it hard to believe that grandma and grandpa had been so cold when you grew up."

Hunter smiled. "My parents were just another one of your mother's accomplishments. I don't have to tell you boys, but she had an uncanny ability to set people at ease, to forgive and teach others to do the same. It was her meddling that caused my parents to return to Florida to be closer to the two of you." Hunter laughed. "I don't think my mother or father knew how to deal with her stubbornness any more than I did."

Chase, the younger of their boys, spoke next. "I'm glad you didn't give up, Dad."

Hunter turned to look at him. "Give up in what? Finding a cure?"

Chase shook his head and wiped a tear from his face in attempt to hide his emotions. "No. I'm glad you didn't give up on her."

Hunter nodded his understanding. "Your mother loved you two boys more than anything else in this world. She believed she was put on this Earth to raise you. I believe she was put on this Earth to save not only my life, but those of everyone she knew." He grew quiet remembering back to the many days and nights they'd spent together. "She once told me that she would lay out in the grass with the two of you when you were young and watch the clouds. While the two of you competed to find the different faces and shapes, she pretended that she could see her parents up there waving down." He laughed again. "She always did say the craziest shit." He paused to swallow down the lump that had formed in his throat.

"But for some reason, the crazy shit she said always seemed to eventually make sense. After she died, I spent many days laying out in the yard when I wasn't working. I looked up at the clouds and I watched to see if by some stroke of luck I would catch a glimpse of her hair glistening in the sunlight. And even though I never did, I felt her - in the wind, in the grass beneath my body, and in the rain that sometimes fell on my face as I lay there. She'd become part of the environment that she loved and it was in those quiet places that I found her, could talk to her, and could know that, somehow, she heard whatever it was I had to say."

When they'd grown silent again, Hunter realized how tired he'd become. "Come on boys, take me to my house so you can get back to your wives and your children. I've done what I needed to do and now I'm ready to go home."

~ ~ ~

When they pulled up to the house, Hunter climbed out of the car and waved at his sons while they drove out to the road and disappeared around the bend. Turning around, he looked up at the two houses that stood on the property.

Through the years that followed the summer he'd met Ellison James he watched as Lily went to college, eventually marrying Ryan and moving to a small town 20 minutes from where she'd grown up. She became a teacher and had four children, three girls, and one boy. Bill remained living in the house that Hunter had spent three months repairing and Ellison and Hunter remained living on the property with their boys

324

until Bill eventually grew old and passed away. Hunter had offered to move Ellison and their sons to a nicer home, one nestled snuggly within a wealthy city or town where they'd want for nothing. But Ellison had always refused, claiming she had everything she would ever need tucked within that wooded lot, minutes from the trails she loved to hike daily. Eventually, when the boys had grown old enough to walk those miles beside her, it became a family affair and Jeremy and Chase had grown up to go into forestry as their mother had always dreamed she would do someday. Ellison's brother, Jake, married when he graduated college and, although he'd completed his degree in business, he realized he wasn't made for life inside an office, eventually quitting his profession to be a tour guide for hikers in the Appalachian mountains. Finn moved away within a year of Ellison and Hunter getting married, an occurrence that Hunter would never say he was completely unhappy about. He didn't want to exclude someone that was important to Ellison, but he never got over his anger towards Finn for having practically abandoned Ellison while her father battled his disease.

Walking up the wooden steps of the staircase, Hunter approached the front door, reaching out to ring the lit doorbell. The chimes inside reminded him of the day he'd installed the damn thing, and the way Ellison had jumped excitedly to have something so simple added to the home she'd always loved.

Letting himself in the house, he realized how much he missed the incessant noise and welcoming barks of the terror mutts Ellison had raised. They'd passed away years after Hunter and Ellison married, however they'd been the best of friends and protectors for the boys during the many years they'd had together. Crossing through the living room, Hunter's eyes flicked to the many family photographs and memorabilia on the walls and counters where Ellison had lovingly placed them. She was always so proud of the family she'd created and she'd talk any person's ear off about the accomplishments of not only her husband, but her boys as well. Laughing to himself, Hunter recognized that if it hadn't been for the light inside her, those accomplishments would have never come about.

Finally reaching the bedroom he'd shared with Ellison for more than 50 years, he dressed in his nightclothes and moved the different letters, journals and photographs he'd rummaged through while preparing for the speech he'd had to give. It was the story of Ellison's life, something, as she'd grown older, that she'd documented and preserved. It'd broken his heart to read her memories of her father's passing, but he could relate and appreciate every terrible experience about which she wrote. He'd experienced it himself when he'd taken a leave from his practice to care for her when she'd become sick and died. He remembered her anger, her futility and her despair and he understood what it felt like to watch the light drain from the person you love. It wasn't supposed to end that way. That's not how he'd imagined he'd lose her. But it's what happened and Hunter had to tilt his hat to life, to recognize that fate and nature were going to do what they were going to do, despite how much you fought against it. He'd wanted to die beside her, but he wouldn't let himself leave the world until he'd destroyed the one thing that had destroyed her.

Lying down, he rested his head against the pillow, pulling another pillow to his side to make up for the loss of Ellison's body. Closing his tired eyes, he curled into a fetal position, allowing his tired muscles and bones to rest.

"That was a great speech. I totally would have agreed with the bitch part. But, as usual, you showed no respect. I remember telling you to refer to me as 'Evil Princess Bitch.'"

Hunter's eyes opened slowly, his mind not comprehending her voice.

"Well, come on. Stop being so damn lazy and wake up. I'm standing right here. Look at me."

When his vision finally focused, he couldn't believe what he saw: Ellison — young, beautiful, relaxed and carefree — leaning up against his wall.

He pushed himself up swiftly, the years of his life no longer weighing down his body. Shock washed over him and he rubbed at his eyes. "Ellie?"

She smiled. "It's about time. I've been standing here forever. You just never noticed."

His jaw dropped. "I must be dreaming. Oh God, El ... you look beautiful."

Pushing off from the wall, Ellison walked slowly to the bed, eventually sitting down beside him. Hunter jumped to feel the mattress lower from her weight.

"You look tired, Hunter. I think it's time for you to retire. You've done what you came to do and I couldn't be more proud." She reached out to touch his cheek.

Feeling the warmth of her skin on his, Hunter leaned into her touch, the few years he'd lived without her never allowing him to forgot what it was like to hold her, to feel her hold him back. Guilt flittered along his thoughts. "I failed you, El. I couldn't figure it out in time." He looked up into her crystal blue eyes. "I couldn't save you."

"But you saved our boys and their children as well ... and so many countless others who would continue to die if it wasn't for what you accomplished. Those people may not be sick yet, but they will be.

However, they no longer have to fear the diagnosis — thanks to you."

He shook his head. "None of that matters … "

"Yes, Hunter, it does. You just need to open your eyes and see what you've done." Reaching down, she grabbed his hand and squeezed. "I've missed you."

He smiled, his cheeks no longer burning with the effort, the pain of his body no longer effecting his movements, or slowing him down. "I never want to wake up, El. I want to stay here, beside you."

"Then don't." Taking his hand, she stood up, pulling him along beside her. She walked him in the direction of the bedroom door. Hunter turned to look back at the bed, his eyes widening in surprise to see the body of an old man, wrinkled and frail, still curled around a pillow.

"El?"

She stopped, looked at him and then over to the bed. Shaking her head, she grinned and looked back at him. "Took you long enough to figure it out."

"So, this is it? What about the boys? Our grandkids?"

Turning towards him, she wrapped her arms around his neck, smiling out at him like she'd done for so many years throughout his life.

"They'll be fine. Our lives are like books, Hunter. Each day is a new page — each year, a new chapter. Just like books, our lives end; but our stories … those are never forgotten. We live on in the hearts and thoughts of those who loved us." She smiled, her face incandescent from an inner glow that emanated from her skin. "Your speech just brought me to life again, in the hearts of the boys and the hearts of the other people in the audience. It was touching." Her eyebrow arched, before she added, "Although, I didn't know about daddy's letter, you'll need to tell me more about that."

Hunter smiled and pulled her closer to him. "So what happens now?"

She laughed, the sound beautiful, brilliant and melodic. "Can't tell you."

"Why not?"

It didn't matter, he knew he'd follow her anywhere, regardless of her answer.

She winked.

"No reason."

The End

M.S. Willis

If you are interested in reading additional books by M.S. Willis or would like to know when new books are being released, M.S. Willis can be found at:

Website: http://www.mswillisbooks.com

Facebook:
http://www.facebook.com/mswillisbooks

Join the Mailing List!!!

If you are interested in receiving email updates regarding additional books by M.S. Willis or would like to know when new books are announced or being released, M.S. Willis can be found on the website or Facebook page.